No Requiem for the Tin Man

A Lou Tanner P.I. Mystery

T.E. MacArthur

LOU TANNER P.I.
MYSTERY
NUMBER TWO

Also by T.E. MacArthur

The Praetorious Agency Files
(A Paranormal Romantic Thriller Series)
The Skin Thief
The Pillar (October 2024)

Lou Tanner, P.I. Mysteries
(A Dieselpunk San Francisco Detective Series)
A Place of Fog & Murder
No Requiem for the Tin Man

The Volcano Lady
(A Steampunk Lady Geologist Adventure Series)
Volumes 1 - 4
Volumes 5 - 8
The Doomsday Relic

The Gaslight Adventures of Tom Turner
The Yankee Must Die: Huaka'I Po
Death and the Barbary Coast
Terror in a Wild Weird West
The Omnibus Collection of Tom Turner

Anthologies
Second Star to the Right (IUPH anthology)
Twelve Hours Later: 24 Tales of Myth & Mystery
Thirty Days Later: Steaming Forward
Some Time Later
Next Stop on the #13

No Requiem for the Tin Man by © T.E. MacArthur.
Published by Indies United Publishing House, LLC

First Edition — First Printing, 2024

Book format by T.E. MacArthur
Cover design by Thena MacArthur

All rights reserved worldwide. No part of this publication may be replicated, redistributed, or given away in any form without the prior written consent of the author/publisher or the terms relayed to you herein. This includes no replication by any electronic or mechanical means including information storage and retrieval systems, without permission in writing from the author / publisher. The only exception is by a reviewer, who may quote short excerpts as part of a review.

The character of Philip Marlowe was created by Raymond Chandler. The characters of Nick and Nora Charles, and Sam Spade are the creation of Dashiell Hammett.

ISBN: 978-1-64456-744-9 [Paperback]
ISBN: 978-1-64456-745-6 [Mobi]
ISBN: 978-1-64456-746-3 [ePub]
Library of Congress Control Number: 2024913948

Attributions:
Veteran Typewriter font by Koczman Balint.
Bridge photo used for cover: Eric Fischer/Flickr
Robot background image created on Perchance.com
Zeppelin image designed by S.N. Jacobson

INDIES UNITED PUBLISHING HOUSE, LLC
P.O. BOX 3071
QUINCY, IL 62305-3071

www.indiesunited.net

Acknowledgements

To Indies United Publish House – Publishers and bastion of patient knowledge. Thank you.

To the usual suspects for all their support and love: *Ana Manwaring* (author and editor,) *Lisa Towles* (author,) *Dover Whitecliff* (author and artist,) *Chuck Johnston* (Beta Reader,) Stephen Jacobson (artist and photographer,) *Jeff Cathcart* (cabana man,) and *Sharon E. Cathcart* (author).

To *Sisters in Crime* (Coastal Cruisers Chapter & the Northern California Chapter,) the *Horror Writers Association* (San Francisco Bay Area Chapter,) *The Authors of Clockwork Alchemy*, and the *Southwest Writer's Group*.

In loving memory of Bill Christianson.

Author's Note and warning

This is a **fair warning** to all my readers: I use language and descriptions here that were grotesquely but commonly in use during the 1930s in America yet are considered (thankfully) inaccurate, distasteful, and just plain wrong today. Sadly, there are people today who would gladly use this language towards people who don't look or think like them. And even worse, many of the circumstances described historically from the 1930s are happening again.

Oh, and yes, I changed Howie (Howard) Johnson's last name. That's because I'm terrible with names and the fact that I named a character Howard Johnson. Apologies to the restaurant chain.

Lady Shamus,
damn right that's me.
gumshoe in high heels.

THE SETUP

Don't ever count on a client falling into your lap. Getting business takes a lot of time, a lot of advertising know-how, and a hell of a lot of glad-handing. You will be kissing babies, accept that fact. Clients simply don't bust into your office begging for help.

-Lou Tanner, P.I., 1935.

I should never listen to my own advice.

Crazy Guy busted in my door, clutching a ripped-up bundle in his arms, and bled all over my floor.

I yelled.

Marley screamed.

Not My Cat, resident feline squatter, puffed up his black tail and hissed like a Halloween demon while knocking over a vase of flowers as he sprinted for safety.

One smart cat.

Two shocked dames.

Crazy Guy shrieked at us, "They're coming! Sweet Jesus, you gotta' hide ... hide before they get ya'! They're coming an' no one can stop them!"

Them? "Who is coming?"

My first thoughts went immediately to the offensive parade goose-stepping its way down Market Street outside. *American Nazis?* There's an oxymoron full of oxy-Morons.

Normally, I love a parade. Not *this* parade.

Seconds before Crazy Guy started decorating my office in red,

Marley and I were watching the spectacle below from the window of the empty office across the hall from my own. Drums, horns, slogans, all shaking the window glass in their frames. Every hooligan or ne'er-do-well with a gripe and a home-made uniform had shown up for this one.

Disgusted, we sauntered back to our own sanctuary to twist the cap off a bottle and send off the workweek with a two-finger salute.

Crazy Guy rudely interrupted our early evening reveling. He looked like hell. Not too tall but boney. Rail-thin arms clinging to a pile of newspapers. No hat but plenty of ripening blue bruises on his face. He'd taken a beating and his red-rimmed, wide eyes told me how terrified he was that more was coming.

Had one of those jack-booted goons chased this poor guy up to my office and would come bashing in after him? What had this wretched man done to warrant being busted up like he was?

I've got a loaded gun for such emergencies and I'm only happy to use it. This poor mook needed all the help he could get.

Have I ever mentioned I'm a sap?

A real, honest-to-God push-over.

Yeah, me, *Lou Tanner, lady P.I.* and occasional volunteer rube.

Thankfully, after two minutes, no one followed after Crazy Guy.

The obnoxious parade stayed down on the main thoroughfare, focusing its ire on the various immigrants and "new arrivals," and other so-called "subhumans" they love to hate, waving their flags and handing out fliers to the confused or intrigued people lining the sidewalks. Mostly lists of who or who not to vote for.

Ah, election season in San Francisco. Nothing brings out violent opinions quite the same way at any other time. For all their issues and candidate promoting, the only thing I figured the marchers managed to do was hold up traffic.

As long as they kept their flapdoodle-con game down there, it wasn't my problem. *My problem* was currently staining my landlord's hardwood floors. *My problem* was not getting kicked out of this office.

I opened my trap to question Crazy Guy when he grabbed me by the lapels and yanked me off my heeled oxfords. In seconds we were flailing around like turtles on our shellbacks, sprawled out on the reception room floor. His bundle, looking more ragged than his shirt hem, clunked on the floor and skidded away.

He reeked to high heaven — I smelled like *Outers Gun Oil*.

He wore rags — I wore my best togs.

Had he waited two more minutes, I would have been wearing *Eau d'Old Forester Brand Bourbon*, a favorite, and the epicurical aromatics of leftover sweet and sour Sam Wo noodles.

Just my luck: the guy has crappy timing.

He clutched me by the shoulders as I sat up. Spittle landed on my blouse while he shrieked on and on, never once blinking during his tirade. That is never a good sign. I generally don't work with *crazy*. Crazy has a reputation for being untrustworthy or unreliable. Both, usually. Crazy is also renowned for not paying its bills. I need my bills paid in full. Right now, that last part about paying was too urgent for me to ignore.

"You … have to hide! They're coming!"

"Who? Mister, who's coming? People from that parade down there? Did they do this to —"

"I can't tell you. I shouldn't tell you. Maybe I'm supposed to tell you. I can't remember. Please … get out of this city. Now while you still can!"

I eyed the front door and knew I could oust him with a bit of effort … except …

I couldn't do it.

Something in his voice told me not to write him off so easy. Something in the terror forcing his bug-wide peepers to stare straight into my soul, appealing if not begging for relief I couldn't deny him. Something about the blood seeping from a nasty cut at his hairline, dripping down his battered doughboy cheeks, that only plucked at my heartstrings.

I'm a real sap alright.

He shrank into a tight human ball, trembling, fighting off some demon in his brain, while only one phrase came out of him.

"Tin Man."

CHAPTER ONE

```
My rules are generally simple:
Don't fall in love, especially with a client,
Don't trust the cops – they don't trust you.
And the end will always justify the means.

-Lou Tanner, P.I., 1935, Letter to Female Pemberton
Graduates
```

If only I followed my own rules and advice with any sense of commitment. Translation? *First class sap.*

Protégée and all-around amazing Girl Friday, "Irish" Marley O'Brien, who has a hell of a lot more going on under those bouncing blond curls than most mooks assume, returned a second later with water, soap, and tissues. We couldn't let him bleed out for a bunch of reasons, not the least of which was that my landlady only needed one more excuse, like stained carpets, to boot me out and replace me with a higher paying, tidier renter. One who can pay the full bill next month, which I could not.

As we eased Crazy Guy up and over towards the couch, the shamus in me couldn't help herself and I launched right in, interrogating the man while he was still conscious. "Who should we hide from?"

I thoroughly expected him to talk about the uniformed men in the parade, stomping away down Market Street. A couple of baseless ideas were flopping around between my brain cells, like maybe he cheesed off someone marching by and they bashed him on the noggin for the grins. But maybe not. If anyone from the parade had thrashed Crazy Guy, they hadn't followed him up to the third floor.

NO REQUIEM FOR THE TIN MAN

Since he was heavier than expected, we accidentally dropped him on the couch. As his coconut thumped against the wall, Marley and I both cringed in sympathetic apology. Closing his eyes at last, though his lips kept moving in a conversation with parties unknown, Crazy Guy rocked his head back and forth, and he clutched desperately to remnants torn from that tattered package. Where the hell had that thing gone to?

I looked around. The package wasn't where I thought it would be. I thought about looking for it but Crazy Guy needed all the urgent attention we could give him.

Over and over, he repeated his warning.

"'Tin Man?'" Marley asked, doing her best to pluck the remaining shredded newspaper out of his locked fingers. To me, she asked, "Slim? What's he talking about?"

"No idea. The only 'Tin Man' I know of was in that kid's book I read a while back."

She managed to get some of the clump from his right hand. "Aren't they gonna' make a motion picture of it?"

"Bet they make it a musical," I grumbled, thinking about having to crawl around under the furniture looking for his package and ruining my last pair of stockings.

The phone rang, causing us both to jump. Crazy Guy didn't notice. Marley grabbed up the receiver and tucked it between her ear and shoulder, signaling to me to keep quiet. Both hands snagged the notebook and pencil she kept handy out of habit. "Tanner Private Investigations."

I recognized the man speaking so loud on the other end he made Marley squint.

"Oh! Hello Agent Hayes," she cooed professionally. "Let me see if she's in." She looked to me for the answer to her question.

Timing. Yeah, it *really* is everything.

Only my new chum, Agent Christopher Hayes of the War Department, would call at a time like this.

Today was all sorts of crappy and would be a terrible day to play the ponies or the lottery.

Politics. Parades. Crazy Guy. Now the War Department's calling? All while waiting for the first paying client in over three months? Yeah, that kinda' luck is the sort of luck you take down to one of those Nevada casino cities if you want to die in debt.

I started to shake my head no — tell him I'm not here.

As if he could see us, Hayes responded. "Put her on the phone, O'Brien. She's there. I know she's there. She can hear me too!"

"The folks in Poughkeepsie can hear you," Marley grimaced while I held back a giggle.

I waved for Marley to give me the phone.

"You sure, Slim," she whispered. "With all this?" her head cocked towards Crazy Guy.

I didn't care who was listening. "Darling, quick, hand it over before a vein bursts in the G-man's forehead and we're accused of killing a Federal employee. You remember what sensitive, namby-pambies they are."

"I heard that," the voice in the phone shouted.

Holding the receiver almost to my ear, I put on my sweetest voice. "Good afternoon Agent Hayes. What can I *not* do for you?"

"Hilarious Tanner. You've gotten less cordial by the week. So, don't talk, just answer my questions."

"You haven't asked any. And I can't answer without talk —"

"You gonna' shut up long enough for me to ask?"

What a schmuck. "Why that would be too easy Agent Hayes."

For a moment, silence.

I sighed loudly into the receiver. I suppose it was better than laughing at him. "Look, it's been a hell of a day and if I'm coming off as sarcastic it's because —"

"You ever meet a Joe named Augustin Gruber?"

This time I gave him a long pause to ponder all while signaling to Marley to eavesdrop on the line. To cover the sharp click on the line when she picked up, I sneezed and apologized. "Sorry about that. A case of the snuffles. What was your question again? I truly want to be cooperative."

"Sometimes you make me crazy, Tanner."

"Only sometimes?"

"Is Marley on the line now?"

Marley shrugged. The ploy hadn't worked. I shouldn't expect

every trick to work on Hayes.

"Of course . What are phone extensions for?"

"Fine. Both of you listen up! If someone asks you if you've ever met or even overheard the name of Augustin Gruber, the answer is 'no.' *Com-pre-hen-dee?*"

Was that his idea of Spanish or Italian? "Who?"

"Perfect answer. You don't know him, you don't know his family, and —"

Crazy Guy groaned, shouted about us being in danger, then fell silent again.

"Tanner, what the hell was that?"

Damn it. With both our phone receivers picking up noise from the same room, of course Hayes heard Crazy Guy. Oh well, with G-man Hayes, it was safer to use the truth. Or at least some version of it. I didn't trust him with everything.

"A client. A *potential* client ... I think ... if he ever sobers up."

Marley glanced my way and mouthed the words, "Nice cover."

"You lying to me, Tanner?"

"Agent Hayes, I'm affronted —"

"What's your client's name?"

"He hasn't told us." Again, the truth. Mostly. Although at the moment, I was certain Crazy Guy's real name started with a "A."

"What does he want?"

"He hasn't given us that yet either. In and out of conversational condition at the moment. But ... should you like, I can always provide you full details, in a report I will submit, in three copies, initialed and signed ..." Then I went for the gut punch, "Of course that's after you supply a copy of the warrant. I hope getting a warrant won't put you into too much hot water with a judge, since it is Friday afternoon, and, well you recall how much judges *love* to be pestered at the start of the weekends ..."

The line was silent again. I pictured Agent Christopher Hayes clutching the bridge of his nose, as if pressure would help with the migraine I was giving him.

"Agent Hayes?"

"Shut up. Just, shut it."

"Hey now! There's no call for that."

"Tanner, for the love of God, I'm not kidding. Listen up! You have never seen or met Gruber. Never!"

I haven't known Hayes all that long, but even I picked up that something was quite seriously amiss. Something far more awful than he was admitting. Guess he didn't trust me much more than I trusted him.

I put my hand above my lips and the receiver, protecting my words from unsanctified ears in the walls for all I knew. "Then I suppose I shouldn't ask about the 'Tin Man' my potential, yet unnamed client was yelling about several minutes ago?"

There was a longer, heavier pause and I got the distinct feeling that this bad day was going from weird-but-funny to deadly-and-serious in a heartbeat.

"Tanner. That's not funny. Hang up. Today never happened."

Ah hell. I never should have gone to church last Sunday, let alone gotten out of bed this week. The hypocrisy had thrown the universe out of whack.

Wait a minute.

Why did he call me in the first place? In a city of six hundred fifty thousand people, why did he believe Augustin Gruber would interact with me? *Now, wait a damn minute —*

"Kit Hayes, explain yourself! You know there's a man who busted down my door. You know who the man is or you wouldn't have called me. Are you staking out my office again? You remember how things went the last time you did that." *God, why does Hayes do this to me? Better question: why do I let him?*

"There? At your office? That was the guy shouting … You're not pulling my leg? He's there … I thought he might have called you or … oh Christ. I'm coming over."

"Bring bourbon," Marley barked at him before hanging up her extension.

"Tanner," Hayes started to growl.

"I'm not going anywhere you or your War Department colleagues can't follow, apparently. I still remember the last time you surveilled me. I remember your colleagues coming and going in my office as they pleased. Not even a 'hello, how are you,' or 'may I please.' You got my office address, so hustle your muscular, tight ass over here."

"Lillian Lucille Tanner!" my name came through his gritted teeth. All three of my names, too.

"What? Afraid a third party is listening in? Some of your War Department buddies hanging out on the roof with listening devices? I'd hate to ruin your golden reputation —"

He hung up.

"Serves you right if they are," I yelled at the dead line.

"Want me to order Chinese? Sam Wo's is open and I can run over to Chinatown to pick it up. We've collected a couple of extra mouths to feed."

"No. Stay put. Lock the door and help me put Augustin's feet up. We'll set him up comfortably. Then shut off any unnecessary lights."

For a while, Marley stared at me. In the fading remnants of the day, shadows crept across her face, stealing the sweet girlishness that usually peeked out from under Shirley Temple curls. Her gray-blue eyes stayed locked on me, and I could read her feelings. "We're hiding?" she asked.

"We're laying low," I corrected with little devotion.

We're hiding.

She nodded to me. Lines deepened around her mouth as her lips turned down. She knows serious when she sees it, especially in me.

I wasn't even trying and I was dragging her into trouble.

Whoever invented the saying, "you could hear a pin drop," never lived in a city. My heartbeat thumped in my ears along with the electric horns of the driverless taxis, 'Crawlers, outside. Traffic was fighting its way past the echo of the parade and all the delays it left in its wake.

Crazy Guy clammed up when the walls trembled. We knew what was happening.

If the shaking was uneven and choppy, it was a quake.

Rhythmic? Pulsing? Then it was another of the charms of modern San Francisco.

Not a quake.

Airship service.

Marley threw her hands in the air and walked back to her desk, grumbling. At least Crazy Guy didn't over react. He tucked his hands tightly under his arms and closed his eyes, rocking back and forth to comfort himself.

Gray balloon envelope filled with combustible gas. Twin-rotor engines. Sparse but elegantly decorated gondola unaffordable to the average Jane and Joe American. German Nazi flag flappin' in our breeze.

Geez. Couldn't someone else provide cross-continental air service? Did it have to be *them*?

The Five P.M. Zeppelin Service from Boston lumbered in overhead, shaking everything underneath it with its huge trans-continental engines. The Zeppelin's engines flared for its approach to the Montgomery Street Aero Station and my office did the shimmy again. The building, blessedly built on rollers after the 1906 disaster, took the shaking in stride.

Downstairs, the familiar mix of human and mechanical life rolled on. Trollies have a particular sound as their wheels glide down the rails of Market Street — clanging bells warning pedestrians and autos alike to make way. Nightcrawlers are different. There's a rush of noise as they scrape along their track and beep with that electronic horn at anything that gets inside of five feet from their egg-shaped bodies. After more than six months in this office, I could report the traffic better than the guy on the radio simply by listening. This evening, I could tell most everyone was unhappy — the parade had held them up from getting to the bars after work.

After all the shaking had subsided, Not My Cat emerged from wherever it was he used to sneak in and out of the office. He sauntered in like nothing was wrong, sat in the middle of the room to clean himself, and stopped to see if the blood was of interest. I guess it wasn't, he stretched out his back leg, revealing his left paw. All his paw pads were black, like his fur, except one pink toepad he liked showing off.

Marley sat on her desk, facing me. "Was I officially supposed to overhear this guy getting all fussy over 'Tin Man' or Tin Men?"

NO REQUIEM FOR THE TIN MAN

"No."

"And neither were you?"

"Nope."

"Never heard of them? Never heard of Mr. Gruber?"

"Those are our marching orders."

She slowly let her head bob up and down, while her mouth twisted into a doubtful smile. "For a couple of bright girls, we sure have a lot of boys determined we should play stupid."

"And you're surprised?"

She shrugged. "Nah. All the same, Slim, I'm getting' mighty tired of it."

"Yeah, Irish, me too." *Tin Man*. That didn't sound so charming. "Oh, Marley? Tuck your Derringer into your waist band. Keep it loaded and handy." I picked up my newly cleaned .38 and spun the chamber. Why? I liked the sound. It sounded solid and confident, even if I didn't.

CHAPTER TWO

It's all well and good to be lucky. But never forget:
Lady Luck can't always be counted on ...
and,
Not all luck is good luck.

-Lou Tanner, P.I., 1935, Letter to Female Pemberton Graduates

Me and Marley waited, smokes in one hand, artillery in the other. I waited on the unlikely but not improbable: a guy to rush in with guns blazing, like it happens in the pulp magazines I read.

This would have been the perfect time to tell Marley. Only I didn't.

I'm dead broke.

No pleasant way of saying that.

I came here to the *City by the Bay* to make my mark in the world and to earn enough scratch to keep me content. My contentment now includes keeping my best friend and colleague employed. Welp, things haven't gone as planned.

So far I've chalked up a lotta' debt and a lotta' dead bodies, including a crooked cop about four months ago.

The Police don't like me, never did, but now they despise me because I was involved in a cop killing. They conveniently forget the *crooked* part in favor of the *dead* part. Doesn't matter how bad a cop is, to them he's still a cop.

If you're lucky, they only run you out of town. If you're not lucky ... well ... they make your life hell until they end it.

I'm not willing to test my luck.

NO REQUIEM FOR THE TIN MAN

Despite the events earlier this year, and the confusion over wo who pulled the fatal trigger plugging that crooked cop, I've been lucky that things haven't gotten too far out of hand.

San Francisco still remains *my town.* We two cling to each other like a pair of drowning lovers on the Titanic. It's beautiful and romantic but ends tragically every time because neither of us knows how to swim — metaphorically speaking. Ah, San Francisco, my unnatural lover. *You're one hell of a lot more satisfying than anyone else out there. Safer too.*

My town. Lots of bills to prove I live here. I'm going to die here too.

I'm the *Lou Tanner, Private Investigator,* printed on the lease and the business cards and painted across the frosted window panel on the front door. This office suite was one I made an insanely lucky deal on. And it was a miracle I wasn't required to have a man co-sign for me. Some folks were only too happy to have *Lou* signing everything without bothering to check who or what *Lou* was. One of these days, somebody is going to notice *Lou* ain't a Louis but a Lucille. Lillian Lucille to be exact.

Good thing my needs, like my rules for living, are pretty simple: keep the damn lights on and pay my staff of one, in full, on time.

That's why I'm impatient for a new case, one that pays some serious coin, as in twenty-five dollars a day plus expenses. That's standard pay for a Private Detective. I'd sell my teeth for such a case. I've already sold off a bunch of things I valued and I'm running out of junk other people want. One good case was all I needed to make up for the last one that went bad. That's all I need.

I made my wish, and surprise-surprise, I got a call out of the blue. Just like that.

A client!

Ever hear the adage, *be careful what you wish for?. I* should have known better. Turned out my would-be client came complete with the wrong kind of baggage: he works with some sort of politician.

Small and local, he assured me. "All the same, discretion is going to be extremely important despite lack national importance.

You know how the newspapers can be. Won't you give me a moment of your time? I'll be by, say, around four-ish this afternoon ... late," the caller said, a man, with a strong whisper that left me feeling like spiders had taken over my wardrobe. I couldn't pick out his accent, age, or any other tells beyond the obvious fact he didn't want anyone else hearing him.

The whole time I was on the phone with the windfall client, my gut kept telling me to hang up. Was it the politician himself who was indiscreet I asked? "No," he corrected, "not exactly." That suggested someone involved with the campaign, or close to the politician, but not the main man himself.

Either way, I couldn't afford to ignore him. I'm flat busted and I'm not sure how I'll pay Marley this week. That means I can't be picky about the next job I accept. In instances like this, *moral* and *ethical* get flexible definitions. Besides, I'm not yet convinced I'd call my line of work entirely honest.

My mentor, Uncle Joe Parnaski, used to say that a lot. After twenty years as a cop then another fifteen as a railroad case investigator? Yeah, he knew what he was talking about. Teenaged me soaked it up like a sponge, every word and trick of the trade.

The crowd lining up downstairs, along Market Street outside the Fox Theater, was dispersing. Everyone loves a parade, right? In broad daylight, one could only imagine who was available to go see a bunch of grown men and women marching around, at the start of happy hour. Any other evening, I'd say "no."

Things have changed lately. And not for the better.

Bombs have been going off. Violence and crime are on the rise. Everyone wants an easy solution. So, today, happy hour be damned, they lined the sidewalks to watch one group who promises to fix it all. Most would never believe this nonsense, but maybe they're the sort who've grown desperate enough to believe now. Or maybe they're people looking for change.

I'm not looking for change — I'm looking for stability.

For the sake of impressing potential clients, I had plunked myself, for one hell of a rental fee, down in the offices above the Fox Theater on Market Street. I'd even picked up some acceptable-looking furniture and the best office girl in California. And I did all of that to make up for some anticipated perception problems — namely, I'm a woman in a man's profession.

Private Investigators don't come in skirts and high heels.

But I do.

My license and a few other important documents filled up my wall, behind the clunky, walnut desk that was good for appearances and for storing booze when appearances and brilliance still didn't fix my femininity problem. Oh yeah, and that big, old desk is terrific for keeping vital weaponry too. Detective work can get a little dicey.

Twenty minutes had gone since Crazy Guy's memorable entrance, when Green Eyes thundered in. Of course he did. He's a G-Man with the War Department and a reputation to uphold. Probably still gets a fancy government car, too. Not a chance in hell he'd get here this fast if he had to catch one of the City's numerous if unreliable, automated 'Crawlers. I think he'd die before letting a 'Bot drive for him. Like many, he's not so big on putting his life in the hands of mechanicals.

He slammed my door open and shut. Apparently Agent Hayes's manners tonight were worse than Crazy Guy's.

There he stood in my doorway, hands on hips, doing his best to fill the whole space like some big bad King Kong.

Didn't work on me. I know better.

Hayes and me — we go back a tad. We saved each other's lives a few months ago, which created a different, *special* kind of bond between us. If you're lucky, that bond happens with people in this business. Too bad, I've sworn off anything serious with the "stronger sex" because in my experience, they aren't. Unfortunately, that's easier said than done, as the saying goes, damn it. "Green Eyes," as I called him much to his embarrassment, was a tall-'n-pleasant package. Thick salt and pepper hair that tended to stand up straight as the Chrysler Building made him look even taller. Hayes was ruggedly handsome, a real Beau Brummell, with a weathered face that spoke volumes and told tales in the lines that deepened with every expression. A knowledgeable face with details I wanted to discover, maybe some time when the weather is rainy and cold, and we happen to have one warm blanket between us.

It'll never happen. I've sworn off falling for colleagues as well as with clients.

Sadly, his daddy never taught him how to dress. Askew tie, uncuffed trousers, and black brogues anyone truly swank would know should have been brown. A beaten old fedora dangled from his fingertips and rapped rhythmically against the door frame — his version of tapping his foot in anger.

Yeah, I'd sworn men off, but that didn't mean I couldn't tease the hell out of him. "Get in here and get cozy, Big Boy. I got the feedbag and you look like you need to graze."

"There you go, Tanner, talkin' like Bugsy Malone. Why can't you talk like a regular dame?"

"I *ain't* so cute when I let on that I'm normal."

"What, you think gangster slang coming out of those lips is cute?"

I showed him my best side and a coy smile. "Down right adorable, and you know it."

Two things will someday ruin me: people desperate for help who can't pay my fees and pretty men. And I confess; were it not for the fact that I keep him at an arm's length, and we argue all the time, and we nearly come to blows every time we meet, I might fall for that world-weary face Hayes has.

No, no, no. No more men who want dinner on the stove and a baby in the oven.

Ah, nerts, all I needed now is for my new client to walk in and we'll have ourselves a real wing-ding.

Marley will have to order take-out after all and there's nothing left in petty cash. Goose-egg. Maybe I can get G-Man to expense it?

Outside my window, people were chatting loudly and heading onward to their next stop, energized or disgusted by the parade of uniformed thugs, simultaneously waving American and Nazi flags. For now, with none of those jackboots coming after Crazy Guy, I was free and clear of them. Out of sight is out of mind, right? The last thing I ever want, or need, is to have contact with that group of hypocrites.

Chapter Three

Whaddaya know – "X" really does mark the spot.

-Lou Tanner, P.I., 1935

"So, there he was, lying on the couch, babbling away," I took a long drag on my cigarette, "and we were trying to decide if he was going to suddenly hop up and say 'surprise, gotcha,' or drop dead at our feet."

Hayes bent over Crazy Guy, twisted his nose up, then stood back. "Drop dead from what, blood loss?"

"Yeah, you're not seeing half of it. Marley cleaned him up. Even little head wounds bleed in buckets. 'Little' doesn't mean it isn't a bad injury. Don't worry. We checked him over to see if there was anything else."

Marley ambled up. "No doubt about it, he is not at home upstairs." She spun a circle with her index finger next to her temple. "You sure this is the man you are looking for?"

"He fits the description," Hayes replied, pushing his hat far back on his head and scratching a bit at his hairline. "Fits it to a 'T'. I'll tell you, if he wasn't so nutty, I'd mistake him for one of those PSSR kooks."

"The what? Who?"

"*People's Society for Social Relief.* Aren't you paying attention out there? A bunch of socialists standing up for folks who think they aren't getting a fair shake at business, jobs, that sort of thing, because they aren't ..." He stopped, recognized his all-female audience giving him "the stink-eye" and changed his tactic.

Crazy Guy's peeps stayed shut while his chest struggled up

and down. Sort of reminded me of a puppy in the middle of a bad dream.

"Lou, you shouldn't be in the middle of this." He was sounding all sweet and caring. "But, why am I not surprised you are?" Hayes growled, planting his hands on his hips. So much for sweet and caring.

Not what I call tactful, that green eyed G-man, but he had the good sense to know when to shut up. Not now, but most of the time.

"Come on, Green Eyes," I enjoyed watching Hayes wince at the nickname, "We couldn't shove him out into the hallway. He's injured. He believes he's in danger. We're good eggs. What else were we supposed to do? Besides, he'd stink up the building and the landlady is picky about that sort of thing."

"Danger, huh? Any chance you still have that Lightning Gun? You know, the one you kept even though I told you not to? The one you were supposed to turn over to me?"

I couldn't help grinning like an inebriated goof. That "Lightning Gun" was handy a couple cases ago. It was one fine heater that lives up to its name. "Don't worry your pretty silvering head. You'll go all white, or worse, all bald. You don't have the right skull shape for bald. You really need …" I started holding my fingers up as if framing a motion picture shot of his scowling face.

"Lou," he growled, "I swear to God."

"Don't get all in a lather. I've got it hidden, in case things get messy."

"You have no idea how big this mess is."

"So explain it to us. We're not a pair of dumb broads. We've already figured out you called us about Augustin Gruber because you have somebody tailing him or spying on us. Your man told you some lug came into this building. You put two-'n-two together and came up with me as his possible destination. That, or you took a chance I might see this poor schmoe and would take pity on him —"

Some punk outside laid on his car horn. The effect was jarring. I'd somehow forgotten there was a city outside for a moment.

"Ah, forget it," I snarled, my previous train of thought racing out of the station without me.

"That's exactly what I want you to do, 'forget it,' but I know better."

Ignoring the G-man, I focused on my sort-of client. None of us could tell if he was down for the count or what, so I gave it a go. "Sir?" I said in my sweetest voice to him. "We'd like to see how you're doing — if you're okay or if you need a doctor. We're only trying to help."

Cautiously, since I know better than to poke at a sleeping tiger, I set my hand on his upper arm. Safe territory. "Just checking on you, nothing more."

At first, he didn't react to me. But then his bean started working and he nodded slightly in agreement. At last! Some sort of response. Maybe it wasn't in agreement, I didn't know, but I wasn't going to take it any other way.

Neither was Marley. She got to work on the cut across his scalp, checking it a second time to see if there was more to it than a simple laceration. Damn, she'd make a good nurse. "It's starting to swell," she whispered.

She was right. The swelling needed to be reduced, but there was no ice box in the building we could pilfer from. I'd have to send Marley down to the drug store — I doubt Green Eyes would go. Then I got a gander at Crazy's arms: there was a whole novel to be read on them. More lacerations. Numerous fresh scrapes and abraded skin. An old bullet scar near the elbow. A few age spots. A bit of a farmer's tan. And needle marks.

Lots of needle marks. Had he done that to himself or were those from hospital stays? Could be both. Could be neither.

The rest of him looked pretty worn out too. His hair was cropped short, and he hadn't shaved today. The last time he shaved, he might not have done it himself. Too many nicks and cuts. The sort of damage you might expect if a barber had to fight his client. Crazy's eyes were a strange but attractive shade of nothing, as if the blue had been fading away with his sanity.

"He's been in a hospital, hasn't he," I whispered to Green Eyes.

"Don't do more than you need to get him moving," he said

without looking at me.

Crazy started to stir. I got to explaining to him that he needed professional medical help, and that being in my office was no bother at all, he could stay put if he wished, said as sweetly and calmly as I could.

Crazy shook his head. "Tell no one I'm here. Please."

"Sir, you need stitches in some of these cuts. We can't do that here. This is just an office. You don't have to tell anyone how you got them —"

"Tin Men!"

Green Eyes stiffened up like Karloff's mummy. His big hand reached out to clamp down on Crazy's mouth, but our patient was out cold again.

"There are no Tin Men." Hayes announced for Marley and me to hear, and not to argue with.

"I gather he saw them."

"Where? Did he tell you?"

"No. He hasn't said."

"Fine. So here's your story: if, and I mean only 'if,' you get pinned down about … the You-Know-What —"

Marley snarled a bit, "Oh for God's sake, we're not dogs or kids where you spell stuff or pretend not to use the real word — in case we might understand. Just say it. Tin. Men."

Green Eyes looked like he was going to birth kittens on the spot. The glare he roasted Marley with should have turned her to a pile of ash. "The Undisclosed, Unmentionable Topic."

"Gee, Mister, do ya' feel better now?" she snapped back.

Ah sarcasm, an intellect's prerogative and one powerful weapon in times of stress.

"You two have heard it from every crazy, former Doughboy up and down Market Street. Some nonsense about bad mechanicals being made by Gerrys during the War. You got that?" He turned to me. "Lou?"

"Oh, one of those tales of the giant soldier robots that blend naturally into the cacophony of the San Francisco skyline, along with every kind of airship, zeppelin, and blimp. Oh, and the Floaters they're using to lift the cables on the bridges. No one would ever notice giant —"

"Damn it Lou."

"You love me, don't you?"

And for half a second, I swear Hayes looked like that proverbial kid caught with his hand in a candy jar. His lips moved. Something sounding a bit like a stuttering denial tried to slip out. But the G-man got his senses back fast, screwed up his brows, and muttered something Mrs. Tanner told me never to repeat, because I'm a lady.

Crazy Guy cleared his throat. He was shaking and licking his lips — a lot. "But I saw them. I did. They were there."

I looked to Marley, who could only shrug and get back to putting pressure on Augustin Gruber's scalp. Crazy Guy mumbled and fussed.

"Hello. I'm Lou. Tell me, where did you see them?" I held out a warning finger to G-Man Hayes making him wait for the answer.

"Mustn't say. For your sake."

A rush of annoyed heat did a marathon up my insides, and it took me a second to remember this guy was not well. He didn't know what he was saying. He wasn't trying to be crazy. He just was.

I had to give a reason to go along with some gentle persuasion. "Look, sir. The Treaty of '29 doesn't allow anyone to weaponize robots or automatons. 'Bots and 'Tons don't get guns. Now, are you sure you saw what —"

"The Pointe …"

Deep breath, soothing voice. Turn on my best Myrna Loy — since I happen to look like the actress. "Sure, the militia gets to use mechanicals for menial labor, but never as soldiers, sailors, or marines, certainly nothing that shoots or kills. Those are the rules. It's the law. And if somebody nearby was making the … um .. Tin Men? Everyone in San Francisco would know. Mr. Hayes here would know. They couldn't hide that sort of thing." Okay, so, I was making that last part up, for Crazy Guy's benefit. Hell, they could be building a fleet of giant dirigibles out at the Pointe or on the Island, and none of us would have a clue. Not even Hayes.

Crazy Guy's body deflated. I couldn't tell if that was from his acceptance of my explanation, or more likely from exhaustion overwhelming him.

"You don't believe me?"

"I'm a detective, sir. I'm a big believer in facts and evidence. You do understand that I'm a detective? You came to my office."

Nodding, he repeated what's painted on my door, "Tanner Private Investigations."

"And you know that 'Tanner" is a woman? Me. I'm Lou Tanner." Let's see how far gone he is from reality.

"Yes." He sort-of allowed a little laugh to creep in. "I think it's obvious you're a gal." Humor is good for the health, they say. Strange, though, Crazy Guy wasn't sounding quite so crazy at the moment.

"Good. Now, let's start with some basic information about you. We'll keep it to ourselves for the moment, if that's okay with you? Just the basics. You know — your name and what it is you need me to do for you?"

He was thinking, for once, about what to say, and since you could practically see the proverbial gears turning in his head, I could tell he wasn't sure what would come out of his mouth next.

Outside the office, the world's slowest elevator clanged into position on the third floor and the doors were pried open. A distinct crash I associate with almost getting killed a few months back. People are surprised at how much upper body strength that gate requires. The lack of grunting or cursing led me believe it was one of my building neighbors who had long since figured out how to make that thing work right. I figured I could ignore it.

I refocused on the man on the couch.

Hayes sat down next to him. "You've served, haven't you?"

"Yes. Yes, in Flanders."

That answered a whole bunch of questions.

"Good. Now, sir, what shall I —"

I cleared my throat. "What should *we* call you?"

Crazy Guy clammed up, his face squishing into that of a toddler who wasn't going to eat his vegetables.

NO REQUIEM FOR THE TIN MAN

Damn it. I couldn't tell who or what I was dealing with from moment to moment. Marley was biting her lip and getting lipstick on her teeth while Green Eyes was pulling on the brim of his fedora.

"Can we call you Gus or Augustin? Gus seems kinda nice."

This was going to be harder than I thought. I needed to stop playing gumheel in favor of playing ambulance corpsman right now. It would do him a lot more service.

Marley hustled out to the hallway water fountain, to refresh the washcloth she was using. Maybe we should put on the tea kettle and use boiled water? I wasn't a good corpsman and this guy needed to be seen by professionals.

I was thinking of what it was going to take to convince him to let us take him to the hospital, when two 'Bots in white paint and white fabric covers arrived, gurney at the ready, led by a broad with a dead wolf pack slung over her shoulder.

"Get your hands off him," she commanded, "Did you hear me?"

CHAPTER FOUR

Why do people think a gat in the hand means a tiger by the tail? Whatever you do, don't pull anything unless you're ready to get bit.

-Lou Tanner, P.I., 1935

Before I could accuse her of poor decorum, the broad walked in — no knocking — marched into my office as if she could buy it and everything in it out from under me. From the look of her, she could. She sized me up with extreme dissatisfaction, the office with absolute distaste, and then reacted to Crazy Guy as if he were an infant she'd lost track of at the circus.

He crawled slightly behind me as she approached.

The broad had a petting zoo taxidermied and wrapped around the upper half of her body. Rail thin body with no hips, which made the blue wool suit hang off her in that sickly-fashionable way that is so very popular this year. I blame Greta Garbo. The woman's stockings were silk and finely made. She had dark blonde hair — shiny and pinned into an up-do of tight perfection, with sharp Marcell waves clutching each side of her head. A little hat sat on top of her locks, offering a narrow shadow across her almost white-blue-eyes. Dark blue gloves covered her hands. She was a fashion plate come alive.

She turned on her heel, leaned out my door, and called into the hallway, "Frederick, he is in here." No expression of urgency found its way into her voice. "He has managed to make a mess again. Bring the gurney, I do not think he can walk." Upper class. Midwest. She didn't have that put-on Mid-Atlantic accent designed for people to use to differentiate themselves from the common man. Chicago very likely. Not a strong accent, but the lack of twangs and drawls identified it. A clipped and formal pattern of speech. More was coming if she ever takes notice of me again. From this point on, I was nothing beyond the furniture.

What the hell, I could go along with the snobbery for now. Might prove amusing. I leaned back and took a long, slow drag on my cigarette, noting all the comings and goings. Green Eyes sat on the opposite end of the couch with his arms folded tightly across his chest.

Frederick came in, sliding gracefully around the white-clad 'Bots and gurney. He personified immaculate. His suit was worth a whole lot of coin and his hands hadn't seen anything vaguely approaching labor, beyond improvement of his tennis swing. His hair was more blond than brown, a dishwater color streaked from the sun, and his eyebrows almost disappeared into his forehead since they were so pale. His eyes were that same watercolor blue that faded into the whites.

Well, it was my office and, in theory, I was in charge here. I pushed forward from my spot only to be brushed off by both the Petting Zoo Lady and her relative. Was Frederick her brother? Same jaw and nose.

Crazy Guy grabbed at my legs as Marley returned with water and a rinsed washcloth. Petting Zoo Lady started to reach for him, but my gal Marley stepped in the way, giving her the darkest glare.

Petting Zoo Lady withdrew her hand as if the water might burn her. "Yes, you can go ahead and clean him up a bit." Her voice was precise. Deliberate. Cold, with a chill to rival a breeze through a mortuary.

"Oh good," Marley growled, "I was waiting for permission to assist a wounded man in urgent need." Yeah, Marley figured they weren't future customers, so she let that sentence snap out like a whip.

"*Client*," I corrected Marley. "Wounded *client* in urgent need."

Petting Zoo Lady sniffed loudly, and Frederick whatever-his-last-name-was looked at me incredulously. "Client?"

"He asked me to take a case for him."

"And what case was that? Can't you see he's sick and

incapable of hiring you?" He nodded at the sign on my window and added, "Perhaps I'll discuss this with Mr. Tanner." He looked at Agent Hayes.

Hayes waved him along. "Not me, brother."

I took a quicker drag on my snipe. "*Miss* Tanner. That's me. And what do you wish to discuss?"

Little Miss Petting Zoo glared at me, and Frederick's eyes grew saucer round and big. I don't know why I enjoyed shocking them, but I did. I could be cold and mean when I wanted to.

"You don't even know who he is," Frederick said after a pause.

"No, I don't. I was just learning all that when we were interrupted. Perhaps if I know who you two are, we can get to the bottom of things much faster."

"We are hardly of any interest to you? And certainly none of your business." She lifted her hand delicately and provided only enough energy to motion with her fingers to the awaiting 'Bots. Their big, round eyes lit up, their white painted bodies straightened, and each clasped the sides of the gurney.

Surprise, surprise. They didn't know not to get uppity with me — gets me all ruffled and such. "Hold up! He came to me, knowing my name, aware of my profession, and asked for help. This is my office, which makes everything and everyone in here my business." My hands were planted so hard on my hips that I thought they might be stuck there permanently. "If you don't like those rules, you can leave my office. But no one comes in here to tell me what to do. And no one leaves unless they choose to leave," I looked down at Crazy Guy, then up at the overdressed pair, "or are asked to."

The 'Bots stalled in unison, heads swiveling to await further orders from Petting Zoo Lady.

Frederick's face showed a brief struggle and his eyes closed. Bet he was counting to ten — I do that all the time.

"This is my brother Augustin," he said at last, having reached a count of twenty. "Allow me to introduce myself." He pulled out a sleek card and offered it to me like a piece of prime cut beef being offered to a raccoon. Petting Zoo Lady rolled her eyes so hard she was possibly looking at yesterday's social calendar.

Nice business card. Linen. Simple. Elegant. "I'm Doctor Frederick Gruber. And this is my ... our ... sister Mrs. Elsa Gruber Weiss."

Frederick? Elsa? Gruber was a rather Germanic surname. Spidery crawlies moved up and down my skin while I forced a professional smile.

Sure, plenty of American families originally came from Germany and Prussia. I'm being paranoid after this morning. Worse: I was being prejudiced. Yet, there I stood, with a man from the War Department, who was trying to hide some military secret from being discovered — and was being annoyingly silent at the moment — while a shell-shocked veteran of the Great War against Germany was trying to use me as a human shield. Add to that, the American Bund, pro-Germany parade that thundered past my window — in broad daylight — for God and everyone to see.

Just because you're paranoid doesn't mean someone isn't out to get you.

But who was I to say who was a good Yankee and who wasn't?

Glancing over my shoulder, I hoped the raised eyebrow I showed Green Eyes said, *you can step in anytime now.*

Frederick was about to respond, when I held up my hand. Turning to Marley, I said, "I think Mr. Gruber —"

"Gus," Crazy Guy offered looking back and forth between me and Marley, and pretty much surprising everyone in the room.

"Gus," I said calmly — kinda' relived too. He looked like a Ben. "I think Gus would like to rest in the big chair in my office. Perhaps these medical assistants could help? Miss O'Brien can look at his wound and he can be comfortable. It's nice and quiet in there. If she deems his wound in need of professional —"

Frederick interrupted me. "We will take him to a hospital!"

One doesn't have to be a professional gumshoe to notice important details, such as the fact that Dr. Frederick Gruber hadn't done anything vaguely close to offering his brother medical assistance. Maybe he was worried about his suit getting lint on it. Or blood?

"Thank you but no. If Miss O'Brien believes my client's wound is serious, I will call for an ambulance with a corpsman." Okay, I was getting uppity, what many men would call 'bitchy,' but if Gus Gruber was that injured, there was no time for nice little drives over to some family doctor who might be out at a dinner show. Maybe I was filling in the blanks unfairly, but I'm a *sap* — a professional, Grade-A, committed *sap* — and there were things that decent people should do for one another.

Elsa Gruber Weiss wasn't buying it. "Oh, Darling, you look terrible," she cooed, appealing to Gus. "Whatever has been done to you?" Her voice was slick as oil on water, waiting for someone to toss a match. As she got closer to us, I could gauge that she was my height and wow, smelled of heavily spiced perfume plus burnt tobacco.

Green Eyes — useless Green Eyes — stuck his hands in his pockets, nodded politely in an almost ceremonial way, and backed out of her path. *What the hell?*

She started to give that *it's-all-your-fault look*, but I cut her off. "No, Mrs. Weiss, we didn't do this to him, if that's what you're implying. He arrived like this. Shall we start over, for Gus's sake? I'm Lou Tanner, Licensed Private Investigator." I offered my hand with no expectation she'd take it. She sort of did, in a limp acknowledgement of my existence. "Why don't we let Miss O'Brien and your med 'Bots help him?" Go ahead, honey, say something that will give me more insight. "Should I also have her call the Police," I baited.

"The Police? Oh heavens, no. Frederick, tell her no. The Police will only make this a public spectacle. My poor brother is not well, so we often have to —"

Her brother Frederick cut her off. Seems he likes interrupting people. "Really, Miss … uh … Miss …"

"Tanner."

"Miss Turner."

"Tanner"

"This is all charming, and I am sure you are good at communing with people of the criminal classes, socialists, the downtrodden, but the best thing for my brother is to get him home."

"So, you're not taking him to a hospital after all."

"Not one that *you* know. Gus requires very specific care. And Elsa wisely had assistants come with us."

Elsa gestured to the 'Bots and yawned a little, as if saying she'd done this all before.

Gus whispered, "Miss Tanner, I don't know her." He was pointing at the woman claiming to be his sister.

My heart sank a little. That right there was a common reaction for the shell-shocked — not knowing where they were or who anyone was. Right now, was I the only person he recognized?

"Dr. Gruber. Where did he serve?" I asked.

"Excuse me?"

"It's clear that he is suffering from long term shell-shock. I'm curious if he was in France or Belgium during the war?"

Elsa pushed past me. "Belgium. He speaks High German, thus they thought he'd be useful there. You are a psychiatrist too?" Her voice could have drowned in the sarcasm, and I would have happily held its miserable head under. "I thought your sign said you were a private detective." Add overt distain to that sarcasm.

"The two professions go hand in hand, and I've seen his condition before."

"Oh? Were you a *nurse* during the conflict?"

"Weren't you?"

I'm too young to have been a nurse or anything else back then, but I didn't like the way she said "nurse," and I didn't like the idea she implied she was too good for the job.

All I got for my retort was a "harrumph" from her and visual dismissal. She signaled for the 'Bots to move in.

"Not yet, boys. You know the rules," I said, holding up my hand and stepping between Gus and the mechanicals, "I told you that this is a private business, and I don't recall inviting anyone else to come in. And this man is my client." G-Man Hayes shuffled his weight, likely preparing to respond. *About time.*

The sister burst into laughter, neither merry nor cheerful. "Client? That again. How typical. Common people will take money from anyone. He is not capable of hiring you, Miss." She hissed that last word like a rattle snake. "He's fully incapacitated. Legally judged incompetent. He is not allowed to make a contract with you or anyone." She waltzed up to about six inches from my nose. I looked her over and decided I had nothing to fear from her or the dead animals she was wearing. "I will call the Police *on you* if you try to stop me from taking my brother home."

"Now you want the Police? Good. We're in agreement. Would you like to use my phone?"

Elsa's realization that she'd contradicted herself played out on every inch of that made-up face of hers.

"She lies!" Gus shouted at me before cowering behind Marley.

"Oh, Darling Augustin. I am here now. You know me. Now Darling, I am taking you home —"

"No! Miss Tanner, I don't know her. I swear I don't."

I was about to put my full weight into escorting Mrs. Weiss's tight ass out, when Gus descended into a fit of madness. A full fit. His arms waved wildly as he cried out about the enemy, trenches, and poison gas.

His brother, Marley, and I dropped down on top of him, manhandling him as he began his seizure. I reached up onto Marley's desk and grabbed up her narrow sign plate. It was big enough to put into his mouth so that he wouldn't bite his tongue and offered something to dig his teeth into.

The 'Bots in white didn't move. Green Eyes moved in, but otherwise didn't lend any assistance. Fine lot of help they were.

Gus ruined Marley's name plate in seconds, but it did the trick. Frederick held his shoulders square and knelt on one arm.

I held down his hips.

Marley had his head supported in her lap.

Between all of us, we knew what to do or pretended with some success. Frederick had certainly done this before. But then, he'd said he was a doctor. At least he started acting like a doctor.

Once Gus calmed down, his sister looked at me, perhaps a little more politely than before. "See what I mean?"

She was right. Snob or not, she was right. Gus was unwell and we weren't prepared to assist him the way he needed.

NO REQUIEM FOR THE TIN MAN

Still, this was my office. I waved the 'Bots over. I instructed them in what they should do, 'cause I was damn sure they wouldn't work it out on their own. And I talked to Gus, explaining how he would be with family.

This time, he calmed down, asking about how things were at home, as though he hadn't been there in ages. He started chatting with Petting Zoo Lady like they were both twelve.

My heart, that goddamn traitor, broke into pieces. I held onto his hand a bit too long. It wasn't fair. So many men went willing to fight a war they believed in, only to have this happen.

God, I'm such a sap.

As much as I felt resentment for the Gruber family invasion, I had to give the 'Bots credit for doing their job well — once they were doing something. They didn't handle him roughly, one spoke softly reminding Gus, in its recorded voice, that he was in San Francisco, and overall acted like human beings dealing with another human. Someone out there did a good job with their response programming.

I was feeling that Gus might be fine when the sister spoke up. "Thank you very much, Miss *Turner*. He is not your problem anymore." She stopped to adjust the hat on her head.

Frederick wasn't nearly so inclined to escape quickly. "I see that you have dealt with his type before?"

"Not too often, thankfully."

"Well," he looked awkward. "I must thank you for the help."

I was happy enough with those thanks, although I truly wanted to know more about him.

Any goodwill built between us vanished when he pulled out a checkbook. "I don't know what the usual cost is —"

I tried not to sound insulted. Hell, it was just like he was leaving some cash on my dresser after a wild evening. "I'd rather know more about your brother."

"Whatever for?"

"Why not? And who knows — he might come back."

He shook his head vigorously. "I'll see to it he doesn't. We'll take further steps to make sure he isn't a nuisance again."

"Look, Doctor, he didn't decide one day to embarrass your

family. He got that way from being in a terrible war. From seeing things no one should ever see."

"I know that!" He calmed down quickly. "I was too young then. I never went to the Front. He was … is … my older brother, though it's hard to tell most days. We do everything for Augustin. Everything." He looked at his checkbook perhaps realizing he'd made a mistake though I doubt it. Putting it away, he still wouldn't offer me his hand. "Miss Turner."

"Tanner." I gestured toward the lettering on the door.

"Ah, yes, of course."

He stared at me for a moment.

Then he inspected my face and the name on my door.

Finally, he asked, "Any relation to Milton Tanner, of the American Intercontinental Railroad? I thought the company was in the most desperate times from gross mismanagement?"

I dodged the question with experienced, tactical precision. "Thank you for the explanation, Doctor Gruber. I wish the best for you and your family."

Truth was, I should have held out for the needed payment for babysitting. Damn my pride.

Marley watched over Gus as he was wheeled to the world's slowest elevator and taken downstairs. Hayes waited in my doorway. I chose to stand in the middle of the hallway like some dope.

And my mind temporarily turned to the topic of the client I was expecting but never showed. Did they fail to arrive at the expected time or were they scared off by all the excitement? I would call, tomorrow afternoon. Reestablish the appointment. Damn it, I needed that case.

Then I turned on Green Eyes Hayes so hard he must have wondered if the 1906 'quake was repeating itself. "You weren't helpful!"

"I was observing."

"Is that what you call it?"

"Yeah, that's 'what I call it.' Wanna' know what I saw that you didn't?" He was smug in a way I didn't know he could be. It was sort of sexy, were it not so damn maddening.

NO REQUIEM FOR THE TIN MAN

"Yes."

"Good. See you at Stan's. Tonight. Eleven."

"What?"

"I need to check on something first. Just be there Lou," he added, waving as he walked away toward the stairs.

"Hayes! Christopher Hayes, you get your iron rodded, tight ass back here —"

My landlady stepped out into the hallway at that moment. "Language, Miss Tanner."

"My apologies."

"Rent is due on Friday."

I shut my yap, fast.

Chapter Five

Keep your friends close, your enemies closer, and your bartender paid in full

-Lou Tanner, P.I., 1935

Eleven twenty-nine at night. Fog wrapped around Twin Peaks and Mt. Sutro like the wet blanket I knew Hayes would throw on the remaining thirty-one minutes of the day. I could bank on it. Damn shame. Maybe I like arguing with the man, but I also would like, just once, to sit and yak with him — civilly.

No. Not civilly. Dizzily. Over the Moon. Big-eyed and bright. That worn face of his needed more than a sucker-punch delivered smooch, it needed a light touch that tried to smooth the frown lines away. Lips needed to sweep across those eyelids before sending him off to a well-deserved night's sleep. My lips.

I wasn't drunk. I'd say, "tipsy" is the better word for it.

If I was imagining Hayes in my embrace, booze had to be involved.

Marley knocked me out of my daydreaming when she propped her head up on one hand and poured a gimlet into her mouth with the other, with as little effort as possible. I couldn't blame her. We were both ready to push up some daisies after the events of the day and waiting for Hayes for over two hours. He's always late. *Men.*

Stan's Bar, my favorite gin mill, sitting next to the Castro Street Transit Tunnel, was uncharacteristically empty. Maybe that was a sign of the times. I kept hearing on the radio that we're doing better as a nation, but … my pocketbook disagrees.

Marley fell asleep with her head on the table and her booze

half guzzled. I might be busted but there was no way I'd send her home in a soulless, unmanned Nightcrawler. I don't dislike mechanicals, I'm indifferent on the subject, but I also take them for who they are. I've got nothing against the 'Crawler system or other 'bot-run services, I decided this needs the human touch. Marley needed protection from slipping on the sidewalk, among other things.

The pair of us hustled our way to the curb while Stan, bless his human beating heart, made a call from the business card I always carry. At least three of the little bullet-shaped 'Crawler vehicles sped by, right in front of the joint. Figures. Anytime you want one, you can't find one.

Skeeter, old pally and one of only five real live cabbies in San Francisco, was there in minutes. Amazing — I swear there are only five taxis and none *of them* are ever there when you need one, except our man Skeeter. If Skeeter ever retires, I'll have to get a car. As was his way, he refused to be paid. I shoved a couple of dollars into his pocket anyway once his hands were full with my sleepy, sloshy secretary.

Marley, strawberry-blond curls still bouncing as she stumbled along with help to the taxi, was on her way home, safely. Me, I kept waiting. I set my timer: a quarter-full pack of Lucky Strikes. The radio belted out a string of notable tunes, broken apart by annoying advertisements for aspirin powders and socks.

Three snipes later, I couldn't see the ashtray bottom anymore.

Green Eyes was a no show for the meet-up he called for. With aching feet and a throbbing skull, all I could think about on the way home was how I would bump him off. I was too tired to get creative, and too sober not to notice. And people wonder why I've sworn off men. Gave them all up for Lent.

The trolly ride itself was as familiar to me as the *Pemberton Correspondence School Manual.* The line runs down 17th Street to Stanyan, connects onto the main Parnassus line, then onto Judah. Easy-peasy. Gotta' love the Sunset District, it looks like the outer urban regions of any city. Neat, planned, single-family bungalows dotting the hillside and the long stretches of avenue from the Park to the Beach. Easy to patrol and maintain order. That was a selling point back in the day. Safety. Plus a few apartment buildings and a dollop or two of businesses to support all those people.

My trolly jerked to a halt. Shaken from my thoughts, I realized I was almost home. My street had a 'Crawler line which would have saved my barking feet from climbing the hill, but the damn trolly doesn't get to use that line, so it sat there on Judah.

The door didn't open.

I leaned forward to the brass receiver. "Please open up. You've stopped at the correct —"

An ear-piercing squeal burst out of the speakers, the folding door whipped open, and I fled from the unit as fast as I could. The trolly appeared stuck on the Judah track but had left me at the bottom of Tenth. I still had enough in me to make it a hundred feet up to the entry to my apartment building. It was the inside flight of stairs that made my knees crack in fear.

Just as I was calling to mind a particularly painful collision between my shoulder and the bullet-laden spray of a Chicago Typewriter, the ground heaved.

Now what?

Too much booze? Another quake?

I lost my balance, falling onto my hands and knees, my hat flipping over my face and dropping in front of me.

That little move highly suggested the last swallow of hooch.

I hoped no one was watching.

Frightened shouts went up from the neighborhood as dozens of lights turned on.

The Nightcrawler and Trolly systems went into emergency shut-down. A little, white bullet-car arriving on tenth went dark and the sizzle most folks don't even notice coming from the 'Crawler tracks stopped.

I righted myself, darted across the street, and up the hill to my front door. I've got a decent view east towards the big park from that vantage. I expected smoke or something. Some indicator that we'd had a substantial earthquake or another bombing.

Nothing. Goose-egg.

Nada. Nix.

NO REQUIEM FOR THE TIN MAN

Industrial area lights were off. No 'Crawler lights were on anywhere. I was betting that people driving cars had pulled over. The City wasn't giving off its comfortable glow at all.

The ground jerked again, then again, in time with an echoing thump.

People fled their homes, heading into the streets.

Call me a paranoiac, but I couldn't help but look to the Pointe. All their blazing lights simply went out. But not before what looked like the flash of lightning. Or rather … explosions.

The pitch dark took over.

Floating above the rooflines — far above the highest buildings at the Pointe — three pairs of glowing orbs. Rocking. Swaying. Glaring?

One pair vanished. The second pair jerked violently, then disappeared. The ground shook once more, a bright ground-based flash, followed by the city-wide *whump!* Neighbors were running, shouting, pointing. My legs wouldn't move even if they could.

The third pair blinked. Blinked! Then vanished.

I swear on my mother's grave: the glowing orbs blinked. There isn't enough booze to fake what we'd all seen.

What the holy hell?

CHAPTER SIX

The smart lady detective has four outfits to her name — if she can afford them. More if she can..
You need a pretty dress that lets you extend your hand for assistance or your legs for attention. A business suit in something memorable but demure. A trouser set for times when you might need ease of movement. And a black wool suit — for funerals.

-Lou Tanner, P.I., 1935, Letter to Female Pemberton Graduates.

In the morning, I murdered some innocent time at the Woolworths counter on Powell Street and ordered the cheapest Special on the menu. Coffee. Eggs. Toast.

Bad decision. I needed grease with my caffeine.

Not only couldn't I escape the chatter about the events of last night, not to mention all the crazy theories as to what it was, but everyone was inordinately loud about it. The blinking lights would turn out to be something easily explained in the bright sunlight of day. At Two A.M., everything is out of whack. I blame the late hour, not the weirdo lights. Those, I decided, were only some search lights bouncing off my sleep deprived brain cells. So, we had a quake and I was sleepy. That made me an unreliable witness — one whose testimony I'd never trust for one second.

I blame Green Eyes too. Why not? He wasn't here to defend himself. He was going to get a piece of my mind, once I squeezed the leftover bourbon and fog out of it. In fact, I'd decided he was reimbursing me for the hooch and Marley's cab. That was time on the clock he wasted. My time has value, even if he thinks it isn't important, since my time was a woman detective's time. I wasn't going to let him get off easy, Green Eyes or not.

There must have been about a minute-long stroll between each thought because my coffee arrived and I'd only worked out a measly two reasons why G-Man Hayes was off my Christmas Card List.

I sure can pick 'em, slogged from one temple to the other, using a machete to get through anything in between. *Men.*

I was seated about six feet away from the booth where I'd offered Marley a job only months ago. I swapped places so that I didn't have to stare at it and lit up a Lucky Strike.

I think I ate about half of my order before drifting off into nostalgia and forgetting my surroundings. Not smart. It was the middle of the morning, one that had started spectacularly much too early.

I had another decision to make. I'm getting good a bad choices these days, this should be a breeze, right?

Either I needed to take the job I had the deepest gut feeling was slathered in political hypocrisy the way my toast was dripping in a layer of melted shortening instead of butter, and I'd keep my place, my office, and Marley paid up, or I'll have to close my business and go home with my tail between my legs. Shouldn't that be an easy choice?

Resting my face on my hand, I managed not to stick my lit snipe into my eye, which on the whole would have felt better than the rest of me was feeling right now. I hate politics almost as much as I hate politicians.

Once I had the morning to shake out the drunken cobwebs and brighten up my cheeks, I'd be seeing things differently. I'd be much more confident and solid. Yeah, doubt and hangovers just love each other.

Uncle Joe was rolling in his grave. Laughing or admonishing me, it didn't matter which.

The job won.

Still hungover, I was about to finish my coffee and ask for the check when two cops ambled in. Dark blue uniforms, wide black belts, heavy-caliber heaters and thick nightsticks, polished shoes. Pretty standard these days.

Then again, maybe not everything was standard. Both of the boys had black armbands around their right biceps. Mourning. I think my stomach hit the checkered floor and I let my face sink further into my hand.

The two blue-suited vultures perched on seats at the counter and eyed their menus like a dead mouse on the side of the road. The younger of the two picked up the scent of death on me, glanced my way, and any bets placed on my leaving without an incident were lost. He nudged his partner and nodded his head my way.

Damn it. Well, I couldn't hide forever even though I sure as hell felt like disappearing.

The waitress dropped off my bill and I took it to the cash register, unfortunately right next to the boys in blue.

"Ain't you that little girl P.I.?"

"Sounds like me, but then, I've been mistaken for Myrna Loy, so you never know. I guess I got one of those faces." Just in case, I kept my "one of those faces" turned away from them while cashing out.

The senior cop stopped smiling. "Heard you were a wise ass."

"Hey," the waitress jumped in, "you keep the language in line. This is a respectful business."

"Beat it, Mabel. This ain't your business."

"It is if it's in my coffee shop."

The cook was looking out over the service counter to see what was going on and Mabel put her hands on her hips.

"Its fine, Mabel," I said before things got hot enough to bring out the brute-sized cook from the back. "I'm heading out. Thanks for breakfast," I added, handing her cash and a tip I couldn't afford to give her but couldn't afford *not* to give.

"Are you," the younger cop asked. "Are you a wise ass?"

"Sure. Definitely a wise ass. But you should see the rest of me in action — I'm told my legs are positively brilliant, though my hair has a mind of its own."

"You're the one Milt Somerset died because of."

No Requiem for the Tin Man

I stopped mid stride. Milton Somerset's face as he died? I see it in my sleep. You never forget the first life you take, even if there's some question if it is your first. Well, I was hoping to avoid this conversation. I shudda' known better. "Somerset turned out not to be up to the standards of the San Francisco Police Department. He killed a young woman in cold blood so he could frame a man he couldn't catch legally. He was on the take. He was in deep. That's not how things are done by good cops like you guys."

The older guy slapped his arm band. "Don't care — he was a cop. We handle our own."

Keep calm, Lulu.

"I wish there had been enough time to hand him over to you. Things ... got out of hand before we could do that."

Mable stepped back as the younger cop slipped off his stool and put his hand on his rod ... that is, his gun. He got close and nasty. "We have codes to live by. Don't matter — he was a cop, and nobody touches a cop." He was edging for a specific answer.

The left-over booze replied for me. "Easy, Junior. I respect police authority but not to the point where I lay down and die 'cause you're not available or haven't decided whose side you're on. There were a lot of witnesses if you want some clarity on how it went down."

"You sound like one of those commie-socialist, bomb-planting PSSR anarchists. Are you?"

"A communist? A bomber? No. A red blooded American? You bet. Not that it's any of your business."

"Rumor says the Fed didn't kill Somerset for you. Maybe you did it yourself."

What could I say — "you're right — I did it?" I was sure I did. I took that man's life. I felled him and he would not get back up. Any bookie would know not to take bests that Junior had ever shot someone . And if I have any hope for humanity, I'll hope Junior never does.

That the Federal Agent, G-man Hayes, ordered me to say nothing on pain of arrest too? That three tiers of overpaid G-managers threatened to toss me in the clink if I breathed a word —

some top-secret nonsense involved with the whole mess? Yeah, I was a good, red-blooded American citizen. I promised I wouldn't tell, but I never liked that agreement.

Of course Junior was frothing-at-the-mouth anti-communist. His boss, Mayor Rossi was too. Not sure what communism, bombs, and anarchy had to do with the People's Society for Social Relief? A bunch of folks trying to get what everyone else seemed to be getting from this big ole world.

Junior was getting itchy.

Now what? If Junior pulls his peashooter on me, do I have to respond in kind? Christ, another cop death bloodying my hands. What about the folks in the room? Stray bullets are known to happen.

Nothing but silence floundered between us. Every face was staring and wondering if they could get under their tables in time. Mabel didn't have anything witty to say and neither did I.

The senior cop put his hand on the younger's arm, looking like honesty had slapped him in the face. "Relax, Jeffries. She's right. You don't have to like it, and we don't have to like her, but rumor says Somerset was crooked and got what was coming to him. Official word is that it was a Fed's doing, ain't that right, sweetheart?"

Me and Junior, we glared at each other. Could have fried eggs in the space between us.

My Derringer left a cool sensation on my fingers. I didn't plan to die today because some horse's ass wanted to prove he was a tough guy.

His fingers twitched at little above his grip. A shiny pin on his lapel — a pair of flags crossed — shot a reflection up into my face.

"Jeffries." Senior stood next to him. "Sit down. We don't shoot unarmed folks in a crowded place, you know that."

Did he? He looked to me like he was sizing up how many holes he could plug in me right quick.

I couldn't help myself. "Where do you shoot unarmed folks?"

"In the head," Junior answered. "Where else?"

Everyone was staring. The woman P.I. and someone threatening her in public. There was only one response for me.

I took my sweet time pulling a pack of Lucky Strikes out of

my satchel, stuck one in my mouth without offering Junior a thing, turned to go while leaving my back fully exposed — *go ahead, you goons, try me, shoot me in the back* — struck the match, lit my cigarette, shook the match out, dropped it in the tray, then looked back over my shoulder at them after a satisfying drag. "Guess that makes sense. You gotta' have a heart to know where it is on the human body if you plan to shoot anyone there. Might as well go for the easier target."

I left my back exposed to them and waited a second more, slipping the pack of snipes back into my bag. *Go ahead, Junior, do something — I'm not afraid.* When nothing happened, I strolled out as though I needed to go shopping for a new hat or something.

Dear God, what had I been thinking? *Hell yes, I'm afraid.* Uncle Joe? That's what he would have done. But then, he wouldn't have agreed to lie about *not* killing someone — certainly not a corrupt cop. He would have fessed up and said, "So what?" But Joe Parnaski was the insider I never would be. He'd been a copper. For Jefferies and Senior, Joe taking out Somerset would have equated to the matter being handled internally.

I was and always would be an outsider.

Although, after this morning, word might get around that a certain dame, with a P.I. license, might not be easily pushed around by cops … or anyone else.

A delivery 'Bot jingled by me, with a squeal coming from its motor box. I jumped a little and almost bit through my cigarette. Okay, so my tough act was more of a cover.

I drew long and hard on that snipe, noting a wee bit of a tremble in my fingers. Nothing I couldn't shake out of them. And if any alcohol lingered in my blood after last night, it was long gone now.

With any luck, I wouldn't be banned from the place. They made damn good coffee.

Heading across the cable car tracks, I sidled through the line of folks waiting to catch the trolly turning on the Powell Street turntable. Heading down Market a block or so, almost to 6th, when some lug slammed into me.

I spun around, gripping my cigarette like a knife, expecting

Junior had snuck up behind me.

But the mook who side-swiped me kept running. Running like his life depended on it.

The air ripped apart!

My hearing shut down. Heat blasted past me in a tidal wave of energy, drowning my senses as it picked me up and rolled me along the sidewalk. Vision came back to me in time to see the cable car trolly land upside down.

CHAPTER SEVEN

Take care of your health, in particular: your ears.
Bad hearing is intolerable.
Selective hearing is a necessity)

-Lou Tanner, P.I., 1935

"How are you not dead?" Marley groaned into the phone.

"Dumb luck. I was a block away." My right ear was still ringing. "Cops told me the bomb was meant to flip over the cable car, but there was some blow out. Yeah, 'some.' Plenty of people got knocked around. Twenty seven unconscious, everybody hurt. Four dead. Conductor on the turntable is alive, barely, but may never walk again."

"You ... talked to the cops? Honest to God, you spoke to actual policemen?"

"Relax, Irish. I talked to them about the bomb? I was a witness, remember? What a mess. I tried to help folks, as if I could do much. The most I could do was hold some hands or put pressure on bleeders."

"That's something, Slim. Are you okay?"

"Yeah, yeah, yeah. Wrecked a pair of my best trousers. I'm gonna go up to the office and change. I'm a sight."

"I'll come in."

"Whoa, slow down, Irish. You'll never get into downtown now. They've cordoned off the whole joint." Marley's such a mother sometimes. She worries too much. "I'm fine. Dumb luck. I maybe have a bruise or two. And things could and almost were worse. I did have a run-in with the blue-boys earlier." I shared my breakfast adventures with Senior and Junior. Before she could scold me like a five-year-old, I changed the topic fast. Marley knows when I'm doing that and has learned not to fight me on it.

"Any news about the noises from the Bay last night? Or are we still on conspiracies and Martians?" I settled back into the cramped telephone booth at the Five and Dime up Powell Street and tried to close the folding door against a brutally loud version of Dick Jurgens's *Lullaby of Broadway* and the unrelenting theories about who planted the bomb at the Powell Turntable.

"They're talking Martian invasion now? Swell!" Marley always sounded more lively on the phone.

"Along with the Germans, the Japanese, and the Bolsheviks. Same folks they're blaming for the bomb today and last week."

"In that case, I'm voting for Martians. We could use something normal around here for once." Marley attempted a giggle but failed. "Last night was likely some unsecured equipment that fell from the bridge construction balloons. I can always ask Sam. Maybe the Hunter's Pointe boys over-stacked something that toppled. Any of the above are in the right place to shake the ground and make a big bang."

"Ten to one, you're right."

"Are we looking into any of the bombings?"

"No!"

"But —"

"That's a case that has flatfeet trampling all over it. It's one thing to provide a witness statement in the middle of a crisis. If I stick my nose in there officially, it'll get bloodied. So, no way. They'll catch 'em." My shoulder hurt like hell. "Did you learn anything about our mysterious Mr. Gruber?"

Lullaby ended with a crescendo and a bit of welcome quiet.

"Not much, which told me a lot more than the facts."

"Go on."

Balancing the receiver on my shoulder and notebook on my knee, her plate scraped as she pushed it aside and settled in at her kitchen table. Her beau had arranged for a phone, in her rooms no less. I guess he likes getting ahold of her. "Augustin Alfred Gruber, according to my upstairs neighbor … a swing-shift nurse over at Laguna Honda Hospital … said he was a frequent drop in. Plenty of troubles. Doughboy with a broken brain. Big with conspiracy plans and sure everyone was out to get him. But anything more than that, she couldn't remember off hand. She promised to do a little snooping for me. Thinks it's real swell she's helping an honest-to-God private detective."

"And?"

"My friend Angie down at HQ said she couldn't find his records but the name rang a bell. She's real sure she's got some file or files on him, but when she looked, nada. Really cheesed her off about not being able to look him up. You know how she is — seriously nutty about being better organized than the Library of Congress. She said she'll give me a jingle when she finds where those records went." Marley cleared her throat. "It's not like Angie to misplace anything, so I'm bettin' someone took those records for a walk and didn't bring them home before eleven, if you take my meaning."

"Missing records … and she's sure she recognizes his name."

"Angie never forgets a name. So … following a reasonable line of logic, if Angie knows that Gus has files with the police and they're now missing, someone doesn't want the world knowing that he has a police record of some sort.

"And police files could be many things, none of which are benign. Arrests, complaints, tickets …" Tapping my stub of a pencil on the notebook was unnecessary but comforting. "I see what you mean about the lack of information." I slipped a Lucky between my lips. Oopsie, no match to light it.

The exhale on the other end of the line told me Marley lit up a cigarette, the same as me, only she was smart enough to have some fire with her. "You said you thought his sister sounded up-scale Chicago? I might know someone out there — from my typing school days. Maybe she can check if he's local and get the scoop on his early life."

"Good thinking. I'm gonna' head back to the office. Clean up and see what's what."

"I'll be in later, Slim. Don't argue. Just take it easy, eh?"

Walking out of the drug store, I kept clicking my ears, trying to clear the right one. It was starting to work. The grumbling increased in volume. As an ambulance rushed by, escorted by a police car with sirens wailing, my heart squeezed for anyone hurt far more than me. The grumbling behind me increased at the same time. Now they were saying it was the PSSR. The People's Society? Yeah, always blame the little guy who normally gets bullied. I didn't buy it. Still …

Things were different in my City by the Bay.

When one's office has been expertly searched, there are always little clues. An item that is not quite in the right place. A chair not where you left it. A visible rim of dust under an object. You can tell if you're smart. It's a game of excellence versus observation.

When one's office has been upended by a bumbling thug, you can tell that too. My office looked like a tornado had passed through it. This time it was overturned furniture, scattered files, and one pissed off feline cleaning blood off his paws. My heart almost stopped. Had someone hurt the cat?

From the look of satisfaction — and yes, cats do have expressions as I have learned — Not My Cat was pleased with himself and wasn't hurt. It was tempting to think he might have done all this destruction, and I wouldn't normally put it past him, but the pried-open drawer locks implied the use of thumbs. Not My Cat, agile as he is, hasn't got any thumbs.

Bloody but adorable paw prints trailed across my desk to end up where my furry squatter sat meticulously cleaning his toes.

"Spill it, cat. What were they looking for?" I pointed a finger at him.

A pair of yellow eyes shifted my way, but the witness failed to answer. Lick. Lick. Lick. "Fine lot of help you are."

Gotta admit, I wasn't peeved. Annoyed at the mess. Definitely cheesed that I had no idea what I had that was so damn valuable to warrant a search. But mostly I was worried that Marley might come in, hangover intact, see the chaos, and loose her nut.

Crime scene? Yup. That means I gotta' walk the scene — notebook in hand. Thanks to the nice floors, I could see some scuff marks that I knew weren't mine, Marley's, or any of my latest visitor's. Any blood there? Not that wasn't cleaned up recently. So Not My Cat didn't slice anything like an artery. Too bad. I sketched out the scene, new scuffs and all.

There was a pattern to how the paper was scattered. Haphazardly. The mook who tossed the joint didn't know how to look. Maybe he knew what he was looking for, but not how. Small drawers and spaces were left alone. Big areas were searched. Whatever it is, it's bigger than Marley's pencil drawer.

The locks in the reception room had been carefully broken open. Inside my office? Not so carefully. So he, she, or they, started out front, ran out of patience by the time they reached my office. The force used to toss things was stronger too. Frustration.

Another clue. Everything stopped by the radiator, partially hidden by the curtains. Ha! Not My Cat's favorite spot to snooze. He, she, or they, startled a cat, tried to pet or grab him, and Not My Cat told them "no" in his unique fashion.

Standing by the radiator, I couldn't see any bloody paw prints. Those started near my desk. He, she, or they, tried to grab the cat, paid the price, dropped the cat, and fled the scene. Hence the scuffle marks. Hence the cat prints scrambled on the floor at the bottom of my desk but casually strolling across it. The danger was gone when Not My Cat got on the desktop. I noted everything.

As if my mother was standing over me and I was in my old room back in New York, I started picking things up. And like those old times, I made note of what it was I was touching and where it was going. The new part of my process was wondering why my office was ransacked by any intruder in the first place and then abandoned without taking any obvious valuables. Guns were still in the desk drawer. Booze was left alone. Amongst papers and files, was something missing?

Damn right I took notes on that too.

By the time I was righting my couch, I couldn't tell that

anything had been taken. Nothing but the locks had been damaged. Without any business, I suppose getting those fixed won't be an urgent necessity.

Even better, neither Marley nor I had been hurt. Not My Cat hadn't been hurt. A pang of guilt gripped my gut. He could have been. Why hadn't he run for that hole he uses to go in and out of my office and the building? Why? Because he's gotten used to me and this place. He thinks of it as safe. What will happen to him if I'm not here to feed him or to tolerate him around?

Not so safe, huh?

I started stroking his fur, which came off as odd to both of us. But before we started getting all sappy on each other, and heaven forbid he started purring, the phone rang.

"Miss Tanner?"

My would-be client. *There is a God.*

"Miss Tanner, I must apologize for missing our appointment yesterday."

"It's quite alright, sir. Something came up for me as well, so things worked out." *Please, please, still want to be my client.* "Would you like to reschedule?"

"Oh yes. Yes. I'm afraid I won't be able to come to you."

"That's not a problem." *Slow down, Lulu. Don't sound as desperate as you feel. Breathe.* "My schedule is fairly open today. What would work best for you?"

"Oh, that's wonderful. Yes. This afternoon is fine."

He gave me an address. Something down in the Cannery District, next to Fisherman's Wharf. Maybe the campaign he worked for was utilizing one of the abandoned warehouses. Can't complain about that. Somebody should be using them.

We hung up and I was feeling like I could take on the world. I had a client. Had my luck gone from dumb, to bad, to good?

Couldn't help it – I snagged Not My Cat by the head and kissed him on his *middle*-forehead and nose. The short growl he produced wasn't serious and I didn't care. I caught him off guard, before he could calculate his best response. "Kibble for everyone," I called back to him, pulling a pocket derringer out of my unviolated desk drawer.

Maybe some crab from the Wharf. Afterall, Not My Cat had protected my desk from a search.

Good kitty.

Chapter Eight

The end justifies the means, right?

-Lou Tanner, P.I., 1935, Personal Journal

I was running a bit too close to 'on time' to be fashionably sensible but feeling otherwise prudent in choosing to wear a smart, stylish ensemble in steel-blue wool, consisting of short jacket, pale blue tie, feminine trousers, and smart brogues — damn all the nasty side-eye I was tempting. It was intelligent wear, which is why I keep a clean set in my office. That wisdom was proven true when I found myself sprinting for a moving cable car.

I was too fixated on being *on time* to remember my current associations with cable car trollies.

I caught the Powell & Hyde just as it passed over the cable crossing at Post Street and leaped on with all the grace of an orangutan attempting Swan Lake. Couldn't have pulled that one off in a dainty frock. Sure, I was meeting a new client, but Mrs. Tanner didn't raise a fool. I can hide a small, backup rod tucked in a pocket hidden in all those folds of a pair of Carole Lombard pants — keeps me free to respond to any ... let's say ... uninvited actions. More than once I've had to tell a potential client 'no,' because he mistook my P.I. license for a permission slip to try something rude.

Sometimes I'm forgetful and not on purpose. I forgot that I'm not the only one who works weekends. A suited man to the left of me kept his crumpled yellow rag up in front of his face as if hiding the fact he was on public transportation. The headlines were somewhat disturbing. Campaign season in the City was in full swing, with the mayoral candidates taking sides and hurling insult volleys into each other's headquarters.

Angelo Rossi, our current Mayor, wanted to keep his job for a second go-around. A Roosevelt New-Deal man tried and true, he had plenty to say about communists, fascists, and other vermin he wanted run out on a rail from *his city*. A progressive Teddy-Republican who somehow thought nothing of using the Police Department to raid every Union or opposition political office he didn't approve of. Today's statement to the masses was that he was Anti-Mechanicals — Pro-Immigration. "Who will clean your houses? Who will cook your meals? Do you really think average citizens want those low-paying jobs," I pictured him saying, in a voice that barked over the radio as often as possible. "Let the new arrivals do that work. That's what they're asking for, they want those jobs. Let the immigrant earn his way into the American Dream just like you."

Of course, there was the other major candidate, one Lucas Landis. All for Anti-immigration laws, supporting Germany's "peaceful intentions and willingness to keep to their own business in Europe," and Pro-Mechanicals. In big type, under the headline, the paper quoted him as saying, "Unclean Foreigners are the destruction of America. Too many taking Americans' jobs. If Americans don't want to do it, let American technology handle the task. Why bring in anything that will contaminate our nation and take money out of your pocket?" I guess being against outsiders, or anyone who looks like they don't belong, is the new insider trend.

I hate politics. Beyond reading the basic statements given by the top contenders, I pretty much ignored the whole mess. Name calling, lie telling, and suggestive hint making. None of it raising to the level of civility I normally expect from gangsters and toddlers.

I haven't decided.

On one side, I'm pro-Union and think the police have better things to do with their time than serve politicians.

On the other, I don't mind 'Bots and 'Tons, in fact I'm sort of indifferent on the subject. I'm also not against immigration, since everyone I've ever met comes from an immigrant lineage somewhere in their past.

Nobody running meets my needs. Oh, and no stunner,

neither party is all that gonzo to support equal pay for women. *Quelle surprise* as my mother would say.

An older woman seated, with her ankles crossed tightly, on the side-facing bench gave me the once over, disapproved of my version of feminine attire, and spent the rest of the trip with her nose in the air. A bad plan for her overall. This cable car line is known for changing elevations quickly — she might get a nosebleed.

She didn't, or rather wouldn't, enjoy the sensation of gripping the brass side-handle, slick from the overnight fog, and feeling the tip of your shoe sliding a tad as the clattering, wooden unit tipped precariously up then down slope. *Ignore the aching shoulder and arms.* Oh, the loss of gravity, when that sense of weightlessness lifts your hair, and you know nothing is keeping the car from going whatever speed the laws of physics will allow, except an ancient, greasy cable circling beneath the street. Cold wind slaps you in the face as the excitement squeezes your heart. You lean back against the fall and maybe — just maybe — lean out to tickle danger's throat with your fingers. Or to snag a golden ring that isn't there. Your hat threatens to fly off, tempting some chivalrous fella' to chase after it.

Then comes the sudden jolt when the conductor yanks back on the grip and the cable below is re-engaged. It's that overwhelming smell of burning fiber and oil that tells you your leap of faith into the thrill of the moment was worth it.

The Powell & Hyde line zigzags northwest until it meets up with Beach Street near the canneries and all those rows of small fishing boats, side by side, squashed into organized chaos. That makes the P&H line a handy commute link if you work at any of the industries down here.

Or, if you're very lucky, at the shiny new building with the view worth killing for.

Brand, spanking new structure. Sixteen floors with plenty of windows to show off the Bay to anyone you need to impress, the Aquatic Tower had been leased out long before construction was completed. Guess some folks don't realize there were hard times going on. Every fancy social wannabe and ambassador parked his lot here. I've never understand the rich.

No Requiem for the Tin Man

The Tower gleamed in the daylight; a serious contrast to the dull, soiled buildings reeking of fish guts and burning coal crowded below its high encircling wall and gates. Filthy hands and gnarled fingers, keep out.

The cable car stopped on an end-line turntable, about three blocks from the Tower above the canneries. All the ladies demurely stepped off first, followed by the women who served those ladies, and then the cannery gals. Most of the working-class men stuck by to help the conductor haul the car around on the turntable for its return trip. The table clunked to a halt and the conductor locked it into place once the tracks were aligned. Droopy-eyed swing shift labor, overnight staff, and midnight clerks were already hustling to crowd onboard, scurrying off somewhere to find a bed.

That's when I heard him: Mr. Shout-'n-Slather.

"I'm an American, a *true* American," he proclaimed.

The said *True American* was on the tall side, a little thin in the limbs, with a diminishing hairline, and a strange ability to make you listen.

He kept going. "I work hard when I can get the work. I don't complain about what I have to do. I do it."

Okay, so he doesn't complain, which warns me that a loud complaint is forthcoming.

"Well, I got something to complain about."

Tada!

"I get up every morning in my America and do you know what I see and hear?"

A herd of pink elephants, left over from the night before?

"An America that has stopped being American."

"He's not gonna' cry, is he?" Okay, that wasn't nice of me to say out loud, but I wasn't feeling nice today. A couple of dark looks shot my way, threatening to silence my opining. G*et in line.* I had to keep my attitudes to myself as Shout-'n-Slather was gathering quite a crowd, and with my upcoming meeting, it was necessary for a good first impression to be sober and lack broken bones from a brawl.

"I know all the facts. Friends I'm an average American. A true American and I'm witnessing some things these days that makes my blood boil. You see them everywhere. Foreigners — with their foreign languages, not speaking American — taking all our jobs and taking all our money. Commies and Socialists egging on unions and using violence to force us to do their bidding. Negroes taking jobs that should be for folks like you and me. Jews in control of our banks and robbing us blind. Chinks and Pansies corrupting our city with their clubs and brothels and filth. It's wrong, I tell you, wrong. We're being taken over and soon there'll be nothing left for us real Americans. They're replacing us by the thousands. So what can we do about it?

"We're going to use our God given right to vote, that's what we're going to do. Vote! Vote for men who will stand up for us in government. For men who stand behind laws keeping those people out and sending those who got in home to wherever they came from. Who know the truth about the Negroes, Foreigners, and – and the Catholic Church too. No real American believes in no foreign God. We are free to worship as Americans."

At least he wants us to vote.

I didn't like the supportive grumbling coming from the crowd. Everything he was saying sounded like the mutterings of a bullied man, pushed to his limits, discovering that rusty knife of his still held a sharp edge.

Bang!

We all jumped. Hell, I damn near came out of my skin. Looking around frantically, all eyes eventually found the garbage can that fell over. A worker kicked it. Yeah, it was nothing to worry about. I don't know about anyone else, but my nerves weren't happy company after this morning.

Shout-'n-Slather appeared to be more annoyed that he was interrupted than scared. He picked up right where he left off. "This is our country, and we got to take it back, one city — one county — one state at a time. This country is being stolen out from under us and we will never be truly free until we are free of it all."

"Whaddaya' mean, free of it all?" Somebody in the crowd put his bravery cap on.

"Yeah, free of what?" called out another.

NO REQUIEM FOR THE TIN MAN

Shout-'n-Slather dramatically counted each off on his fingers. "Free of Negroes who don't know their place. Free of polluted foreigners from dirty countries who don't belong here and won't speak American. Free of Catholics, Masons, and Jews. Free from those who would force women to take jobs they aren't qualified for — take them out of the home where they should be. Where they are safe, and we can protect them. And free of the sodomites who drag us down to the depths of Hell. We need to exercise our right to freedom and save this Christian country and our race before it's too late!"

I started calculating how much my bail money I would need if I walked right up to that ignoramus and slapped him around a bit. I could take him. Then again, did I want to be on the wrong side of law enforcement right now?

The answer was a resounding 'no.' My imagination filled my coconut with a crystal-clear vision of my welcome down at police headquarters, complete with a greeting they'd enjoy right down to their brass knuckles and nightsticks. Uppity dames accused of cop killing don't get the dainty treatment.

Someone cut short a comment that would have offended even my Uncle Joe. The man next to me tried to cover it in a white linen handkerchief. His pristine and imaginative suit with the carnation invited any number of guesses why he thought so poorly of Shout-'n-Slather. He glanced over his hanky, eyes almost apologetic, then, taking notice of hostility growing around him, looked for a quick but dignified route to escape. He wasn't a big fellow by any measure, except for his bravery this morning, and he used his minimal size to disappear into the crowd.

"More than that! We need to be free of those people who want to give a man's job to mechanical thing so that they don't have to pay an honest wage. Yet at the same time, willingly send us, living flesh and a men, into wars overseas."

Ah, there it is. Now we've come to the true heart of it. Ultimately, it's always the mechanicals, isn't it? Did Shout-'n-Slather come back from the Great War with a screw loose? Although, he didn't look quite the right age. Maybe it was a brother or father?

Maybe that family man didn't come back at all, and now Shout-'n-Slather had no one, no job, and nothing better to do but blame others. I had some sympathy — I lost my family too, although not to war. There are no words to express the sorrow or to prepare you for the crippling grief that comes out of nowhere, with no warning, for the rest of your life. But it's a lousy excuse for hate. There is no excuse for the crap he was spewing.

He was right about one thing, only humans go into battle. The Treaty of '29 made sure there were no weapons for robots or automatons. And I figured he'd move over all his hate-filled spittle to them. The ultimate victim to bully. All those 'bots and 'tons, who can't and won't stand up to abuse. It's not in their programming.

"They want us to die in foreign lands so that they can live here in luxury, being served by foreigners and mechanical beings," he added, gesturing towards the gleaming Aquatic Tower.

I needed to go. The only things boiling here were tempers. Too bad you can't use evil thoughts as a hand warmer.

"I don't want to die in Europe, like my father did," Shout-'n-Slather added.

Ouch. Okay, so I'm a push-over for a sob story, and for half a second, pity yanked at my guilt.

A bunch of folks stopped wandering off.

I guess Mr. S&S understood his audience more than I gave him credit for. "That's right. 'Bots for delivering the milk to our kids, rather than an honest milkman. 'Bots building factories and then working in them, while good men stand in bread lines and beg for nickels and accept hand-outs. But come the war in Europe, the one that's being stirred up, that's when they send the sons and brothers of this land to die in the trenches. They've got it all backwards. Send the 'bots to war and let us have the jobs."

How about no war at all. Yeah, nobody's thinking of that one.

A shiny automaton walked by, looking as human as they are meant to, and though I know that it felt nothing like fear or embarrassment, I guess I gave it credit for the emotions anyway. It was modest, shiny, and innocent appearing. Stopping, the 'Ton scrubbed the ground, swept up used cigarettes and heaven-only-knew what else, and rattled along its way. On its back was a little knapsack filled with the civilized rubbish it had collected.

None of the folks listening to the speech even noticed it. That's how common and every day they are. I noticed, with much relief, that no one decided to attack it. I'd seen that happen too. Pathetic and always unprovoked. I guess 'real Americans' want jobs, only not the ones that are menial and filthy and wouldn't pay much to begin with.

I walked away, in disgust, with some idiot calling after me, "Hey Myrna, whatcha' doin' outside of Hollywood?" *Yeah, real original. Like I've never heard that before.*

I get that all the time, and it isn't any better the tenth, twentieth, or hundredth time. So, I got as far away as I could. Just because I agreed that we could save lives by not sending live soldiers into battle didn't mean I agreed with the rest of his horse manure. I lit up another Lucky and thought about Augustin — Mr. Crazy Guy. If we had sent armed 'bots to Flanders instead of men, who would Augustin Gruber be today? Is there ever an excuse to waste so much life? Is anything worth wasting a life over?

With the Depression starting to fade for some, the rest of us still faced the truth about the cheapness of our own lives. Not so much how we value ourselves, but how those around us do. I'm always wondering, does a woman Shamus deserve twenty-five-dollars a day plus expenses, just like one of the boys. Once I pull out the license or stick my nose in somewhere it wasn't invited, any courtesy offered to ladies is off the table. I become one of the boys.

Stretching the muscles around the scar tissue I earned from a bullet a couple of cases ago, I know I have my answer. Yeah, a female gumshoe does earn it. This one did. I can die from flying slugs and pounding fists like any fella. Maybe I value myself too highly, but I'm not making that my problem. Mother would be appalled, but I've grown out of the *everyone-else-comes-first* part of my womanly life.

Okay, okay, so I like to walk, smoke, and internally pontificate. I only wish I got paid by the philosophical musing.

As the cable car rumbled past me from the turn-around, I had one of those moments when my brain got to the point, the reason I've been obsessing about life — value — and meaning. Agent Hayes had demanded that I give him the blame for killing SF Cop Milt Somerset. That was the very thing tugging at my gut and hammering at my sense of right and wrong. It was also the reason I was treading lightly these days, when it came to cops.

There isn't a thin blue line in this city between the police and the population: it is a thick, stone edifice painted official flatfoot blue, with signs that say, no trespassing. I'm a trespasser — an interloper. There are codes within codes at the SFPD and I had stamped all over them in my pretty Newberry's heels.

Sure, I could also chalk it up to being a dame. Or, that I wasn't an old, tried-'n-true investigator with a long list of contacts and friends. Or, any number of things. But my wager was that my caseload dried up due to the San Francisco cop problem I had now. You know, because I need one more thing to wipe out my livelihood.

A young woman surprised me, yanking me out of my philosophy. She handed me a single sheet of paper, folded in half. The outside listed an address, nothing more. "You look like someone who might appreciate this."

When I started to open the sheet, she stopped me gently. "Open it later. Away from *this* crowd." She nodded over in the direction of Shout-'n-Slather. "I don't like what he has to say either."

And with that, she smiled and sauntered off, looking for others escaping the vitriol of the sidewalk preacher.

It was probably religious stuff. I poked it into my purse and forgot all about it.

On North Point and Hyde, I stopped to finish my Lucky long enough to remember what the hell I was doing here.

Cars raced each other and swerved around the Nightcrawler cabs on their tracks. Train whistles echoed everywhere as freight cars rolled along Bay Street towards the Mission Street yard. Must be lunch because I couldn't hear the 'Floaters' working on the new Bay Bridge, connecting the City to Oakland. Couldn't see them either. Those big balloons carrying Rivetmen up and down the bridge girders are pretty damn noticeable. There's a job that requires skill and bravery.

No Requiem for the Tin Man

Sam, Marley's beau, was a Rivetman. He had to be nuts. Not a job for me: I hate heights.

Upwind from the cacophony and stench of the canneries and fishing boats, nestled quietly in view of the new Tower, was my destination. A warehouse repurposed. And I wasn't sure I liked the new purpose.

Correction: I *despised* this repurposing.

I doubled checked the address.

Damn. This was it.

My whole body turned into an ice cube in a hooch glass.

The building was a nice old century brick, with windows on the top floor and big sliding doors on the bottom. All those doors were closed except one near the north side, now prominently decorated to draw attention.

The main entrance looked more like a ravenous maw sucking everything it could into its dark gullet. The monster was well guarded by two tall men, dressed in black military-style uniforms with shiny black boots, shiny black belts strapped across their chests, and shiny black guns. All around them milled people of varying sizes and shapes, all with one shared characteristic: civil uniforms. Not to be confused for the Salvation Army or the Knights of Columbus, these folks looked like an army unto themselves.

I was breathing but couldn't catch my breath with a baseball mitt.

This can't be right.

Men and women both dressed in white shirts, black ties, and black trousers or skirts. All the dames put their hair up in Heidi fashion, braids crisscrossed on top. Some gals pulled their hair back as tight as they could, to the point where their skin stretched like a drumhead, removing any evidence of smile lines around their eyes and mouths.

People put on regalia all the time, for all sorts of reasons. Hell, I was wearing my shamus uniform, complete with an emergency heater in my pocket. Those uniforms didn't disturb me half as much as the three flags and the huge sign identifying the warehouse usage.

One of the flags was becoming an all-too-common sight these

days, showing its ugly red and black colors on everything from the Market Street parade to Zeppelins docking at the Montgomery Street Station. The second was the Stars & Stripes. The third was a strange one in blue with the face of George Washington stamped in white ink.

As for the sign, it was made of sail canvas, emblazoned with six-inch letters declaring the space to be the Headquarters of the German American Federation. Beneath those prideful black letters, only slightly smaller, was *Amerikadeutscher Bund.*

The American Nazi Party.

This can't be happening. Nazis. *No, no, no!*

I'd stopped thinking about them or any experience I had with them. *No.* That was the past. I shoved that memory to the back of my head so hard it almost hurt. Gone. I told myself over and over, until the truth had no place to breathe: it never happened. Never.

I had the sudden urge to punch something … or throw up … or … or to run.

Nazis.

I'd seen them in the newsreels before the last picture show I'd gone too. Real ones. Stomping and marching all over Germany. Forests being ripped out to make way for tank factories. Bavarian women being told to stay at home and make babies for the future of the Fatherland. Of *that man.* The one so confidently grasping the awe of an entire nation.

The newsreels never said they were here, but a few papers did.

And here they were, right in front of me. Bragging about their presence in my city with signs and banners and piped-in music. Pompously flouting the image of the first President beside a symbol of their cancerous madness in Europe. My friend and news supplier, Howie Evans, had long ago warned me about these guys.

Were they even Americans?

I stared again at the address. No doubt, it was where I was to meet my new client. Oh hell, what political campaign needed a private dick like me? The Nazis? Nobody told me …

I wanted to turn away. I couldn't. All I could was picture Marley, trapped again in an office where her boss pinched her ass, called her "honey," and held her paycheck hostage to his desires.

NO REQUIEM FOR THE TIN MAN

There might be cruel laughter as my business name was scraped off the door of the office, the trash can filled with my useless business cards taken to the incinerator. Everything ... every part of my dream and hope ...

Hold up, Lulu. Don't panic. I'm not working for the campaign, but for a person. Maybe this is something ... something ... I don't have all the facts. But nothing I'm thinking brings the warmth back to my hands.

Yeah, I shut my eyes. And yeah, I hoped that when I opened them, I'd see something better. This was the only client I had? The only promised source of income —

"You better not be going in there," the voice growled in my ear.

CHAPTER NINE

On a private note, don't expect to be on equal footing
until you've kicked a few shins and
stepped on a lot of toes.

-Lou Tanner, P.I., 1935, Letter to Female Pemberton Graduates.

Agent Hayes took me by the arm and spun me around. Even through the worst of the last case, he never looked at me *like that* before. His grip was starting to bite into my skin. It was wrinkling my suit too.

Looking down at the address, then the warehouse, then Agent Hayes, there wasn't any way to wiggle out of this. "I *am* going in there, although I admit I wasn't expecting ... *this*. Politics, yeah, but not ... *this*."

"What the hell is wrong with you? Why?"

My hearing started to fizzle, like I'd stuck my noggin in the bay. Hayes was here. He couldn't possibly think I was going in there because I *liked* these goons. "A job," I muttered, staring at the crowd near the entrance. "I got a call. It sounded like some tail and tattle work needed. Nothing was mentioned about ..." I was fumbling. I don't fumble. My hat damn near flew off I shook my head so hard. The underwater sensation didn't go away but my moxy came back like a crashing wave. "What's it to you? Look, big guy, it's not like I'm joining their sick party. I don't have to like or agree with everything my clients do. They need to agree to my fee and —"

He had the temerity to grab me now by both shoulders. "You are not going in there."

Ya know what? Two things will make me do something, even

if I don't want to. Even something stupid. A threat to the life of a friend and being told what to do by someone who doesn't get a say in ordering me around. Nobody orders me around. "It's just a job," I snarled back.

"It's career suicide."

"Oh yeah, like I have much of a ..." I stopped to take a breath and lower my voice before someone noticed we were there. "As if I have a career to kill? Look G-man, beat it. Unless you know about a bomb in there or a raid on its way, I'm going in. Holding my nose, but I'm going in there to meet a client who needs —"

"They're Hitler's cronies!"

"And Hitler can go take a powder from the universe. I'm not working for that creep. Some fellow, in there, needs me to do a little work for him. You and I both know that means somebody thinks his wife is cheating and he wants grounds for a divorce. Or he wants some relief and to be spared a whole load of embarrassment."

"So you'll help a Nazi?"

"I don't know that he is a Nazi because I don't even know who the schmuck is. You don't either, because neither of us has met him. I know the voice that asked for the meeting, that's all."

"If your client is in there," Hayes thumbed hard at the building, "Then he's a Nazi."

Deep breath, Lulu "I'm not looking to work for the Nazi Party. But I need the job —"

Hey, since when do I need to explain myself to this Boy-o?

His face grew red and his brows pressed down over those big Green Eyes. *Damn it.* I didn't want him mad at me. I didn't want him disappointed in me. My heart felt squeezed as though Hayes himself reached in and crushed it like an eggshell. He was leaning down, pushing himself into my personal space.

And I looked away. Why? I don't know. "Look, I'm going in there to see what the man wants. I have the right to say 'no' if I want to." Which I already knew I wouldn't, because I simply couldn't. I'm that desperate.

All of a sudden, what I needed more than Hayes's approval, was a shower. A scalding hot shower and a bristle brush to wash off the scum I felt glomming onto my skin.

But what I needed even more than that shower was next month's rent and Marley's salary. There was more to my desperation — I'm not completely blind to my own foibles but sometimes the means justifies the end. Rent, apartment, office, Marley. Simple. My needs met.

"Since it's for them, let's assume the answer is 'no.' So, don't even bother going in."

My God, this guy is dense as granite. I pulled away, hard. "Look! I'm willing to help a guy who wants out of a bad marriage or needs to know he's in a good marriage. If he's willing to pay twenty-five dollars a day, then he can afford to pay me to be blind to his stupid political choices and to be stupid about his political choices."

For a moment, Green Eyes opened his mouth to protest.

I stopped him. "Shut it. Unless you have a paying job for me, I need to take this job." I didn't have to explain shit to him, but the words came out of my mouth without my permission. "I have bills and I don't have Uncle Sam paying me to stand around and harass civilians or scratch my keister or whatever it is you do all day! Take it on the road, Hayes, we're done here."

With that, yanked free of him and I marched away. I wished to God I felt proud and holy, like I'd taken down Goliath with my little stone.

I didn't.

His eyes were burrowing into my back and I swear I felt every dig of his righteous shovel.

Closer to the building, the view to the back parking lot was clearer. I was sorry that it was. A row, the length of the warehouse, of single-rider, personnel carriers awaited use. They glistened where water clung to their freshly washed exteriors. Just like tanks, cut in half, trimmed down to size for one, plenty of room for later gun placement, and thick treads that could run over any terrain — rural or urban. They suited the uniformed theme of the group, but made my knees weaken.

Passing under the sign and the flags, I slowed to adjust the shoulder strap of my work bag. While my hand was still up that far, I let it rise further until my fingertips slid along the fringed hem of the U.S. flag. The wind whipped it away, far away from my touch.

Message received. Too late.

I was already heading into the monster's lair.

Inside the building, my insides knotted up even more. The lobby was floor to ceiling propaganda. A wide set of doors opened into a space converted into a dark auditorium. Uniformed youth used flashlights to guide attendees to the hundreds of folding chairs lined up in front of a metal stage. Patriotic swag draped every horizontal line. At the back of the theater, a scaffold supported a cadre of men and women — in uniform, of course — working electric equipment and huge spotlights pointed towards royal thrones on the stage.

Another outrageous image of George Washington was sandwiched between the American and Nazi flags behind the wood and red velvet covered chairs. Party members — I supposed they were party members — milled about the stage, waiting to take their seats, a mix of uniforms and civilian wear.

The roar of the din was deafening. Folks knew one another. The Corridor I cowered in was packed with even more uniforms. Everywhere else, civilians stood around reading pamphlets and chatting as if this were some sort of deranged Sunday Church Luncheon.

My head was still swimming in the bay and my fingers were going numb. My stomach was somewhere down by my knees.

This was enemy territory, presenting itself as casually and warmly as a kindly old lady about to pull a butcher's knife on you.

I only had the address and office number. I was pointed up the stairs to a set of doors, to the den of my client. Might as well have been climbing a scaffold to my death. Their uniforms smelled funny. This stairwell smelled funny. The whole building stank — or was that me. The stares were intense, and it sure as hell wasn't because I looked like a movie star.

Well, I'll be damned!

At the end of the upstairs corridor, was Mrs. Elsa Gruber Weiss. Hair up. Frown down. Uniform buttoned tightly to the throat. Anyone near her was waved away so that we shared a twenty-foot by ten-foot space alone. "Miss Turner. I was surprised when I learned you were coming."

"*Tanner.* Lou Tanner," I said, discreetly keeping my badge to myself. "If you'll excuse me, I'm here to meet someone, specifically."

"Not my brother, Augustin?" she enquired with a nastiness I was neither surprised by nor threatened by.

"No."

"Ah, he is no longer your client?" *Did she just bat her innocence-eyelashes at me?*

"I'm afraid I can't discuss the particulars of any of my cases with you unless it concerns you directly."

"Regardless of the fact he is my brother?"

"No, I cannot. You wouldn't want me to be sharing every intimate detail of your case with anyone who asked — if we had such a case?"

Elsa had perfect teeth which she quickly bared then hid behind dull rose-colored lipstick. "I'm sure your answer will make Herr Landis very happy. He worries about people talking too much."

"*Herr* Landis?"

"Of course. We celebrate our German ancestral connection to the American dream here. But, if you prefer, Mister Landis."

"Mister Landis?" I genuinely tried not making that uncomfortable laugh and bit the inside of my lip instead. "As in the leading candidate for San Francisco Mayor, Lucas Landis?" *Oh my God*, I wasn't only in deep, I was about to drown. The next possible mayor of my city needed me to spy on one of his staff?

"The same." She stepped forward and started to place a pin on my lapel. It matched the one she was wearing, in a slightly smaller size. Gold, enameled with a small American flag and a huge black swastika over it. Her pin caught a spark of light and flashed into my eyes.

I hadn't meant to, but I knocked her hand away.

"It's only to make you fit in better, Miss Turn ... Tanner."

"I don't need to fit in. I'm here on business," I said through a forced smile.

"Mr. Landis wants this discussion with you to be discreet. For that, you need to look like you belong here."

I doubt it? "Then perhaps he should have come to my office or met me somewhere less populated."

"And perhaps you should have worn something more professionally feminine."

"I'm quite comfortable, thank you. Professional, and capable. If Mr. Landis would like me to leave —"

Elsa shrugged, rolled her pale blue eyes, and sighed. "He is the leading candidate, as you said. His time is demanded by many. And believe me when I say this, he simply can't go somewhere and meet with any woman anytime he wishes. He has a reputation to uphold." Every word slithered out at me, purposely striking me in the sore spots.

Okay, my response came out fast, well before I could give it proper consideration. "I have a reputation to maintain, too, Mrs. Weiss. I'm picky about my clientele. I haven't said 'yes' to Mr. Landis yet."

The noise in the auditorium faded into a distant drone as we focused to a pinpoint on each other.

Finally, the dull-rose lipstick parted, presenting perfect teeth in a perfect smile, again. "I'm sure as you wish to keep your smart office, and your shanty Irish secretary, and wherever it is you live, you have already decided. We have chosen to be equally flexible in our choice of … " she looked down her nose at my trousers, "professional. Let's call this a mutual contract of convenience though not of admiration."

"'Professional' being the most important word."

Her eyes brightened a bit. "Indeed, yes."

"Good. I am willing to assess the situation if Mr. Landis is."

"Outstanding," she said, reaching forward with the pin.

"Don't even think it, Mrs. Weiss." I gave her my shoulder, temperature on the frozen side.

That's not a line in the sand, sister, that's a solid brick wall.

CHAPTER TEN

As a woman undercover, you're going to be limited in the roles that you can play. Sadly, women who travel and are allowed to be professionally curious are always expected as journalists. Just get used to that.

-Lou Tanner, P.I., 1935, to female graduates

"Come in, come in. How good of you to come." The man at the window was far too enthusiastic as he pounced on my hand to shake it. As I opened my yap to say something, he squeezed my hand several times — too hard — and turned away from me. "Gentlemen. This lady is a journalist from New York."

Ah, we're going with that cover story again? I must have a reporter's face. Okey-Dokey. What the hell, I'm the one who whipped it out to save my backside the last time. I was wondering what he and Elsa had cooked up as an explanation for my presence.

Several oppositional glares turned into hopeful yet cautious stares. I suppressed any startled-deer expression as I grit my teeth into a concrete smile for the small crowd of uniformed men waiting in attendance.

"She is writing up a few kind words … I hope," he added, giving me an obvious wink, "It's about time we were given an even-handed delivery for our platform. Far too often, the old guard newsmen and their biased newspapers have silenced fresh voices so that they may stay in control of information. Information is power, gentlemen. Power."

Mumbles of eager agreement encouraged the churning in my stomach. For the sake of my cover, I kept grinning like an idiot.

NO REQUIEM FOR THE TIN MAN

He continued proudly, "Miss *Heinreid* will give me the opportunity to present the *American* German Bund —"

"*Amerikadeutscher Bund,*" Elsa corrected through a stare of death at me. I wasn't sure what she was correcting.

"Yes, yes, Frau Weiss. *German* American Bund." He produced a dazzling smile for me from somewhere up his sleeve. Maybe he had a rabbit up there too. "Miss Heinreid and I likely agree though, it should be American German. But that is a discussion for another day." His tone was lilting and cheerful. "We are not just an extension of one nationality supplanted to these United States but an expression of modernism. An expression of true Americanism."

Ugh. Politician. I only wished he let go of my hand. I was on the verge of chewing it off.

"If you would allow us some brief privacy, *bitte,* we shouldn't be long. *Danke.* Thank you."

I didn't need the Times Square ticker tape roll to tell me what was going on in the little, dirty minds of at least half the men in the room. So, I'm pretty. And he's a big man in his world. Shouldn't that mean we're going to have some nookie on his desk once the door is closed? They apparently don't understand tiny nuances of life, like dames and joes can get along without doing the Tumble-'n-Mamba.

Elsa took her sweet, disapproving time waltzing out, the last one to close the door. In the sudden emptiness, Landis let go of my hand and took up a handkerchief to blot the sweat he developed on his face and neck. At the first opportunity he put his big oak desk between us. Maybe he was thinking the same thing his colleagues were and he wanted to protect his own reputation? I can't say I blamed him. I'd read some of the so-called reports on politicians over the years. "Smear Campaign" is a good name for it, and it takes little to get one started.

"A drink, Miss Tanner?"

Not Miss Heinreid? Not *Fraulein* Tanner? Nothing about the weather? Good. Stright to the point. "No thank you, Mr. Landis. I think it might be best if we get right down to business."

"Of course," he said, gesturing to one of two nice chairs positioned in front of him.

I sat and took in the whole staged scene. In order from left to right, haloed from behind like a heavenly Renaissance painting: the state flag of California, the American flag, Lucas Landis in splendor, the Nazi flag, and the made-up George Washington flag. He knew what he was doing: posed thoughtfully, his chair a bit higher, wider, fancier than any other in the room, all the objects on the desk tilted toward him. *Perfectly staged.*

Politician or actor? Or were they the same thing?

The man himself was lean and meticulously dressed in a tailored gray suit of medium weight wool. His silk tie and pocket handkerchief matched in black. His light brown hair was swept over a high forehead and pasted into perfection by a generous application of pomade. Under his long, thin nose waited a trimmed and waxed moustache that slightly covered his upper lip, giving him that constant appearance of satisfaction. Even larger than Elsa's was a gold pin glistening from his lapel.

He cleared his throat. "You'll forgive me if I confirm a couple of points?"

I shrugged. "That depends on what those points are, Mr. Landis."

He nodded. "Are you at all affiliated with the PSSR?"

Oh, *them* again. "No."

"That's good. I'm sure it will turn out to be a rumor, but I am hearing that they are the one's behind the bombings."

"I'm hearing rumors that several groups are being suspected."

"They have the most at stake." He cast his line to see how I might take the bait.

"They also have the most to lose should the associate them with death and destruction."

No nibble. I came here to work for a person not a party. He looked about ready to start asking all sorts of other personal questions, so I cut him off at the proverbial pass. "For the record, Mr. Landis, I don't belong to one political party or another when it comes to my work. I don't take sides and I don't get involved. I am professionally neutral."

"Interesting. And unusual."

"Not for a Private Investigator."

"And what does your husband think?"

Nice try again. Obvious, too. "I'm not married. Never have been. I have a college education in the Arts, I'm a graduate with honors from the Pemberton School of Private Investigation, yes — my father was Milton Tanner, no — I'm not seeing anyone, due to a lack of time, yes — I am of voting age, no — I'm not telling you who I am voting for in this upcoming election, and no — that decision will neither hinder nor help with my dedication to this case. A case is a case and a contract with a client, Mr. Landis." I swept imaginary crumbs off my trousers. "But you knew all that, already, didn't you?"

He gave me one of his better, charming smiles. "At least I didn't ask your age."

"Thirty-one."

He barked out a short laugh, gathered up his wits, and changed the subject back to the matter at hand. "Miss Tanner, as described on the telephone, I need this to be handled as a very sensitive matter."

"And I understand why. Any job you need a private detective for won't look good as a news headline, certainly not for a mayoral campaign running on integrity and honor." I nodded to one of the campaign signs resting on the floor to the side of the desk. "Regardless of the task, I'm confident your Chief of Staff wants to control all reports and propaganda. That means, everyone tows a straight line."

"Astute. Yes. And … this is not precisely an innocent situation that can be easily explained. In fact, if I may be blunt, it's the sort of situation any political campaign desperately wants to avoid. The absolute antithesis of our platform."

"You suggested infidelity … by a staff member —" I began.

He huffed. "Oh, that would be preferred. No. It's worse. So much worse. You see, Miss Tanner, it's *my* own wife."

Bravo. I did not see that one coming. He'd suggested otherwise. Shame on me for taking his word for it. I kept my expression calm.

Landis checked his clean fingernails. "I know I indicated

someone else was involved, but you can't expect something that explosive to be said over the phone. For exchange operators to overhear and such?"

"Hence your insistence that we meet face to face." But of course. And, not enough time to figure out why I was meeting with the most important man in the building. Possibly in the whole city. "If this were some member of your campaign staff, your Chief of Staff would be dealing with it."

"Indeed. In fact, my Chief of Staff has no idea why you're here. None of my staff does, except for Elsa, who brought the whole possibility to my attention."

Oh brother. This was deeper than the Grand Canyon. And me, without a parachute. I kept my lips pinned together while Landis shoved a newspaper photo across the desk. The bombshell that stared up at me with gray-scaled eyes was the epitome of Teutonic beauty.

Strange he didn't present me with an actual photograph. A quick glance around the room let me see that there were no photographs of his wife anywhere yet there were gaps in personal items, where a photograph might have been.

His index finger tapped on a figure behind her.

"You are acquainted with *Arzt* ... excuse me ... *Doctor* Frederick Gruber?"

I've gotten pretty damn good at keeping my face neutral over my few years on the planet, but that little reveal almost got me a second time. This case was full of surprises. Couldn't lie to Landis. Chances were, Elsa had told him that Frederick and I had met.

I was darn sure Landis and the Grubers knew a hell of a lot more than I did, both before and after Gus arrived in my office. The figure in the photo, behind Mrs. Landis, was unmistakably Frederick Gruber – Gus and Elsa's brother.

My nerves were dancing to that all too familiar tune: *You're getting' played, Sweetheart.*

"I did meet Dr. Gruber, along with his sister, just the other day." To see where this might go, I left my maybe-client, Gus, out of the discussion.

Landis slouched into his chair, something I didn't think he knew how to do. "So she said. She mentioned some *kerfuffle* during the parade that kept you two from speaking about my case. She … Elsa … took it upon herself to visit you first, before me. She is concerned about appearances, especially with the campaign and our political movement gaining such positive momentum. We represent something so new and yet so common sense." He leaned towards me, eyes wide in excitement. "What we can do to bring America …"

"Mr. Landis. Stop. Please."

He waited, his hand quivering a little at the midpoint of expressing his ambitions.

"I see I need to clarify something now and I believe this will be mutually beneficial: I am not interested in politics nor in policies. I don't want to know about or be involved with your movement."

Panic has a certain expression, and I was watching it invade Landis's face. I guess he thought I was only making professional sounding noise when I told him this the first time.

"It's always best if I don't become involved with my clients," I continued, before I accidentally caused him to have a coronary He'd never know how much I'd learned that truth on my last case. Steering wide of entanglements with clients was simple intelligence, and I sure as hell wasn't taking the time to tell him the juicy details. He'd have to take my word for it. "Neutrality and, as you noted earlier, even-handedness, are essential to my work. I must be available in wit and wisdom to make every necessary observation." I read that in the *Pemberley Private Detectives* manual I think. I felt like giving him a shovel before he choked in my volumes of near-Shakespearean overkill. But, what the hell, he's a politician — if he can dish out one of those ambrosia salads of words instead of fruit, he better be able to take it, sickening sweetness and all.

"I see your point."

The drop in his tone told me he might not, but I didn't care. I too have a dazzling neon smile.

"Do you believe your wife is having an affair with Dr. Gruber?"

He slumped again in his oversized chair, folding his hands

across his chest. "It's a possibility that could destroy my campaign. If it's true and Rossi ... my opponent ... ever finds out, well, I might as well quit."

"You want to win," I added coldly.

Landis sat up. "More than that, Miss Tanner. I want to know. I need to know. Please, I love Regina." He picked up the photo and looked at it lovingly. Too lovingly. "I need her by my side when I win this race."

"What if she is unfaithful to you?"

"Then at least I'll know, and I can move on."

"Without her."

"Yes," he said almost as a question.

Move on? Guess you don't need her by your side too much. "Very well, Mr. Landis. I will find out if your wife is being unfaithful to you. I will do so under the strictest confidence. My fee is twenty-five —"

He waved me off. "You'll be paid."

"I'd like you to be certain of what you will be billed. I charge twenty-five dollars a day, plus expenses."

"Ambitious for a young woman."

"Standard for a Private Investigator."

That statement seemed to do the trick. His shoulders and head relaxed a bit. "*Danke* ... Thank you."

I picked up my bag to leave when he surprised me one more time. "Miss Tanner. I genuinely love my wife." He stood up, slowly, almost defeatedly. "I don't just want to know if she's taken a lover. I *need* to know. A man wants to have faith in those around him. As a politician, that's not what I have come to expect. I accept those conditions as part of the political life. But my wife ..."

Landis turned his back on me. Was that a dramatic gesture for my edification or to genuinely hide his emotional vulnerability from me?

Landis's voice softened down to a whisper. "I don't trust easily. I shouldn't. I can't. That's why I need you to find out."

"You trust your campaign staff?"

"Not as far as I can pick them up and throw them." He faced me again with an expression I couldn't quite read.

No Requiem for the Tin Man

For perhaps a bit too long, I observed him. I didn't like him. I don't like politicians as a general habit. And I sure didn't like his cause. Yet, here was a guy, married, insisting he wanted to know if he was being made a fool of. If his love was being used and thrown away. Was that such a bad thing? Don't kings hurt too?

Landis slid an envelope out from under his desk blotter. My hopes jumped that an advance payment might be in there, but honesty kept me glued in place. I don't normally ask for payment up front. Once he presented it to me and gestured that I should open it, I found a handwritten list.

"My wife's and my schedule for the next few days. Mine is more likely to change at a moment's notice. Nature of the campaign business."

I stood up and asked, "How would you like me to contact you with any questions or conclusions?"

"Through Elsa. That is the best way. Any journalist would end up working through her as well. It will appear natural." Maybe he read my mind a bit. "Don't worry about Elsa too much. She's old school. Old European manners. She comes off cold as stone, but she's brilliant. Organized, determined, and obedient. I ... and this campaign ... would be lost without her. Forgive her, her unfriendliness."

"This job of mine sometimes demands a great deal of forgiveness," I said, shaking his hand. It was damp and clammy.

Or was that my hand that was cold?

"Oh," he suddenly brightened. From a limited pile of shiny objects, he carefully withdrew a gorgeous, gold cigarette lighter. Fashionable and small. No lettering, but a delightful set of lines running up the front to emphasize a point at the top where the spark wheel awaited a thumb. There were several that showed their backsides from where they lay, each enameled with the same flag and swastika as the pins everyone wore.

"No thank you, Mr. Landis. No need for gifts. I'm strictly Twenty-five dollars a day —"

"Plus expenses," he finished for me.

He was listening this time. How refreshing. I only wish that sensation could wash away the rest of the scum I felt drenched in.

Outside his office, I couldn't help looking for the fire exit in the back. I couldn't bear leaving through the front. Enthusiastic cheering erupted from the crowd in the auditorium. The microphones provided only so much amplification. The speech was cracked and broken.

I was grateful I couldn't make out every detail.

"Looking for the servant's door?" Elsa finished lighting her cigarette with one of those gold lighters. I guess everyone Landis liked got one.

Oh, what the hell. "Yes, actually. I don't want to draw too much attention."

"Oh, that can be solved by wearing one of these," she held out the pin from earlier.

"No," I said, exaggerating the pronunciation.

After pocketing the pin, Elsa shook her head, and gracefully took her snipe out. "The … what you might call *the back way out …* it's this way." She pointed to a dingy staircase.

I was never so glad for a dark, grimy set of steps that smelled like someone used it for a toilet. At least the bottom door opened. I startled several uniformed youths but made my escape otherwise unnoted.

Chapter Eleven

First rule of detective work:
run away when the first question you ask is,
"What could go wrong?"

-Lou Tanner, P.I., 1935

A cheating spouse. I figured that was what my new case was about. Not a huge stretch for anyone. I had not, however, expected it to be the Candidate-of-the-Hour's wife. Jeez, had I hit rock bottom or what? Politics. Still, it was a case that could have legs to run a lot farther on than this one mystery. Holding my nose and working for someone I'm repulsed by but very well situated with the Swell Set, could still get me future work from the people who had plenty of cabbage to toss. I could make a good name or repair damage done and put more experience under my belt. I might even get back into the good graces of the police department.

Most importantly, I wouldn't have to let Marley go. She'd never have to go back to work for cheap bosses with wandering hands. Or marry herself into anonymity and unending boredom.

Isn't this where the hero asks, *what could possibly go wrong*?

Something popped!

I froze. I guess it would be a while before sudden, loud noises didn't bring back reminders of this morning. I've been in vehicles that have crashed, been shot at by a Tommy gun and taken a bullet,. But a bomb, randomly set by someone intent on harming or killing? That came with its own set of horrors.

My earlier glee had departed for destinations unknown. I was far too cognizant of everything wrong around me. Getting on a trolly wasn't on the menu right now. I walked.

Eventually, I crossed under the Union Pacific aqueduct right on time as the *Northwest Moderne* blasted by, dumping steam over the sides onto the pedestrians below. A double blow on the whistle let the folks at the Montgomery Aero and Rail Station ahead know that they were arriving. The clanging bell made sure there was no guesswork about that. Twenty-five minutes late by my reckoning. I suppose that's not too bad — Daddy wouldn't have liked it if his railroad lines had run so far behind, but such things weren't his worry anymore.

Nor were they mine.

At Fourth and Market was Howie Eva's newspaper stand. This was a routine — dare I say ritual of mine. I'd even go so far as to say it was a comfort for me. And I needed some comfort right now.

Evans himself was bent over, unwrapping stacks of the Chronicle, the Globe, and a few other local and national papers, and making room for the afternoon editions. He stretched up, groped the shelf above his reach, and then held out a small stack of product he'd obviously been saving for me. My favorites: Black Mask and D&S Detective Magazine. Pure fantasy that reminded me of how average and dull my daily life could become. The newspapers reminded me of how dangerous my daily reality had become.

"I have friends with eyes and ears," he said softly, without looking up.

"You always have." I set my meager coins on the lip of his cash register. "You notice that I never ask."

"I like to think of it as a professional courtesy. One inquiring mind to another." A pair of piercing black eyes looked me up and down. "Somebody told me I should be worried about you."

"Because I might be in trouble?"

"Uh-huh."

"When am I not in trouble?"

Evans stood and planted his hands on his hips. He was a tall, negro man with worn features and more than his fair share of war scars. "You invite twice as much trouble as you're allotted."

No Requiem for the Tin Man

"It's more fun that way."

"Some trouble isn't worth it."

I was getting a little aggressive with the page turning, regardless of how much I wanted to stay calm and sassy. "Going somewhere specific with this, Mr. Evans?"

"Just sayin'. I know you well enough to recognize the difference between your clientele and your friends. Not everyone can do that. Or is willing to."

Well … shit. The word got around pretty damn fast. *I wonder if I have Hayes to thank for that?* "Strictly clientele, Howie, strictly clientele. And I wouldn't bother if I didn't need …" God, what were the right words that wouldn't confirm my status as a bottom-of-the-bin, undoubted heel? "If I didn't …"

"In need of cash?"

"No, no. Not a loan. A favor. An item to borrow." I couldn't look him in the face out of shame, but my shame didn't stop me from asking. "It's only for a quick tail job. No politics. Zip. Zero. Made sure it was clearly understood I wasn't interested in any 'cause.' Got a little uppity on a couple of them too."

"And they still hired you?"

"Yeah."

"Why?"

Damn good question, but somehow I felt a little offended. "Golly gee, thanks. It couldn't be that I'm damn good at what I do?"

Evans was startled. "I wasn't being insulting."

"Of course not. But you just pinned down the nagging sensation I've been having. Why *me*?" I lowered my voice and began leaning on and tapping the top of a stack of newspapers. "Did you just tell me that you have some highly reliable friends, Mr. Evans?"

"I've known them for a long time. They trust me. So, I told them not to read anything into your business. Is that reliable enough?"

My hands grew cold. Guilty. That's what I felt. "Thanks. hope I didn't get you into any trouble with your friends. They're not wrong to be … concerned. I kinda' got caught with the proverbial trousers down when I found out who they were, if you catch my meaning." Yeah, shame drove down the tone and volume in my voice. "Things are … tough right now."

"No bother. As long as you are paying attention and keeping them at professional arm's length. I know you will."

"Again, thanks. Well, I think I used up my last favor card."

"Not at all." He dropped a pile of papers onto the top of others and cut the twine tying them together. "Ask away."

On cue, because I believe that my existence is nothing if not designed for the movies, two soldiers wandered up. Hunter's Pointe Militia soldiers. Black pants, black shirts, thickly-belted jackets, black ties. Black gloves and boots. Both sported a broad billed cap — in black, of course. What is it with black uniforms these days?

There must have been ham hocks and bacon in the redwood branches, because I was staring at militiamen out and about on an average day. In broad daylight. Weren't they all allergic to light? I was sure they only came out at night, in packs of ten. These two looked as casual as a lazy Sunday afternoon picnic.

Evans stood up. "Good afternoon. Are you gentlemen looking for something in particular?"

Neither spoke to him.

I waited, leaning against the side of the stand, pretending to read one of my magazines. Moving slowly, I pulled my hat down a bit so I could surreptitiously observe from out under the brim.

One, with golden blonde hair and dulled blue eyes, pulled a note pad and pencil out of his pocket, and wrote down what I could only guess were newspaper names. "You carry the Globe but not the American National?"

Evans didn't miss a beat. "American National has declined the opportunity to be sold here, but I can recommend a convenient place nearby where you can get a copy."

"I can see why," Golden Boy sniffed. "You know the Globe is coming down hard on the Pointe militia, damn hard, don't you? Or don't you read, boy?"

My mature friend was the epitome of patience. "My personal tastes tend toward a lighter fare. Less depressing these days."

"So why do you carry the Globe?"

"I believe in freedom of speech, and the reader's right to choose as they please."

"But you don't carry the National?"

Golden Boy's partner nudged him. "He told you. They won't let no nigger sell them." He pulled out a pack of cigarettes and a gold lighter. I recognized that lighter.

"That is correct," Evans replied politely.

Golden Boy didn't say anything else but stuck the snipe in his mouth, finished some notation, and turned to leave. "Say, you ain't one of them People's Socialist bomb lovers are you?"

"I don't know what you are referring to," calm and cool Evans replied.

The partner's lip curled. "*People's Society for Social Relief. Should have called themselves Not-white People wanting White People's stuff without earning any of it.*"

"Hmm." Evans pretended to ponder the notion. "That wouldn't create a neat acronym, would it?"

Golden Boy's colleague glared daggers at Evans for a minute.

I found my hand had wandered its way onto the little heater in my pocket. Evans might be patient but I wasn't feeling so broad minded.

Golden Boy turned back, and his eyes fell on me. He gave me the once over so intensely it felt like someone working a bakery rolling pin over my skin.

"Broads wearing men's trousers and niggers hawking communist propaganda. Where the hell is *my* America?"

It wasn't a question, and even if it was, it wasn't a question we were permitted to answer. Golden Boy and his friend walked away, almost daring us to try something stupid. Now, I can only speak for myself, but I guessed Evans was with me in really, really wanting to try something stupid.

I was wrong. You could have pushed me over with the solid, serene, almost amused look on Howie's face.

"Mr. Evans, you look entirely unsurprised."

He half smiled. "That's the third *uniformed* visit I've had. I'd take it personally if I hadn't heard that other newsstands are experiencing the same thing."

"Pointe Boys with nothing better to do?"

"That's what I figure."

"I guess they're getting more base leave than before."

"Or they're planning something."

"Mr. Evans, are you being paranoid or pessimistic?"

"Both." He shook his head and swung a heavy, string tied pile of papers to the top of a stack. "With a heavy dose of hopefulness that I am wrong."

"I don't like that they're out here," I sniffed. "It's not as if they're official military. They're auxiliary. Supposed to be ready in case something happens. But these guys, they do what they want and dress it up as patriotism. No war department to answer to. A bunch of boys all gussied-up and playing soldier."

"They're not the only ones. Political groups, social groups … it's the latest thing, all the rage. Everyone has a uniform and the clearest idea of who 'us' and 'them' are. And none of them wants to do good … not really. Certainly not for folks who need help and all the good they can get."

"Uniforms," I said with a level of disgust that made Evans raise an eyebrow. "You'd think they'd forgotten the war. But then, we have short memories, don't we?"

Looking to me while I still fingered my derringer, Evans shook his head with amusement. "You weren't planning on shooting them, were you, Miss Tanner?"

"Mr. Evans, I don't like bullies and I've had my fill of them today."

"And it isn't even three o'clock yet." He folded his arms across his chest. "So, what was the favor you came to ask for? After that little scene, I'm in a generous mood."

CHAPTER TWELVE

It's called Keyhole Peeping. A Tail Job. Snooping.
It still pays coin and maybe does some good.

-Lou Tanner, P.I., 1935

Skeeter the Taxi Driver isn't just handy for rescuing us from bars after late-night rounds of pickling. When I know I can pay him, he's my ride. I'd need him today. I had a wayward wife to tail. But first, I needed to check on someone still tugging on my gut.

And, I had to admit, the cable car system wasn't looking too good right now. My imagination was filling in blanks in my memory and the more I looked at a trolly, the worse the memory became. Every time that bell clangs, I had a sudden vision of a trolly flying through the air.

The hospital at Laguna Honda was supposed to be the finest facility built after the Great War with the peculiarities of the survivors in mind. The best in compassionate care for those who returned all screwed-up. Approaching the hilltop fortress with its strange Tudor-prison looking façade and the cadre of military police securing its gates, the place sure as hell suggested another atmosphere altogether. Crenelated stone-work lined the rooftops and the barred windows seemed a bit too narrow to my eye. Was it a hospital or a Citadel? I was waiting for the volleys of stones from enormous trebuchets to begin at any moment. Skeeter muttered something and declined my invitation to repeat it.

Behind me, the City was humming away with indifferent chromed wings and deco themed skyscrapers. The Intercontinental Zeppelin was ten minutes early and prodding its nose into the spire of the Montgomery Station. Fading fog and overworked steam engines had filled the chilly air with a wash of blue watercolor that turned the whole view into a poster for tourism.

I gave the Floater crews another five weeks and they'd be done with the Oakland - San Francisco Bay Bridge and Aqueduct. Cars, fresh water, high-speed rail locomotives, and local Key System trains crisscrossing the bay. No more running around the bottom of the Bay, adding miles and hours to get from one city to the other that were only 8 miles apart on a map.

Between Marin County and the City was a twin sister to the Bay Bridge. Plenty of traffic could pour in from the north. Now that's progress.

Turning back to the hospital, my insides regressed, and depression swallowed me whole. Damn. If I'm feeling this way at the front door, how do the patients feel?

Proverbially girding my loins, I marched into the place like I owned it. That usually works with security and guards. They don't like messing with a lady who has that much moxy. Today, I was playing the lady. Nice business suit, a tad severe, Go-to-Sunday-Meeting hat, gloves, librarian glasses … the works. I made certain I gave off the impression heads would roll if I was so much as moderately delayed by a second.

It worked.

The average age of the military security man couldn't have been more than twenty-years-old. That's what we get for sending two entire generations off to a war that wiped them out. All we have left to defend us are the old, the unwilling, the broken, and the much-too-young.

Inside the dungeon was more like a beehive. Everyone active and fussing. Orderly 'Bots with built-in patient chairs rushed around each other in a frenzy of tight schedules and dispassionate pre-designated paths. Humans in those chairs held on for dear life. Some closed their eyes and gripped the arms of the speeding rides.

I've been in taxis like that.

A 'Bot rolled in front of me. Instead of a chest, it had a gigantic board with rows of flipping letters and numbers. "Please

NO REQUIEM FOR THE TIN MAN

state your business," a pre-recorded voice stated. A tiny, brass microphone extended to me.

"I am here to visit a patient." Keep it short and clear.

"Room number?"

"I do not have the room number."

"Patient name?"

"Augustin Gruber."

The wheels on the 'Bot's board began flipping furiously. One by one, although not in logical order, they stopped, until showing me the floor, ward, and room number for Gus.

"Thank you," I said, out of habit.

"Please have a pleasant day, Miss Ta …" It cut off with as strange sound and left before it could finish its sentence.

I wasn't certain, but for some reason I felt known … too well known by that mechanical. That made no sense, and I tried to let the idea go. But I'm a stubborn sucker and once I get an idea into my head, well, I've been known to kick it around until its beyond recognition.

And usually, I'm right to keep on that thought.

Not at this time, of course. Clients first. I back-burnered the creepy feeling.

The elevator was a caged cell of gold ornamentation, tarnished, and in need of repairs. Still, despite clanging and banging in several distressing moments, it deposited me on the correct floor.

I'm taking the stairs back down.

Finding Gus's room wasn't too hard. The floor was mostly empty of visitors. Only the remnants of the War were there: defeated victors, cowards, and heroes. Men staring into the distance, not seeing the reddened clouds and sunrise, but the fields of Flanders. Men waiting to become specters in the cold hallways beyond or around the corner.

Gus's room had a soothing voice coming from it. Inside, a gorgeous woman sat at his side, holding his hand, and speaking to him in a sickly sweet sort of way.

Mrs. Landis. Mrs. Regina Landis. Hair up in an innocent sweep, if a Harlow bleached blonde can ever be innocent. A blouse covered her neck demurely with a soft bow, and a figure-flattering, dark wool suit covered most everything else. The tilt of her simple hat couldn't help but emphasize her sulky red mouth and allow her bright blue eyes to glow like police lights out from under the shade it provided.

The notion jumped in my brain that I was seeing a lot of blonde haired - blue eyed folks these days. Gus fit the same bill.

She stopped speaking the moment I reached the doorway. I was lucky that my life didn't rely on the nature of her stare, otherwise I'd be stone cold dead.

"Are you lost," she asked, in a silky voice even I found alluring.

"I'm an acquaintance of Gus." I glanced his way, hopeful he might remember me. This might get a bit awkward ... more so than it already was ... if he didn't recall having a tizzy in my office.

Gus appeared confused. "I ... I think I recognize you," he slurred. His eyes couldn't quite find me as if there were three of me and he was deciding which was real.

Think fast, Lulu. "You weren't at your best when we met. It was a couple of days ago."

Mrs. Landis's head snapped towards him, her eyes wide. Gus simply looked at the olive-drab blanket covering his legs. "I wasn't at my best, to be sure." He picked at the threads for a moment. "I apologize —"

"August! You don't need to apologize!"

"Your friend is correct," I added, moving in closer. "No need to apologize. It was a difficult day for you."

I guess the closer I got, the fewer of me there was for him to track. Medications, such as sedatives, can work on the old bean that way. He was high as a kite but low as a stone. Gus wasn't going anywhere.

He was at least washed now, a strong whiff of medical soap floated my way. Remnants of dishes and utensils implied that he might be fed, if he'd actually eaten. He was clean shaven too, not to mention his hair was cropped even shorter than before. I suppose that's what happens when you get involuntarily admitted: bathed and shaved.

When his head flopped back and he lifted a couple of fingers to examine the non-existent texture of the ceiling, I thought Mrs. Landis might cry. "You've never seen him like this before?"

"Not ... like this," she muttered out from under her hands. She would smear that pretty makeup job doing that. Maybe she didn't care so much.

I perched myself at the end of the bed, mostly to watch the scene play out. Might as well. I couldn't run off without causing some questions to get into her head, and I sure wasn't tailing her any closer than this. Mrs. Landis sat with her face in her hands. To my left, a chart hung off a hook at the end of the bed frame. With Gus enthralled by the roof and Mrs. Landis having a sob or two, I took a gander at the doctor's notes.

Doctor? *My, my, my, call me surprised.* Dr. Frederick Gruber.

So the family doctor was the doctor of record. Wasn't there something ethically wrong about that? I guess money adjusted any question of medical ethics. I'd have to get Marley on it, but my gut was already telling me that this was one hospital Dr. Gruber had free reign and control over patients.

Flipping through the pages, I noticed that the handwriting was horrible. Even with that, I "noticed" something else: a change in his meds. The scribble was different. I couldn't begin to guess what the medications were, but I could see that they were not the same ones he'd been prescribed earlier..

Mrs. Landis comported herself and tucked a few stray strands of hair back into place. "So, Elsa isn't coming herself today?" The words were loaded with distain.

"I wasn't sent by anyone. I'm here because I met Mr. Gruber the other day."

Big surprised eyes stared at me. "You're not with my husband's cause?"

"No." Instinct told me to refrain from any commentary or explanation — let her fill in the blanks. Right now, my opinion about the "Cause" was neither relevant nor helpful. I had no idea if Mrs. Landis was a believer or not. If I want to avoid an argument, perhaps it was best not to say anything disparaging. Yet.

"Great," she snuffled again. "Then Elsa will be here soon. You probably don't want to meet her. She's ... ah ...overly fond of her brother. You know ... protective."

Gus played with something in the air. "She doesn't like me."

Mrs. Landis set her hand out on his arm. "That's not true, August. Your sister loves you."

He made some sort of noise that might have been stifled laughing. I almost made the same noise.

Instead, I decided to play my opinion cards tight to my chest and keep asking directed questions. "He does seem to be out of it, doesn't he?"

"I've never seen him like this before." She watched me with a side-eye as I put away the chart. "You a nurse?"

"Who me? I'm a nobody. I had the fortune to meet Mr. Gruber. Gotta' say, that scribble didn't make much sense to me."

"Doctors are notorious for bad handwriting. Frederick is the worst."

First name basis. Hmmm. Shall we try something? "So, Mr. ... Gus, behaving this disoriented ... it's new for him, isn't it?"

Mrs. Landis nodded.

Let's see what she knows. "That explains the different scribble." I reached over to pluck the chart off its hook again and showed her. "New medication. Maybe it isn't right for him. But don't ask me. I could be wrong. As I said, I'm not a nurse and I'm certainly no doctor."

She took the chart from me like it was the only food she'd had in days then gripped it like a life preserver. The pages whipped up and down. Her baby blues got bigger by the second. "You're right, Miss ... uh?"

"Heinreid," I lied without batting an eyelash. *And no,* I reminded myself, *I don't feel guilty for yanking a little on her leash. Why should I? Even if she isn't cheating, she married a Nazi. Probably is one too.*

"Why," she asked to no one in particular, forgetting that I was in the room with her. "Frederick, why?" came out as a whisper so desperate my ironclad heartstring got strummed. *Damn it.*

No Requiem for the Tin Man

The chart hit the floor.

Her pretty, made-up face landed in her hands again. Sobs fell out from between her fingers.

Gus lost interest in the ceiling and petted her arm.

I felt like a real louse. Fine, I'm no Philip Marlowe, that's for sure. He'd never be bothered by using a witness or even a client. All it's taken is a little throb in her voice and I'm the easy push-over.

Ten minutes later, my handkerchief was soaked and stained with mascara and war paint. Gus was on the verge of sleep and Mrs. Landis was calmer.

"Look, Lady, you don't know me from Eve, but I like Gus." That was true. "I got no designs on him. I wanted to check on him. What's all this about? Maybe you'll feel better if you —"

"Oh no! I can't say anything. Please don't take this the wrong way. It is so lovely of you to care. I'm being silly and everything is fine."

Sure it is. Why is it women, like us, always say it's fine when it isn't. Come on, sister, spill it!

She folded my hanky and handed it back to me. "Thank you, Miss Heinreid. I believe you are correct, the new medication isn't working as it should. And if a non-doctor can see that clearly, it must be truly obvious. I'll ask Frederick to change Gus's medication back to what it was before and he'll be fine."

"Will he do that?"

"Oh, yes. Yes, he will."

That was rather confident of her.

The clock tower rang out the hour from over at St. Francis. Mrs. Landis checked her wrist watch. "Miss Heinreid, at the risk of sounding rude, I think you may want to leave. This is about the time Gus's sister comes by. Elsa. She is exacting. Prompt. No errors or deviations." *Was that sarcasm I heard?* "And I don't think you'll like her."

I don't think I'll like having her see me here, talking to the Mrs. Can't say I'm excited to see Elsa anyway.

Gus started waving me off. "She doesn't like me. Just wants my package."

"Gus!" Mrs. Landis scolded. "Don't be so vulgar in front of Miss Heinreid."

"Everyone wants it." He curled up like a child and closed his eyes.

She returned to me. "I am so very sorry. He isn't like that."

"I wouldn't think so. Has to be the medications."

"Yes." For the first time, she brightened, in a startling, genuine way. I couldn't put my finger on it: maybe it was the softness in her expression or the relief in her voice. Overall, her muscles relaxed. She wasn't scared of me. "Thank you." After demurring a bit, she stunned me by adding, "I'm glad you came by. Not only for Gus, but I'm glad I met you, Miss Heinreid. Most of the people I meet are … well, let's just say I'm not the reason they are saying 'hello.' My husband is the star of the show."

I shook her hand, stammering some sort of niceties that would have made my mother proud, and blubbering along about how I hoped her day would go …

Yup. I'm a sap.

I left the room a little wiser. I had more information, but somehow I was further from an answer than I thought I'd be. Didn't help I was beginning to like Mrs. Landis. If she was having an affair, I was of a mind to wonder if maybe she wasn't due some comfort. Landis himself was slippery, but then, he did seem to love her. That love was tempered with his love for his career, a fact alone that could make things tough between them.

What did it matter? That wasn't my job. I wasn't here to judge.

I'd barely egressed the room when Elsa, with a pair of tough bruiser-like boys arrived from the opposite direction. I considered loitering across the hall until one of the toughs took up a guard post outside Gus's room and the door was shut.

It sure didn't take long before the shouting started, not that I could tell what was being said. The voices were strictly female. I figured the fellow inside with them kept to himself. Smart move.

The door opened allowing Regina to stand in the frame. The circles under her eyes appeared much darker than before. She took one long, deep breath, then turned back to the room. "If you care about him, you'll let him go to the Marin Institute. It's beautiful up there."

"This hospital may not be much to look at, but at least the administration is run by pure, old world families who understand what is right and correct. Frederick is allowed to care for Gus here. And up there? You'd let him be touched by a bunch of Jews."

"Elsa!"

"It's true, Regina. I won't be surprised if they have Dinge or Dago nurses soon. I won't allow it! This country is being —"

Regina slammed the door and the screaming match continued.

I could only loiter close by for so long before it was obvious that I didn't have much business there.

A nurse with a no-nonsense-glare ordered me along, and my inside surveillance was over.

Lingering outside the building, working on a pack of Strikes, I timed Elsa's stay. Skeeter was reading one of my magazines. Twenty-three minutes later the Teutonic Queen emerged with Mrs. Landis reluctantly in tow.

Things were getting interesting.

The two tough birds moved in to get all frisky with the wife. She was having none of it. Good girl. I wouldn't put up with that pawing. Neither did her chauffeur waiting with a beige Packard. The assured gesture from Mrs. Landis and the subsequent response told me the chauffeur was all hers. Okay then. Didn't hurt he was about four inches taller than Elsa's boys. That would help if things got nasty.

Elsa put her foot down.

Amusing. That didn't achieve what she wanted it to.

Mrs. Landis maneuvered past everyone with a flourish of her fur stole and marched to the Packard. The chauffeur glared at the tough boys and sprinted past his boss to open her door.

Since I'm being paid to follow the wife, I knew which vehicle to keep up with. I loaded up in Skeeter's cab, told him to follow the Packard, and we were off.

Chapter Thirteen

I may have sworn off relationships, but I'm not dead.

-Lou Tanner, P.I., 1935, Personal Journal

Even in my nice suit, I wasn't dressed for access to the upscale joint across Stockton Street.. I certainly didn't carry enough coin on me to grease any palms to get in either.

The café on the other side of the street was more my cup of Joe — literally. A high-class coffee house, perfect for business people expected to rush in, get their breakfast and coffee, then hurry off to work. A cross between a coffee cart on Sutter Street and a fine diner. Overpriced, to make sure a certain class of clientele was drawn to it.

The café's window seating consisted of a row of stools and a long, oak table, allowing for even faster escape during the work morning. Midday, I decided to take up residence with a book, coffee, and cigarettes on one of those stools to watch my mark. Excellent view into the dandy restaurant over yonder.

The waiter first offered Mrs. Landis a window seat, which she absolutely refused, then an interior table. The confused waiter removed all but her cutlery and another set from the chosen table. I could see her well enough, through the Venice-lace curtains, so long as no one sat in the rejected window spot.

My coffee arrived via the hands of a tall, dark-red-haired fellow, with a sharp, smooth face, deep hazel eyes, and a coy grin. I don't recall table service in joints like these. "Thanks," I purred out, shaking a smoke out of my deck.. This could be fun, if I didn't take it seriously. He was pretty. *And pretty is my weakness.*

Holding up my cigarette, I asked, "got a match?"

No Requiem for the Tin Man

Red leaned his long, slender body over the server's counter, lightly fussed for a moment, and returned with a lit match. Holding it for me, he allowed the other side of his grin to turn upward. I liked how the fire reflected in his eyes.

Lowering my eyelashes and dipping my chin while exhaling, I looked up at him over my cheaters. "Say, you don't mind if I stay a while, do you?"

"We're not busy. The lunch crowd moved through already."

"Well. I don't want to get you in trouble with the boss."

He leaned against the window table, all casual-like. "I am the boss."

"Oh, I like that. That's even better."

"I notice you keep watching the place across the street. Hoping to get a reservation? Or maybe a job over there?"

"Any reason to think I couldn't do either?" I retrieved the pack and offered him one of my Lucky's. Afterall, he is the boss.

"Can I have it for later? I got to set a good example for the kitchen crew. But I wouldn't want you thinking I'm high-hatting you either."

"Please," I held the pack closer.

He took the proffered snipe, not with his lips — too bad — held it reverently, and nodded in appreciation, then tucked it into the shirt pocket under his apron. *Nice flannel.* He thanked me for the snipe with an enjoyable smile. "This is interesting. Not much ever happens around here, though there are some notable things, otherwise not much. So now I'm curious. About the other place? You have to know somebody who knows somebody. They don't let just anybody sit in there."

"'Bet they're picky about who gets a window seat too. Gotta keep the reputation tight."

He gave me a sharp, knowing nod. "And they only hire men. Used to be a men's club, then someone's wife got upset, and they started letting the ladies in for lunch. Otherwise, it's for the boys and only the boys."

Glancing across the way, I could see Mrs. Landis getting some coffee but gesturing sharply, then checking her watch.

"She goes there often," Red said, out of nowhere.

"You know that?"

"A fella notices when a looker like that is a frequent visitor in a place with limits. Or here."

"That's pretty good. You like to keep an eye on things."

He gave me a once over as if to prove his skill. "I sure do. But not just lookin'. I figure things out too. Like … you're not here for my coffee, are you?"

I took a sip as if to prove him wrong. Gotta' admit, his coffee would be worth the trip downtown on any day. "You got me. But I think I wouldn't mind coming back if this here is your average cup."

He settled his tongue behind his teeth and narrowed his eyes. "You're watching the woman across the street. Maybe hoping I know something or I've seen something. Okay. That tells me a few things. I know they're hiring women into the police department, but something about you doesn't say cop. That could make you a jealous wife?"

I paused him with two fingers then reached into my purse. He was suitably impressed with the shield-shaped bronze buzzer pinned to the flap of my wallet. "You are good, Mister. I'm a shamus. Bonafide Working a tail job."

"A real honest-to-God lady Private Dick. Now I've seen everything."

Not everything. I took off my cheaters and pushed my hat back a little bit.

"Say," he added sweetly, "you're not half bad, lady. Kinda' remind me someone."

"Yeah, I get that a lot."

He was thinking again: narrow eyes, tongue behind his teeth. "From the look of things, she's waiting for someone who's late."

"Agreed. And you know that because?"

"It's not the first time her lunch partner has been late."

"I'm willing to bet she doesn't appreciate the fashionably late entrance."

"Never does. Remember I said nothing much happens around here, except for some notable things? If Little Miss Notable doesn't slap him for being late —"

"*Him?*"

"Oh, definitely *him*. If she doesn't slap *him*, get up and walk out on him —"

"Which you are going to tell me she's done repeatedly before?"

"Twice before. If she stays, it will take him a bit of time and bubbles to calm her down."

"Interesting. Does he have a particular look?"

"Of course he does. Rich. Playboy. Tall-ish, but not as tall as me. Dirty blonde hair, cut long in the front, short in the back. Like a Swell wears it these days. In his thirties, though I can't tell if he's in his early or late thirties. Likes to be dressed well. No backbone when it comes to the Looker. He might … might have a mustache. Not sure."

Yeah, that sounded just like Frederick Gruber. "Interesting again. Go on."

"Then they'll have lunch for the next hour and a half."

"And I'll have to stay here the whole time. You don't mind do you?"

"Not at all. Oh, one other thing. If a black Packard pulls up, there'll be fireworks. If a beige Packard pulls up, it's hers."

That was quite a lot to chew on, or in this case, sip. Still, I took Regina Landis to be more on-the-ball than that. A public feud or two. That was sloppy for someone trying to have a quiet affair. Someone with a famous husband. Unless, of course, she wasn't trying to be so quiet about it. Or she doesn't care who knows what she's up to.

I fluttered my eyelashes at Red. No reason, I just wanted to. "Who owns the black Packard?"

"Don't know. I don't often get a clear view of the fire-setter. Mostly I hear the excitement, then see the guy get in his jalopy and drive off. She follows after him but doesn't leave."

"And they let the lady back into the joint — after all that fuss?"

He winked at me. Damn cutest thing I'd seen in a while.

"Trust me. I know my neighborhood. The lace curtains and matching tea service over there doesn't mean diddly. The customers are supposed to be respectable. Doesn't mean the owners or employees are. They're the sort who know when to look the other way."

"Red, you ought to consider a career in detective work. But don't stop making coffee." I sipped, slowly blinking my eyelashes at him over the rim of the cup. "This cup of Joe is too memorable."

A little bit of drizzle and fog got themselves together to make a baby rain. One of those tikes the parents adore and think is the most beautiful child in the world, but everyone cringes when they see the multitude of photos. Around here, light rain equals slick roads and a feeling of slime on everything you're wearing.

I was glad for the warm company.

Correction: warm, smooth, and handsome company.

While Red was off giving his attractive attentions to another customer, I dug into my purse for a match. I couldn't interrupt him now. Nearly cut my fingers on a folded piece of paper. Sticking a cigarette between my lips, I unfolded the paper, the one handed to me by that gal near Fisherman's Wharf. An invitation to come listen to speakers in support of the People's Society for Social Relief.

So, the PSSR had infiltrated Mr. Shout-'n-Slather's crowd looking for like-minded folks. How I'd rated with them was a curiosity I'd have to contemplate later. For now, I chuckled a bit.

"You thinking of going?" Red asked over my shoulder.

"Too busy. Don't get me wrong, I'm all for the working man … and woman. But truth is, I'm a lousy joiner. Always forget to pay up on my dues, never any time to get involved."

Red shrugged, took my match, and lit if for me. My gut took a note for me. He hadn't batted an eyelash at the advertisement. Maybe he was anti-union. Maybe he was pro-union. Maybe, he didn't want to take a stand at all. If so, I could appreciate the wisdom in that.

A sweet Desoto Airstream coupe pulled up across the street. The kind of jalopy that was far too pricey for the average Joe. Swank. Pearl colored with chrome. Meant to be seen. Yeah, the driver wanted everyone to know that he had dough and was willing to flash it.

So, it came as no surprise to me that Dr. Frederick Gruber leaped out, looking swell and sheen. I swear, the drizzle parted like the Red Sea for him as he dashingly dashed into the restaurant. Red gave a low whistle behind me.

"Know him?"

"Him? Yeah, that's the Swell I told you about. He's one who's been on the receiving end of her ire before. But the ride is new. There's some serious sugar in those wheels."

"New car. Someone's showing off."

We both leaned down and forward, to see a little better past the curtains across the way. Sure enough, Frederick was escorted over to Mrs. Landis's table. Oh, how the apologies were flowing like a drywash flood in Arizona. His hands pleaded. Her folded arms refused. His clutching fingers and attempts at taking up her hand begged. Her back leaning tilt said she'd had as much as she'd take of him.

This might get interesting, were it not for the fact I'd been in her shoes before. I filled in the blanks where I couldn't figure out the words. She stood up, listening to excuses, knowing full well that one lie was covering up for another. Sure I was assuming, but it was the way he leaned in. It was the way he moved in a practiced manner. Too slick. Too smooth. Like the car. If she was already his mistress, who was he trying to impress?

She stood up. Correction. She jumped to her feet, hands balled into dainty fists.

Red and I both caught our breath at the same time.

Would she slap him?

Not this time. The lady decided to keep her dignity and merely walked away.

I hoped she left him stiffed with the check.

As I followed her rush to her chauffeured car, I pondered my own feelings. Were they interfering? Was I adding to the observations based on my own experience? I didn't know why Frederick was late. Maybe the Desoto wasn't his. I needed to find out. And it didn't do me or my client any good to fill in the blanks without evidence.

What did I know? Red had seen him there before, with Regina. He was brother to Gus and Elsa. He was rich, at least in appearance. A Doctor of some sort. One that had visiting rights at the hospital, including housing a patient under his direct care. And Mrs. Landis and he did things together. They'd been photographed together. She'd taken umbrage with him before. All of that suggested an affair, but only circumstantially. It wasn't proof. I needed hard evidence of an affair or of a volatile friendship, either of which was equally probable right now.

Once the chauffeured car passed the little café, I waited for Frederick. I wanted to see his reaction. He left money on the table. She *had* stiffed him. Still not evidence of adultery.

The man who exited the restaurant wasn't the jaunty, carefree doctor who walked in. Every line on his face dragged downward changing it to one of those Greek masks worn by the tragic character. His eyes glanced around the street as if he needed to see if anyone had witnessed his humiliation. I kept my book in one hand, snipe in the other, and both up near my face. An old but effective trick.

Frederick trudged out to his expensive showpiece jalopy and sped off.

Enlightening but, yet again, no evidence. Sometimes it isn't so much a collection of hard clues but soft perceptions that add up to tell the story.

With reluctance, I bid farewell to Red and headed out into the San Francisco spit.

Chapter Fourteen

Trust nothing and no one.

-Lou Tanner, P.I., 1935

Nothing like walking into the aftermath of a storm. Especially *inside* my own office.

Coming up the world's slowest elevator allowed voices from my floor to float over to me. Down the hallway, I could tell one of those voices was Marley. No problem. Didn't recognize the man's voice, but he wasn't threatening her. My guess, it was Sam, her beau.

Sure enough, it was Sam Mayfield. I opened the door to Marley cleaning yet another trashing of the space, Not My Cat dashing out into the hallway, and Sam scowling — arms folded tightly across his chest.

"Again?" I asked, stepping around Sam.

"I wondered," Marley replied from the floor where items were scattered. "The files were tidy but not quite right." Backing onto her heels, she glanced over at us. "Slim, you remember Sam?"

"Sure."

His scowl broke. "What happened? And what do you mean again?"

"Someone cased the joint," Marley answered for me.

Sam blinked. "Cased? What?"

"Someone came in, tossed the placed looking for something. They didn't find it the first time and I suspect they didn't find it the second time," I answered for Marley.

"They didn't."

For a full minute, Sam rested his nose between his fingers.

"You realized the pair of you sound like a Cagney movie, right?"

All we could do was shrug.

Marley started to stand up and tried to explain while he rushed to assist her. "It's the lingo of the trade, honey. It's expected."

"Not from a pair of ladies."

I tossed my glasses and hat onto my desk. "Most people don't assume we're ladies. We're in the wrong profession, don't have enough money —" I choked off the last before continuing, "to be rich folks, and run in the right circles. You are sweet to think better of us."

Not My Cat sauntered back in.

"Is the cat okay?" I asked.

Marley and Sam stared at him. "Why?"

"He's the hero of the hour. He chased off whoever trashed the place last time. Scratched some bruiser up pretty good. Say, how do you know that they didn't get what they came for this time."

"Sam chased 'em off. They left empty handed." She pranced over to Sam and kissed him on the cheek. "He was swell. They were running outta' here."

Sam blushed.

I tried not to laugh. "Thanks! I'm getting' a little tired of seeing this place turned upside down. I have no idea what they're looking for."

"I don't know either, Slim. We don't keep cash. Nothing of serious value. Guns are on us or …" she pointed, "still there where we keep them locked up."

Sam's scowl came back.

I felt something whack my ankle. Not My Cat was flopping around, switching from taking a swipe at my feet and batting under my desk. "Hey, cut it out." I moved my feet.

Marley thumbed over toward the hot plate. "They spilled the coffee. I'll go get some water to clean it up and make a fresh pot."

As she left the room, Sam put out a hand to stop me. "This has got to stop, Lucille."

Nobody calls me Lucille anymore. "Lou. And I agree. Better locks —"

"No. Marley can't work here anymore. And this nonsense about her become a Private Detective ... you put that idea in her head."

About six retorts came to mind, all competing for me to use in that minute, but all I did was glare at him. Finally, I said, "Nobody 'puts ideas in' Marley's head. She decides on what she wants. She carefully weighs information and comes to a conclusion. She's not an empty headed —"

"I never said she was 'empty headed.' I'm just saying she's easily persuaded. She follows you around like a love-struck teen who wants to please her hero. She'll do anything to —"

"Whoa! Do you really believe that? She isn't the weaker sex."

"She's the fairer sex and I'll do anything and everything I can to protect her. And I don't want her following you into a grave."

"Well, boy-o, you may want to check with her to see what she wants."

"We're getting married. She won't need a job after that. I'll take care of her. I don't want you getting her killed before the honeymoon."

When Marley arrived with the water, the crushing silence must have been stupefying. She chose to say nothing and went to make coffee.

Not My Cat kept playing with whatever he'd knocked under my desk. I'd look later on.

Once coffee, not as good as Red's, was steaming out of a cup for each of us, Marley busted through the quiet. "Green Eyes called. Demanded to know where you were."

"What did you tell him?"

"I told him you were off today. He hung up on me."

"The crust that man has." Oh my, was that me making fun of G-Man Hayes? "Anything new in the news?"

"Everyone is still talking about the quakes and freaky light show above the Pointe."

"Still hoping for Martians?"

Marley giggled.

Sam gave her a bit of side-eye. "Me and the boys workin' the

Bridge say the Pointe is experimenting with some sort of battlefield light that will make it easier to fight at nighttime."

"Gotta' admit, that's the most sensible thing I've heard yet." And Sam ought to know, being a team supervisor with the Rivetmen finishing the structure. "What do you Boys on the Bridge think about the quakes?"

"It's San Francisco." He shrugged. "Maybe the Pointe fellas used rockets to get the lights up high enough. That doesn't cut it in my book, but it's better than little green men are coming."

"I prefer Little Green Men from Mars," Marley teased. "Especially since I don't trust the Pointe. Why night lights for battle? Or don't they sleep?"

I settled back in my chair, feet up on my desk. The coffee mug warmed my chest as I held it in place and rocked the chair. "I saw those lights. But I had fire-water in me and I'm not sure I trust me as a witness. It was late too. I sure want to know more or get another look — a sober look."

"How did today go?" Marley looked particularly bright eyed.

"Pretty basic. Like I said, a tail job. Nothing scary." Wowzer, that was a big fib, but I couldn't tell her … yet … who the client was. If banking on Marley's strong ethics wasn't enough, the conversation with Sam cemented it: neither of them would be thrilled with the client.

I wasn't thrilled with the client.

"Good," Sam muttered.

"Either of you following the politics right now? I, ah, haven't been so keen on them. You up on who's who?"

The cat popped up from under the desk with a piece of newspaper in his mouth, as if to join in on the conversation. He spit it out and began slapping it around the floor.

Marley watched the cat for a moment. "Rossi versus Landis is what it's down to. The papers were full of political name calling and a bit of actual talk on what they might do for us schmoes. This latest distraction with the lights an' all, now that's what everyone is jawing about." Marley dug out her pack of snipes.

Sam retrieved his lighter, adding, "Every editor says that all the current aldermen and cops are corrupt. No one is strong enough to do anything. Rossi is on defensive, blaming fascists and communists. Unions, mostly, though I don't know what we have to do with lights at the Pointe and earthquakes or any ground shaking."

"Floater's Union?" I asked with a big smile.

"The Brotherhood of Civil Structure Builders Union," he snarled back, while lighting Marley's cigarette. "Landis, of course, is promising the Moon. He'll stop it, he promises He says its out-of-control or conspiring immigrants."

Smoke wafted up from my lips. "Landis is in charge of the German American Bund. Aren't *they* all immigrants?"

"European immigrants ... with money. That makes them okay. They're *new arrivals* and that means they belong. Everyone else is a dirty, polluting immigrant out to steal everyone else's money." His snarl stayed in place, and despite our earlier conversation, I could see some good points to Sam. "Truth is, the anti-mechanical movement is stupid. Think about it. What would we do without them? There aren't enough people to do all the tasks we're used to having them do. They do it for almost no cost. No one wants their jobs — certainly not at their non-existing pay scale. If we have to start paying 'em scale? The cost to the average Joe'll be too high. So why be against them? Regulations that make sense, sure. But turning them all off and junking them? Stupid."

"Stupid, but not that much better than Rossi's stance. He's pro-immigrant, yes? He's saying the same thing. They'll do the jobs we don't want to do for pay we won't accept. Does it matter who we kick to the bottom and undervalue? We're still in the wrong."

"At least Rossi recognizes humans first. Maybe that's better?"

"I suppose it is, Sam. And yet —"

The phone rang, much to all our collective surprise. Marley reached over, grabbed her pad and pencil, and snagged the receiver. "Tanner Investigations."

Marley kept nodding and "uh-huh-ing" until she glanced over at me. Rolling her eyes, she concluded, "Yes, Mrs. Weiss, let me put Miss *Tanner* on the line. Will you please hold for a moment." She pushed the receiver into her hip. "Oh Miss *Turner*," she mocked in a whisper, "would you mind taking a call?"

"What is with these people?" I gestured for her to hand me the phone while we changed placed.

"Mrs. Weiss? Lou Tanner here. How may I help you?"

"Oh good. I'm calling to receive an update on your progress."

"I've just started."

"So, you have nothing of value."

Ugh. "I've established general patterns of behavior —"

"Of course," her voice was slightly annoyed. Something else: her Midwest, Chicago accent was missing. Her "r" was longer and words were much more clipped than ever. "You wouldn't be familiar with the lifestyle of someone such as Regina Landis. I hope you found something interesting … to someone such as yourself."

"I find much in life interesting." *Such as your assumptions.* "At this time, I am not able to report anything in particular. I will, however, continue as my client has contracted me to."

"And that is?"

I waited. So, Landis told Elsa his concerns, about his bringing me in, but not the details of the case? "Confidential."

"Oh come now, Miss *Turner*. Lucas and I are both —"

"I'm very sorry, Mrs. Weiss. If my client wishes to share details with you, it is completely in his purview to do so." Both Sam and Marley stared at me. "I, however, cannot discuss any part of an agreement between myself and another party. I am strict in my definition of confidentiality."

"Well! There's no need to be uppity about it."

"I'm sorry if I offended you."

Marley's eyes rolled again. Sam kept jerking his head back and forth to look at the pair of us.

"I am offended. You would do well to consider how you treat your betters."

"Thank you for your advice, Mrs. Weiss. I'm certain that my client will take you fully into his confidence and will be satisfied that the decision was left to him." I didn't allow her to start ranting. I already knew who she liked to attack in those rants. "Was there anything else I could assist you with?"

No Requiem for the Tin Man

The line went dead.

So much for upper class manners.

I caught my Irish Girl Friday and her Beau up on the other half of the conversation, sans the client's name, that they didn't overhear and enjoyed their hostile opinions of Mrs. Weiss.

"Snob," Sam muttered under his breath. "Talk about high hatting."

Nodding, I took Marley's pencil and paper, wrote a few words, and showed it to both of them.

<u>Relax, then check for listening devices.</u>
<u>I think we've been bugged.</u>

We sat there in angry agreement and silence. Smoking. Drinking our coffee. Listening to the cat swatting a piece of old newspaper around the floor.

Where did NMC keep getting that trash?

Chapter Fifteen

For men, it's called Gut Instinct and it's held in high esteem.
For dames, it's called Women's Intuition and
apparently adding lace curtains makes it worthless.

-Lou Tanner, P.I., 1935

You sense it when someone is watching you. The hair on the back of your neck stands up. People across the street look at you and then something behind you, then at you again.

Some Schmoe was tailing me, and I needed to ditch him, toot-sweet. But there was a catch — isn't there always?

I was heading home after another day of work, up the steep incline of 10th Avenue. It had been a day of shopping — for Mrs. Landis, not me. I got to follow her into all sorts of nice boutiques. The big ones. I'd be spotted in the smaller shops. In the big ones, I knew a couple of the in-store detectives and after today, I know a couple more, whether I wanted to or not.

The disguise of the day was pretty much the same as yesterday. A mustard yellow dress with matching coat, rose-colored hat with a wide face-shading brim, mid heel shoes, simple jewelry. Not enough glamour to draw attention and yet enough not to get thrown out of the hoity-toity salons.

My dogs were barking by the time Mrs. Landis had relieved her sorrows with cash and headed home. Skeeter, my Taxi man, was hungry, so I sent him off to his wife to put on a much needed feed bag. I thought I might stop to get a sandwich at the deli on Judah, but looking at the line out the door, I decided otherwise.

Then I noticed: that Schmoe was tailing me. *Me.* I thought I was the one doing the tailing. I'd hardly be able to take off in an uphill run. And as much as I wanted to dart into the lobby of my apartment building, that would only confirm where I live. I go to some great pains to keep that on the hush.

So, I did what any dizzy dame might do: I dropped my keys, gave my best *Oh Gosh* startled look to no one in particular, bent down to pick them up while getting a look back down the sidewalk, and locked eyes with the schmuck on my tail. He didn't know how to do the *Oh Gosh* maneuver. I think the skinny, tall, Horse faced palooka only has one look: annoyed. And he was wearing that one hard-core. He started up the street after me. I pitched myself forward and out into traffic.

Wheels screeched and horns blazed as I wiggled around cars that barely missed me. How I made it alive to the opposite side of 10th is a point of amazement to me. Its times like these I believe flexible hips are a lady's advantage. But I didn't take the time to ponder a gift from the universe. I ran like hell, back down the hill. Horseface was right behind me, and his annoyed look was shifting into cheesed-off, right quick.

I had those flexible hips but he had long, long legs. Every straightaway was his chance to gain ground on me. I got down to Judah and made for the regular trolley. There would be enough people on board to make killing or kidnapping a bad idea. Too many witnesses can put a professional gunsel out of business fast.

The local tram, headed downtown, was one block ahead of me. All I had to do was get past a fruit stand, two old buzzards chawing over the latest Seals game, across 8th Street, and I'd be on board.

The old buzzards kindly tipped their hats as I blew past them. One of them must have stuck his foot out because Horseface took a sudden tumble. All I caught was some cussing and a pair of old men apologizing to their verbal abuser.

I was home free. The tram started to move.

A black sedan pulled right in front of me. Huge. Shiny.

I slammed into the passenger door and bounced back, somehow managing to stay on my feet. The front and back doors opened and three men emerged. Dressed just like Horseface.

I backed up and leveled my stance. I could take 'em. My heart was pounding in my throat and my hearing was a clattering of jumbled noise, but my brain kept telling me I could take them.

Horseface moved in behind me. Okay, four. I could take four — sure I could. And I had good reason too: I could see Horseface better now, and I could see scratches on his nose and one across his cheek.

"Miss Lucille."

What the hell?

"Would you please get in." The voice came from the dark interior of the sedan. No voice I knew.

The big guy on my right? It was the way he was standing. Begging me to kick him in the column right between the want ads —

"Miss Lillian Lucille Tanner."

"If I said 'no, that's not my name,' wouldn't you be a bit embarrassed after all this." I gestured at the Brunos.

There was some movement in the car. "Indeed. But, I don't think we're wrong. Miss Lucille, or would you prefer Miss Lou?"

"Miss Tanner. I'm a grown woman," I snapped, "who can more than take care of herself." I didn't take my eyes off Big Guy.

"No doubt. But you are an unmarried woman, and everyone with any modicum of manners knows that an unmarried woman is addressed by Miss followed by her first name. Are you going to continue making an unseemly presentation of yourself? I hope not. Please do as you are told and get into the vehicle."

"No," then I added, so as not to be 'unseemly,' "thank you."

"I assure you, you will not be harmed."

"An assurance from a stranger who has sent four bruisers after me is not substantial enough to protect my delicate reputation."

"They are not damaged."

"They will be if they so much as twitch."

The sigh that shot out of the car was the epitome of frustration. "I am certain Milton Tanner would be quite ashamed to know that his daughter was behaving so inappropriately in public. It is disappointing alone that you have taken a profession, any profession, and such a poorly chosen one at that. He would never have allowed it. A husband would never allow it."

My hackles were up as the speaker slid out of his vehicle. Slender, polished and as classic appearing as his sedan. Trim, neat, and tidy. I put him at 6 feet, maybe 1 or 2 inches plus. Not more than 200 pounds. His suit cost more than the value of all the fruit behind me, stand included. He slowly lit his cigarette wedged into an ivory and gold holder. His face was like marble, smooth and unlived in, yet I could see that he wasn't particularly young. He held out his hand, not for me to shake, but for me to grasp. "Come along."

"No."

"Obstinance is not attractive."

"Neither is arrogance."

Horseface let out his own sigh, or whinny, and said, "he just wants ya ta gab wit da Mayor, sweetheart."

I glanced over my shoulder at Horseface and the small crowd gathering behind him. "Interim Mayor Rossi wants chat with me? Could no one have said something, such as, 'Miss Tanner, Interim Mayor Rossi would like to speak with you. Would you mind coming to his office this afternoon?' To which I would reply, 'but of course. I'm free this afternoon at two, and I would be delighted.' See, boys, that's how the not-unseemly conduct civil conversations."

I felt a little twinge of satisfaction when Horseface blushed a bit.

Mr. Fancy Pants looked me up and down with a mix of distaste and interest. "'Interim Mayor?' I thought you said you weren't interested in politics."

"Excuse me?"

"You said —"

"I know what I've said in the past few days. And I did say that. During a meeting behind closed doors with a client."

"A rather dubious client."

"With a reasonable case that does not include his politics." My whole face squished up in an unintended sneer. "You work for Rossi and Rossi had you bug Landis's office. That's illegal, you know."

"Miss Lucille —"

"Running on the platform of integrity, are we?" I said as loud as I could while sashaying my way over to the car door. "I don't like crowded cars. Have the goons follow in a 'Crawler. Oh wait, Rossi is anti-mechanicals. Have them take a taxi. If they can find one. And if they can fit."

"Get in the goddamn car," Fancy Pants hissed through his teeth.

I stood in front of the heavy oak door, with its polished brass handle and gigantic name plate, and mentally tapped my foot.

"Please go in, Miss Lucille."

Two can play this game and frankly, I was feeling like a real creep today. Albeit an immature creep. I'll own that title, good with the bad. So I waited.

After a short moment, Fancy Pants strolled over and opened the door, mockingly sweeping his hand to direct me inside. As I swanned through, I noted three men seated inside, glaring at me, so I turned back to Fancy and said, "Why yes, I'd love a cup of coffee. Cream please. No sugar." Before his outrage could slip out past the snarl, I gave him my backside to sneer at and walked straight up to the Big Man behind the enormous desk. *The* Big Man.

I was meeting with power brokers. This was the right time to pull out every trick of the trade that I learned in finishing classes. Mother didn't send me away to special school, but she made damn sure her girl knew all of society's rules. Witty repartee with all the sizzling slang I loved didn't cut it with these boys.

Two stuffed shirts sat in the nice, padded chairs arranged in front of the Big Man's desk. Advisors? Confidants? City aldermen? Big men themselves? One was dressed in money I'd never see any time in my adult life. He must have felt armored against any repercussions from judging the likes of me.

The other I recognized as a face from the papers although the name that went with it escaped me. He was in a fancy, smartly-clean Hunter's Pointe uniform, with plenty of gold braid and ribbons. If I was guessing right, I was locking eyes with the Commandant of the Pointe, a big man in his own right.

Both mugs were in their late fifties, the fella dressed in civies carried a rich man's paunch, and looked quite at ease with the power of their immediate neighbor.

Surrounded by American, Californian, and other flags, the Big Man, Angelo Joseph Rossi looked rather small, and older than I expected. A round head, bald crown sided by thin, neatly barbered hair whiter than the walls. His moustache too was thin, to the point I had to look twice to make sure he had one. A natty dresser, yet Rossi looked exhausted. I understood politics could do that to a man. If they don't come into the game withered and aged, they leave it that way. Or in a pine box.

Centered on his desk was a model of the City. *My city* — though I didn't think the Mayor would appreciate the distinction I made. In his model, *the Oakland - Bay Bridge* was complete and had his name written in pen across the upper deck. Underneath were erasure marks and what I could see were the original marks naming the bridge after the looney but loved Emperor Norton. I guess Rossi didn't approve of the first naming choice.

There were several other public-looking works I didn't quite recognize in places I knew. Since this wasn't the time or place for my civic commentary, I kept my yap shut.

Rossi leaned across his desk, a third larger than Landis's, and waved the unknown Pointe man out of his chair. With mumbling reluctance, the Commandant surrendered his seat to me and went to go lean on a table.

I locked up my features into an unmovable expression of "don't screw with me." I'm well-rehearsed.

"Miss Lucille —"

"Excuse me, Mr. Mayor. I'm Miss Tanner. I would appreciate being called Miss Tanner."

The Commandant who'd abandoned his seat to me stood up straight. "That's Mayor Rossi addressing you, missy. You don't talk to him like that."

Oh how my eyes wanted to roll back and stare at yesterday, except there wasn't much to look at yesterday. Other than Red, but I couldn't let him distract me. "I asked him to call me 'Miss Tanner.' I referred to him as 'Mister Mayor.' Is there something wrong with that? My finishing instructor was quick clear on such rules. Was yours?"

Rossi leaned on his arms and chuckled under his breath for a moment. "Miss Tanner, what my colleague means, is he thinks you ought to be scared out of your wits and on the verge of begging for mercy."

I managed to get one eyebrow to lift. It's hard to get anything to go up when the rest of your face is turned down so damn hard. "I never go out without my wits, scared or otherwise. As for begging, well, never got in the habit. It's so unseemly." More chuckling came from the Mayor and his crew, minus one. "Mr. Mayor, since you've gone to so much trouble to … acquire my attention and to illegally wire-tap a conversation I had —"

Rossi didn't move, except for his eyes, which darted towards the door. I guess Fancy Pants wasn't supposed to let on that the big man was spying on his political opponent.

"Sorry, Mr. Mayor. Your associate let something slip. Like I said, I don't leave home without my wits."

"I think you did. I think you left them home two days ago, when you walked into that den of evil."

"You think Lucas Landis is 'evil?'" Eyelashes batted.

"Don't you?"

"I try not to make morality judgments on paying clients. I've learned in the last few years that early assumptions can get you false results."

"It can get you into trouble, young lady."

My turn to lean forward with some serious drama. "It can do even more, Mr. Mayor. I've learned it can get you killed."

"Did he threaten you?"

"Mr. Mayor?" I asked with mock incredulity. "You tell me. You were listening in."

No Requiem for the Tin Man

He slouched backwards, leaning on his elbow on the right arm of his overstuffed leather chair. "Mr. Hampton did the listening. I merely received his report."

Hampton? Perfect for Fancy Pants. "Ah, so, if anyone asks, *you* didn't unlawfully spy on the Landis campaign."

"Exactly. Just as *you* aren't a member of those war-mongering, fascist traitors because *you* aren't working for them, you're working for Landis."

"Not quite the same. I have no interest in gaining personal advantages from Landis's campaign or party. I want nothing to do with them. I work for the man, only. I'm sure that to you, that is a very thin line of distinction. To me, it's a wide ravine. One does what one must to sleep at night."

"And to pay the rent? What if I offer you double what he is going to pay you to give me the results of your … what do you call it?"

"Tail job," I replied with some enthusiasm. I do, after all, love my profession.

"Quaint. Yes, 'tail job.' How would that work?"

Truth lives in the eyes — Uncle Joe taught me that. Rossi's eyes told me a story of wanting to have all the gossip, all the dirt, all the nastiness. There wasn't a flicker of gratification there, simply a craving. I could understand him and his need.

"It wouldn't," I said flatly.

"You *are* one of his followers," the Commandant growled.

"No." I allowed myself to blink while I smoothed every nerve and breath. I also decided I'd keep my conversation strictly with Rossi. He struck me as the only reasonable one. That might be what he wanted. They might be playing good guy — bad guy with me. I frankly didn't care. "Mr. Mayor, I took a job. I entered into an agreement. I have no idea if Landis will keep his part of the agreement. I presume so, and I have my reasons for believing that. As such, I intend to honor my contract —."

"He's a Nazi."

Okay, so the wisenheimer forced his way into the conversation. Who has the poor manners? "To my disgust, it turns out that many of his supporters are, as you say, fascists, authoritarians, and other ugly political factions. Hence, I'm not working for them. I am not working for his campaign or ambitions either. I have a perfectly legal and honest contract with a citizen that does not violate any of the codes or regulations of my business. The details are confidential. And I will not breach my contract."

The men in the room huffed, as if laughing at me or disbelieving me ... to their detriment.

And I continued to ignore them. I'm well-rehearsed in doing that too. "If I let you buy my honor today, who will trust me tomorrow? I work for people, not political parties or corporations."

"You see! She's a communist! Just like that negro she spends her time —"

"That's enough, Carlotti!" Rossi shouted, slamming his big paw down flat on his desk. "I'll have none of that in my office."

Carlotti, so that's his name. Now I remember reading about him. Anti-union all the way. Pro-Police. Defended all the violence during the Great Strike. Applauded the injuries and pain the unionists suffered — said it was all their own fault. Lips firmly plastered to Rossi's backside.

"Angelo, that nigger is one of the PSSR. They're all communists. All of them. And this one," he pointed to me, "is one of his little comrades. She and her family were union backers at the railroad —"

"I said, that's enough." Rossi's face darkened. He turned that deep, burning red skin on me. "Is that true? Are you friends with a negro communist? Are you pro-union?"

Ya' know, you can either try to shout down zealotry or accept its presence and move around it like the pile of horse manure it is. Any way I tried, I wouldn't change Commandant Carlotti's mind. Yet, I might change Rossi's view, because if I didn't, I wasn't leaving the room as a free woman. I wouldn't do so good in the slammer.

Think, Lulu. Think, then speak.

"Mr. Mayor? Are you angrier that I am acquainted with a negro man or that the man in question may not agree with you politically and is black?"

No Requiem for the Tin Man

Well, that caught Rossi off guard. "I ... I don't care if he's negro. He could be ... purple ...polka-dotted ..."

"Don't give me that bunk. We both know it bothers plenty of boys in power that negro men have thoughts, let alone exist. They think their own lives are better if people they deem unworthy remain silent, invisible, and disposable. I'm trying to ferret out whether you and Commandant Carlotti are two of *those men*. If you are, then I am the one who's angry — and very, very offended." I'm told I'm a little bit scary when my voice drops in volume and tone. "I'm a voting citizen, too. You might not like how I choose to vote if I find out you are one of *those men*. Can you afford to lose my vote?"

The quiet alderman must be the peacemaker in meetings like these as he jumped in. "Now, now. Let's all keep our heads."

"Why?" I asked. "I know the man you're referencing. He is a veteran of the Great War, having served his country in Flanders. He runs an honest business and pays his taxes like everyone else. God knows how much bull ... garbage he endures because of bigotry." Okay, I didn't think before I spoke that time, but I didn't regret any of my words either. "Commandant Carlotti, if you persist, I can only conclude you are a bigot."

The silence in the room was numbing. And satisfying.

"As to the other questions, which are, at any other moment in time, none of your damn business, but you forced the matter, didn't you? No, I am not a communist. Communism is not overly fond of women who want to be more than breeders of more communists. As you can guess, I have ambitions of my own that go far beyond birthing mouthpieces for the next generation of politicians. And yes, my parents, specifically my father, were in support of the railroad unions, even when he owned the railroad. The unions we dealt with stood for honest pay, worker safety, and regulations. I can't see one thing wrong with those ideals, and I question the character of anyone who does."

The mumbling around me was loud, but Rossi took in my words in silence. His face not only lost its flaming color but faded to the shade of dull putty. I liked that. It was a refreshing change of pace.

I didn't wait to be given the royal dismissal, so I stood up without permission. Rossi was on his feet, less out of respect I think, and more out of habit. Still, even that little gesture was refreshing too.

"Mr. Mayor, regarding your offer? For several legal and ethical reasons, I must decline."

"So be it. But consider the offer still out there. I have a feeling that you'll find your client disappointing. His followers even more so."

"Obviously not the only disappointment I'll have today." I shot a glare over to Carlotti. "It's a chance I take with every case." No one offered his hand to shake, so I nodded and retreated towards the door. Had I won?

"Oh, Miss Tanner. One thing."

What now? I bit a little into my lip as I faced the Big Man. "Mr. Mayor?"

"We're investigating the police department. Seems they weren't so up and up during the General Strike a year ago."

"So I've heard." I snapped out at him.

"Would you be interested in providing testimony against any particular employees?"

"Living or deceased?"

Rossi paused to think. "Living. The deceased aren't of issue right now."

"Then, no thank you. I have no current complaints. I dislike their behavior in starting riots and committing violence against striking workers. However, I only read about those, I did not witness them. Any testimony of mine would be based on hearsay and therefore of no value." Head tilt. "Is that all, sir?"

"I think that will resolve several questions."

"I'm glad to hear it. Oh, and Mr. Mayor, I won't need a lift back to my office. I would take it as a kindness if you didn't try to replace the listening devices I've already removed from there. The one's placed by Mr. Hampton's rather large employee. You know, after he destructively searched the place and he didn't find whatever it was he was looking for? It's not entirely his fault that I found what he planted. He was rushed. You see, it's all in his face."

NO REQUIEM FOR THE TIN MAN

With that I opened the door to find Horseface and Fancy Pants waiting. I pointed to the scratch marks on Horseface's cheek and nose. Big, ole cat scratches.

CHAPTER SIXTEEN

Amendment to prior saying:
Keep your friends and your bartender paid up.

-Lou Tanner, P.I., 1935

If you know anything about San Francisco, you know that its fog has a mind of its own. Friday night, nine o'clock, and the chill was blasting down Market, playing hide and seek with the buildings of the downtown district.

Bless his heart, Howie Evans had locked up his stand early for a Friday and was waiting with my wheels.

Now, I'd asked to borrow a motorbike. I expected something small, well-maintained, and affordable. Something I could replace if things went wrong. Something that puttered along but could make some speed on straightaways if desired. Evans unveiled his beloved wheels, or so he called them, pulling the cover off with a flourish like a magician revealing the surprise at the end of the trick.

It took me a minute to get my damn jaw off the sidewalk. "Where the heck did you get that?"

For a moment, he appeared startled. His lips pursed together, and he got lost in thought. "Maybe its best if I keep that to myself."

Oh, Howie. Please don't be one of those PSSR ...

My nerves were still rattling from the bomb. Folks were saying it was the PSSR. Yet, nothing about the PSSR sounded violent.

Yet.

My, my, my. That Road-to-Air Rocket was simply gorgeous. "Howie, I can't take that," I stammered.

"Why not? Best ride west of —"

NO REQUIEM FOR THE TIN MAN

"If something should happen to it, how could I ever replace it?"

He raised one of his big paws. "I know the risks. You're following a lot of money on a case that could be tons of trouble. Then there's the weather. I'm not lending you some flimsy, slapped-together road rocket. This is my baby." He patted it, pride filling his smile.

"But —"

"Nor am I lending this to an idiot. If something happens, it's because you couldn't stop whatever it is from happening." Then he had to go and say it. "I believe in you."

He drew his fingers along the sleek lines of the motorbike as I gathered up my jaw and shame from the ground. A Henderson KD Streamline Aerolift-Motorbike. Midnight blue. Looked black in the shadows. Multiple lines of thin chrome striping that begged my fingers to indulge in some tactile caressing of my own. Dark tan leather seat. Part land vehicle. Part hovercraft.

Shaped like a bullet in want of a trigger.

"Filled 'er up, just for you."

"Mr. Evans …"

He waited patiently for me to stop tripping over my tongue.

In the distance, through the fog, the Ferry Building clocktower began chiming. Nine fifteen. I needed to hustle my fanny over to the Opera House. Mrs. Landis was due to leave when the show was over.

Straddling the cycle, I appreciated the nod of confidence from Evans. This wasn't one of those two-wheelers left over from the war, like those I'd sneak a ride on during oppressively hot nights of my childhood. This was the height of modern thinking and aesthetic engineering. Three quarters of the dashboard controlled land movement. The last quarter, marked with danger-red buttons, was for dislodging the vehicle and rider from the Earth. Were I not committed to a case …

Hooked to the satchel strapped across my chest was the one prize crucial to my survival, regardless of the vehicle's make and model. The last thing I needed was to crack my skull open let alone be recognized. Best bet was to put on the old helmet I'd acquired from a neighbor. A half-dome of metal painted dull brown, padded on the inside with well-worn leather. Fly-boy goggles covered my eyes and cut out some clarity in my vision, but not *too* much. Ear muffles flopped down on both sides, and stayed pinned in place once I secured the strap under my chin. Hot, sweaty, and a little itchy. Nothing short of a higher caliber projectile was getting through. And hopefully, my brains would stay in.

Mixed with the old airman's jacket, gloves, baggy trousers, and boots, there was little to identify me as a woman. Suited me fine. The cycle itself was showy, but I figured at this point the night would conceal most of it.

The motor growled like a chain-smoking tiger. Pretty much what I anticipated. And that was with the loving care of Howie Evans. It was made to be flashy and loud, but he'd calmed the creature's roar.

I had some questions for my friend, who felt more like an acquaintance all of a sudden. I seemed to know less about him than I thought. But those questions would wait. He was a good man. There was no room to argue about that.

Trying not to spin out the rear tires or make Mr. Evans wonder if he'd made the worst mistake of his life, I gunned the engine and sped onto Market Street — wheels grounded. The Aerolift function was for an emergency maneuver, although I confess, I secretly wanted to take this baby flying, were it not for the fact that I hate heights. I wanted the sensation of the reverse grav-pulse engine kicking in — in a fantasy where I'm not acrophobic. That would be real power! Instead, I kept my head on and my ambitions landlocked. I had the last few minutes of a show to catch.

Loitering across the street from the Opera House, the applause from what had to be the second curtain call drifted all the way out to those in waiting. Must have been a pretty good show. Not a Wagner fan myself. I went to a performance once with my father and mother. You know, to be enriched by the experience. The music was strong. The costumes great. And I could never imagine what it took to sing like that. Yet I remember something …

The three of us. Walking away from the New York theater. All dressed up. My dad in a tux and topper. Mom in a gown. I remember wearing one of my first truly adult dresses. And a poppy brooch, for the Doughboys coming home. Something. My dad wasn't comfortable. Something about the opera. Not the music. It was the story or the words. He said he'd tell me about it … later … when I was older.

I exhaled some smoke from my Lucky Strike. Yeah. Later never happened. Now Mom and Dad are both gone 'cause somebody forgot the rules of the road.

"Taxi!"

Oh look, there they all are. Here I thought San Francisco only has five cabs total, but it turns out they congregate around the Opera House like bookies around a boxing ring.

People were streaming out of the Opera House. That long, sharp nose. Blond hair. Fashionable figure. Regina Landis.

Spotting her wasn't all that hard. She was dressed to the nines and ready to demand all the attention and reverence due to an Empress.

Surrounded by mainly older couples, she was clearly there to represent the Landis name. Alone, but focused on her job. Plenty of glad-handing was accomplished and she was a pro. Exiting the other side of the building, likely by design, was the Rossi contingent. Reporters scrambled to cover both political parties *relaxing*.

Lucky gal, Mrs. Landis. She had a private car. Everyone else was scrambling for the six taxi's in waiting or dashing out to the main avenue to snag a 'Crawler before the Nightcrawler system was overwhelmed with requests. Some neatly dressed Bruno with the look of a German heavy weight boxer stuffed into a Teutonic-gray sausage casing opened the car door for her. Not the usual guy. Not the one from earlier today. And not the usual beige Packard. A dark colored sedan.

Mrs. Landis, alone, climbed in. The beefy chauffeur never

looked at her. He practically goose-stepped around to the driver's side, squeezed in, and revved the engine to life. For that one brief moment, I might as well have been in Berlin. A clang from the Market Street tram rescued me.

As the sedan pulled away, I turned the motorbike, and followed — behind a taxi — with the headlamp off. The plaza and streetlights provided enough brightness to make it seem like daytime. I figured I could keep fairly invisible until I absolutely had to turn on that lamp.

Pemberton's *Manual for Private Investigation* is quite clear about tailing suspects. But, since Pemberton's is a correspondence school, the practical lessons were up to the student to arrange. For hands-on training, I needed only to pluck from a variety of memories with my Uncle Joe. He was always taking me places, following this suspicious person or that guy actin' all cagey.

At first, the route was simple, though I thought it was the long way. Maybe Mrs. Landis wanted some time alone. I kinda' doubted the new chauffeur was the chatty sort.

The sedan turned up Fell Street from Van Ness Avenue and sped up. Other than wanting momentum to get over some of the hills, I didn't see a point in going so fast through a residential neighborhood. Didn't matter, with Howie's Aerolift-motorbike, I could keep up. It might growl and snarl at stop signals, but it loved those hills and skimmed along the road like a cobra. I had to control every urge not to put this thing into the air. Now *that* would draw attention.

We skirted along the length of the Panhandle, trying not to be oblivious to the temporary encampments of lost or damaged war vets. Well ... I tried not to pretend they weren't there. I couldn't vouchsafe for the people in the sedan.

I skidded to a stop, deep inside the Park. No cars. Definitely no sedan.

Fog clung to the treetops. A distant putter of cars on Fulton or Funston Streets echoed off the marine layer. Not far away but muffled by the dense greenery. Breezes swayed the redwood monoliths, giving off a feeling of giants watching ... waiting.

Gave me the creeps.

I allowed a glance or two upward. At any moment a pair of round, engineered eyes were going to open and stare back at me. Eyes, just like those from the other night. They'd be as tall as the redwoods, wouldn't they? Maybe taller. Had those eyes the other night looked at me? Seen me? Or ...

Dogs were barking. Nearby neighborhood mutts, no doubt.

Leaves scattered across the pavement.

I wanted the hell out of there. Not because I didn't like the Park, I love the Park in daylight, but because I was scaring myself needlessly.

The sound of squealing wheels comforted me. I dunno'. Maybe because it was sound that I was making as I got moving. A sound I knew. A sound I controlled —"

A Garbage Collection 'Bot stopped right in front of me. It appeared out of nowhere.

I cursed and swerved.

A huge *clunk* followed.

I stopped and the damn mechanical stayed in place, blocking my way.

My first thought was that I lost the scent of my quarry. Then, *oh my God*, what if I damaged Howie's Aerolift cycle? What if I damaged the garbage 'Bot? Would the Park Services Bureau fine me? As if I didn't have enough expenses right now.

The 'Bot basically consisted of two huge arms, a dome that tilted back to let it pour everyone's unwanted dreck down it's gullet, and wheels. Simple. Ugly. Efficient. It set down, or rather dropped, the other garbage can it emptied, followed by a familiar *clunk*. My nerves let out a sigh of their own. "Hey fella," I don't know why I called it that, "watch out for drivers."

"Please ... excuse ... the altercation. Are you injured?"

"No. I'm delayed. I have to go."

It cut me off again. "Please ... confirm ... you are not injured."

"What? Fine. No, I am not injured." I moved forward.

So did the 'Bot, blocking me. "Please confirm."

Confirm? "Okay, 'Bot. Confirmed."

"Please confirm … you are not injured."

"Are you trying to cheese me off?"

"Please confirm … you are not injured."

This was weird. It wasn't letting me go. I moved left. So did it. I moved right. So did it. "I confirm, I am not injured."

The pause made me wonder if it was thinking of a new question. "You … should not be … in the Park … tonight."

Eh? "I'm not staying. I'm driving through."

"You … must go home. It is … safe there."

My gloved hands were growing numb all of a sudden. "Do you know me? Or why I'm here?"

The 'Bot did not answer, which it should have.

I was willing to guess at the answer. "Were you programmed to stop me?"

"No."

"Were you programmed to stop anyone following a particular vehicle?"

"No."

"Are you attempting to stop me?"

"You must go home."

Okay. Let's try this. "You have not completed your task with the two garbage cans here."

It looked at the cans and not at me. I gunned the Aerolift-motorbike's engine and made a wide sweep around the 'Bot. Out of his reach and out of his range. If I had to, I was willing to hit the Aerolift feature of the bike to escape, but the 'Bot stayed where it was. No chasing, only watching after me.

CHAPTER SEVENTEEN

'Bots and 'Tons are supposed to be cute. Right?

-Lou Tanner, P.I., 1935

Damn 'Bot.

That was the third time some mechanical gave me an intense awareness of being known. It happened once too often to be ignored, but too inconvenient to deal with right now.

Forward? Had to be where the Landis car went. Nowhere else to go. I aimed down the street and revved the engine. I controlled the bike until I caught sight of a pair of head lamps in the distance. Nobody else was out here. It had to be them.

A pair of signs lit up from my lights. Tiny from my position but landmarks all the same. Speeding along with little light of my own, I found those signs. "Music Stand." "Museum." Both off to the left. The sedan passed them by.

It was turning right, just ahead. That would be Funston Street. I had to hurry if I was to keep up. Funston was a busy thoroughfare. I could lose them.

Out of the park, into the chaos.

They turned onto Cabrillo and disappeared into a sea of traffic. Everybody's driving a sedan these days. They all look alike.

What the hell.

I gunned the motor and began whipping in and around every obstacle. I dared any copper to follow me now. One flatfoot with a whistle made to slow the traffic. He stood in the middle of 23rd, directing cars. He was a blur — I was doing sixty when I passed him.

The traffic thinned down to a few cars and a 'Crawler once we got beyond 25th.

By the time I reached 47th Avenue, I reached another important epiphany: I'd lost them. And I was now the only vehicle on the street other than the 'Crawler. I could see the ocean, so unless Mrs. Landis and her driver were expert divers, there was no way they kept going. Okay ... I'd passed them. Without smoking out the wheels this time, I retraced my path back down the avenue numbers.

Northbound on 40th, a pair of taillights shut off amongst the row of parked cars. I cut the motor and rolled past line of sight with the lights off. Beyond view, I hopped off and pushed that beautiful street glider back to 40th and down close to where the sedan was parked.

Through the back window, the glow of the chauffeur lighting his cigarette provided his location. The brief light showed me Mrs. Landis was not in the car.

Leaving the Aerolift cycle and tip-toing along the parked cars in the shadows, I kept checking on the driver. If he saw me, the jig was up. But that was one of the many advantages of working in the dark of night. The drowsiness of the late hour helped too. The chauffeur rested his fingers on the bridge of his nose and yawned widely.

In an area built up with stucco homes jammed together, all repeating the same or mostly similar frontages, it turns out the occupants repeat each other's schedules and sleeping habits too.

Sandwiched between the bay window stucco, a bay window stucco, and another bay window stucco, was one little bungalow. Wood siding, front porch, craftsman style. Lights on. Not the porch light or a walkway light. Only a fine glow of activity inside the living or parlor space. Someone was up late and receiving visitors.

Remembering Howie's look of trust, I backed the Aerolift cycle into a generous space between two family cars and waited. No cigarette for me. Too risky. Might give me away.

The chauffeur leaned out the window, scrutinized the bungalow, threw his cigarette out, and did the last thing I expected: he drove away. Just like that. Gone. Wasn't he waiting? Maybe he went for coffee, but don't professional chauffeurs bring it with them?

NO REQUIEM FOR THE TIN MAN

With the street not quite as full now, even my little spot felt too exposed. I needed a better hiding place for Howie's Aerolift cycle. On the corner was a simple Ma-'n-Pa store. A tiny alley ran down the back. I could see where they had a few things piled up under tarps. From the pooled water, littered natural debris, and some leaky oil spills, clearly whatever was under there, hadn't been moved in some time.

The flying horse, aka motorbike, fit. Nice and unseen. Now I wouldn't have to worry about that being stolen or even remarked on.

On the chance the chauffeur might come back, I took the opportunity to get closer to the house, slinking low between parked cars and bushes. Just because the lady went into a house didn't mean this was proof of an affair. I needed evidence. My folding camera was in my coat pocket, and heavy enough that I'd know if it wasn't there, yet I checked anyway.

With the way everything was sandwiched together down the block, there was only one way to get around to the back. A tiny dirt space that led to a wooden gate. Most of these places fronted onto cement sidewalks and streets. Barren and plain. In back, however, they had gardens and lawns, kept away from the prying eyes of outsiders. Although the bungalow was different from its neighbors in architecture, I suspected it hadn't strayed too far from the overall design concept by having a nice, big backyard.

I love it when I'm right.

A small, one step-up patio extended from a backdoor that was slightly ajar. Wood that hadn't been kept up well, but still held up two matched lounge chairs. A tiny, round table for cards or smoking.

In the movies, there's usually a scream that follows the gunshot.

Not this time.

I heard three shots, fast, matching in power and location.

Gun in hand, I ran up the step and into the house.

I stumbled my way through a house I didn't know, and found the front door. Opening it only gave me a fleeting view of taillights vanishing into the distance.

That didn't guarantee that all the gunslingers had run away. I closed the front door with me and my minimalist artillery on the interior, listening, with no success. My heartbeat overwhelmed most of my hearing.

Down a hallway, a light was on. A popping joint and a shuffle across the carpet. Someone was in the lit room. I crept forward, on high alert. The scent of cordite permeated the air. A shadow moved. The bed squeaked. A thump — something fell.

A fast check of the room gave me a blurry picture of two things: a man sitting on the bed and a woman lying on the floor. The man muttered and laid himself back on the floral duvet cover, taking an interest in the ceiling. At his feet lay a .38 Police Special. That pungent cordite they use in ammo was close to overwhelming in this tight space.

Keeping an eye on the man, I checked the woman on the floor. I was hopeful she was still alive. No pulse. The woman's skin remained warm, not that I expected her to turn stone-cold in the scant minutes after she'd been shot.

Her elegant gown was pushed down past her waist underneath her prone body. The hair I recognized, in all its glorious upsweep. All the clothing on the body or tossed across the bed too. The skin of her back was flawless except ...

Three closely clustered holes that indicated penetration of bullets into her heart and lungs. Didn't matter if they went in from the front or back. Same result. She probably wasn't alive by the time she hit the floor.

The man sat up, playing with a piece of her jewelry. A necklace.

Well. If it was an affair, it's over now.

Regina Landis was dead.

And Gus Gruber did it. Maybe.

I backed up to the doorway. I needed to look at everything – to take it all in. Even Gus, sitting there on the bed, lost in some medicated fog.

An eleven-foot by eleven-foot room. The closest thing to a master bedroom a bungalow could offer. Not particularly tidy. Too much floral print and heavy feminine touches. Matchy-matchy pillow shams and curtain swag. The carpet was well used and hadn't been cleaned recently. Bits of leaves and detritus scattered around.

Starting at the left I used an old trick Uncle Joe taught me: with only my eyes, since I didn't want to leave trace or disturb anything, I noted everything down the wall, including the tacky, padded headboard and the faux painting above it. Two nightstands on either side. At the back wall, louvered folding doors opened to a thin closet that was an add-on. Sweeping back towards me again, was the bed, Gus with Regina's necklace, a pair of men's shoes, the .38 between Gus and the shoes, and a dresser next to my hip.

Up again through the center of the room, in front of me, was Regina, the end of the bed, a narrow table covered with unopened mail, another pile of unopened mail scattered on the floor along with the contents of Regina's open handbag, and a big pool of blood.

At the back wall again was the door to the toilet. To its right was a covey, where I could see a dressing table with a three-mirror table, sets of perfume and makeup, and a matching stool. Last to my right was a narrow table with two fake plants and an equally fake Chinese vase with a poorly painted dragon on it. Whoever decorated this joint had no taste whatsoever.

I crouched to take a look at the mess on the floor near Regina. I hated to ignore her, but … well … there are things I had to do. The mail looked, more or less, like coupons, notices, and postcards from abroad. Paris. Rome. Berlin. Munich. Amongst that wreckage was a silver tube of lipstick, possibly a European manufacture. A tortoiseshell cigarette case with her initials in silver on it. A compact to go with that. Stubs from the theater. A set of keys. One of her husband's gold lighters. Two delicate, embroidered in silver and blue thread, handkerchiefs. And one big wad of cabbage. She was carrying close to ten grand if I was guessing right. What the hell was she doing with that much loot on her? It wasn't as if she needed to catch a taxi or 'Crawler home … in Timbuktu.

Maybe I could carefully step over to the closet. Whose clothes were in there? That could tell me plenty, but first, I had to do something I was hoping to avoid for a long, long time. I needed to reach out to the Police. This was a homicide and they had to be called.

"Gus," I whispered, not hiding my anger.

He held up the necklace and tried to examine it. His fingers couldn't achieve the dexterity needed. Was this a man who could hold a gun, let alone fire it three times? Or was he in shock?

Again, pain split my vision in two. I fell forward onto Regina. My gun loosened in my grip, but I didn't drop it. I rolled over and held it both hands, squinting through shooting, stabbing head pains.

At first, all I noticed were two shadows.

Then one.

Footsteps pounded away from me and out of the house. The front door slammed.

One? Two? Some goon cold cocked me and the feeling that my head was split open was nothing less than I deserved for not making one hundred percent certain the house was empty.

Was it one? Or two?

It could be thirty for all I cared. I got up and sprinted to the front door. Neighboring houses were lighting up. They'll call the Police. Good. Poor Gus. He wasn't going anywhere in his condition, and I knew what the Police would assume. If someone else killed Mrs. Landis … one or two someone's … then I had to catch them and bring them back. The police would never believe me otherwise.

Peering out the front door, I searched the street. Parked where Regina's car had stopped briefly, another car had filled the space. A pearl colored, Desoto Airstream coupe. I knew that car.

Movement? Yes!

A shadow turn the corner onto Cabrillo. It was traveling damn fast. That was the perp. Forget the Desoto for now, I took off, wobbling on my feet at first, then getting a rhythm that Cole Porter would have been proud of. I reached the corner.

Almost a block down, the figure was cloaked in shadow. Their good fortune. They must not have known I was following as they had slowed their pace to a fast walk.

I may be a sap but I ain't stupid.

I didn't shout. I didn't yell. I paced along with them. As long as I could see them, I didn't need to catch up … yet.

They turned north again.

Once I was out of their visual range, I cut into a jog, then ran to close the distance between us.

Rounding the corner myself, I stared down 38th Street.

Nada. No one.

I crouched down. My head and balance protested. I sneaked behind a parked car and looked down to see if anyone was getting into one of the cars.

Sirens filled the air. The Police were arriving back at the house.

As for me, I couldn't see anyone. Checking the other side of the street, I found no one again. Not getting into a car. Not on the opposite side of the street.

They'd vanished.

More sirens.

I couldn't go door to door. That was the cop's job. And I had to get back to Gus. I had no evidence in hand, but surely something was left behind. Hell, the crack on my skull might be something. I needed to tell them what I saw.

All of 40th Street was filled with cops.

At first, the beat cop wouldn't let me through. I tried to explain that I knew what was going on. Tried to show him my buzzer, to prove I'm a legit P.I. Nope, he was having none of that. So, I did what any good shamus would do: I waited for him to get busy with some pretty pair of legs in her nightgown and headed over to the Ma-'n-Pa shop to circumvent him.

A hand closed over my mouth.

The men that dragged me away were strong and in no mood to let me go. I tried. Someone's chin met my elbow without polite introduction. Shins were damaged.

I tried.

I failed.

CHAPTER EIGHTEEN

Note to self: perhaps I'll get back to letter writing, or journaling, or whatever. First, I need time to think. Second, I need to stay alive.

-Lou Tanner, P.I., 1935, Personal Journal

Green Eyes slammed a familiar yellow rag down in front of me, hoping to scare me.

He didn't.

The paper did. The headline was a doozey:

CANDIDATE'S WIFE MURDERED

Escaped lunatic held as killer.
Accomplice sought.

Landis in mourning, promises increased
police powers as Mayor.
Law & Order for all!

"Escaped lunatic?" I said, not asked. "Is that what they are calling Gus Gruber?"

"They can say whatever the hell they want to say. Or whatever suits the people who influence them. Happily, and only by sheer dumb luck, they don't know *who* his accomplice is."

"Oh for Christ's sake, Hayes, it wasn't me. You should know that by now."

"I should. But can you prove it? What the hell happened out there tonight?"

He might as well had cuffed me to the chair and turned a bright lamp into my eyes. This was an interrogation — a real one. "I chased the accomplice, or the killer, or the witness ... I don't know who or what they were. Lost 'em on 39th. I was on my way back to talk to the Police when —"

He held up his big, calloused hand. "I know."

"You do? Then what am I doing here?"

His voice got awful quiet and sad. "Not getting slapped to death in the clink."

Ice flowed out through my chest. He wasn't wrong. "Thank you. But Detective Rollins wouldn't let that happen."

"Bennie? Bennie Rollins is only one man. Besides, he might not be the one assigned to the case. He might not be in the office. He might be on holiday in Palm Springs. Did you ever think of that? Good odds says your one and only pal among the cops isn't even assigned to this escaped lunatic case or that you have anything to do with it."

"Gus Gruber wasn't in an asylum. He was over at the hospital, under his brother's care. You saw him when he was in my office. Nuttier than a fruitcake, sure. But he wasn't violent."

"Lou, he's a former soldier who has all the ... training. He was found at the scene with the murder weapon in his hands and the body at his feet."

"Is it the murder weapon? Was it tested by ballistics? How about fingerprints? Were his on the weapon? Where on the weapon? On the trigger or only the grip?" I watched Hayes trying to wear a path in the wood floor behind his desk. "Call me picky, but it takes time for ballistics to be matched. Prints don't happen in a couple of hours. A good combing of a scene? It's too soon to be announcing an *in-the-bag* case."

I was met with that kind of silence you only expect from the grave. I pulled that odd newspaper closer. "Say … it's not even four AM yet and this edition shouldn't be out until six, so what gives? How do you have a copy of the morning paper before it's on the street?"

While Green Eyes went to go stand by the window with nothing to yammer about, I gave the story a thorough read through. A pack of hooey. No one says why Mrs. Landis was there. Not a peep about an affair — no surprise about that. Landis or his Bund pals made sure that was kept on the hush. No one claimed to see anything except the asylum escapee who went on a raging killing spree and was found with her body. His name is being withheld, along with names and details about who else he knocked off on this so-called *spree*, so the press came up with something oh-so-unbiased to call him. *The Asylum Killer*. Original. Some news hawk must've stayed up all night to come up with that one.

There had to be significant signs of a second person in the house besides the killer. Why else did the cops know to be looking for me or anyone else?

I must have been thinking out loud.

Hayes shook his head. "Chief of Police says they have more than enough evidence to convict Gruber … you know … making a show of going after the killer with all they have. No stone unturned. Hell, even the Commandant of Hunter's Pointe is weighing in, but I suppose he has to, being Mayor Rossi's buddy."

Sure they are putting their all into this, it's one of theirs. Nothing in the rags about me, the chauffeur who dropped off Mrs. Landis, or Gus's relationship to candidate Lucas Landis was mentioned, so this was going to be a first class handwashing. The politicians all announced their stance on law and order, the threats posed by the insane, how the other guy is wrong about crime, blah, blah, blah.

"Hayes. Do they suspect *me*? Or do they suspect *someone*?" I kept watching him for tells. I could clean him out in a poker game — that experienced face of his was an open book. A novel. Not a pulp or dime rag, but a serious novel. "You put two and two together?"

"Not just me. I was told they got a call. An anonymous caller who described you to a 'T.'

"A witness that described me?"

"Yup. Called to say Myrna Loy was seen running out of the bungalow after shots fired."

"That's awfully specific considering it was dark and I'm not exactly dressed to be recognized."

"Yeah. But it won't take long for the cops to make two plus two add up, same as me."

"On the happenstance they don't come up with an answer of five? Let's see," I started running my own numbers. "If some smart fella like Bennie is on the case, then he'll talk to Lucas Landis, who will say he has no idea why his wife was there."

"He'll lie."

"Like a rug. Dead wife or not, he's not telling anyone he's a cuckhold with his political future on the line. But he too will throw the cops a bone: me. He'll tell them he hired me to follow and ... maybe watch his wife. Maybe for her safety, or some cock-'n-bull sob story like that. Viable. A smart cop will wonder if it was the P.I. who was at least a witness if not an accomplice, right?"

Hayes produced the most satisfying snarl. "Landis is in mourning but not allowing that to slow down his manly need for justice."

"I wouldn't put it past Landis or any of Gus's family who are part of the Bund, to then point out that I knew and ... was sympathetic to Gus."

"Two plus two equals seven. But it gets them what they want. A cause that everyone can get behind. This country is still mourning the losses of the War and then the Depression. Who wouldn't set aside any disagreements and stand with a man who lost his wife to murder. And if Landis can be the one who brings revenge?"

I wanted a cigarette.

I wanted a drink.

I wanted a bath.

"I was starting to wonder why —" Nope. I didn't have enough evidence. What I needed was to get back to the crime scene. To look around with a set of eyes that hadn't already decided what happened. Maybe Gus did do it. I wouldn't like that, not one bit, but I had to be ready for that answer. He was cuckoo. Not his fault. They don't hang crazy, they lock it away so no one has to see it. Don't they? Or do they need a body to remind everyone to keep to the straight and narrow?

Gotta' admit, Hayes couldn't have wound himself up into a tighter ball of anxiety if he thought about it and gave it the old college try. I was reading his stance and the verbiage said he wasn't sure about me yet. Something was crawling under his proverbial skin.

I wish I was surprised. I'm young and potentially naive enough to be, so why wasn't I? "Hayes?"

He didn't answer me. He looked miserable in fact.

"Kit Hayes."

He managed only to turn his head and show me deeper-than-usual lines under his eyes.

"None of this," I lightly slapped the paper, "is true, beyond Gruber being in the same room with the victim. You know that, right?"

"Yeah."

"And if you know that, then why am I being held here? Don't get me wrong, it's a nice office, for a government flatfoot."

Three long strides brought him back to his desk and he landed his full weight onto his hands. I could see flecks of gold in his green eyes. "Because I need to know you won't disagree with that cock-'n-bull story outside of this room."

I was stunned. Genuinely stunned to the point of not being able to come up with something smart to say. "That 'cock-'n-bull story is gonna' hang Gus Gruber for murder."

"Better him than you."

"Hayes," I shouted, not meaning to. "I can't put my finger on it, but I swear, I don't believe Gus did it. And the fact I chased someone who clocked me on the brain out of the house only confirms my suspicion."

His head drooped as did his shoulders. "They have the murder weapon."

"So they say. I say, they haven't had enough time to do their investigation thoroughly."

"I agree. You're lucky we nabbed you before you volunteered yourself as a punching bag."

I leaned back so he could see my whole face. "Hardly. My prints aren't on that gun. I'm not stupid enough to touch evidence. But a guy with a broken head, who might be disoriented by finding a woman's been murdered, might be dumb enough to pick up the murder weapon. See, you and I, we know the rules. Joe Average? He doesn't."

"Make up your mind, Lou. Are his prints on the gun or not?"

"I don't know! That's what a proper investigation would find out. Not some coverup so Gus Gruber steps off for Regina Landis's murder. I don't even get why the cops are putting so much into going after Gus."

"That's what happens when you kill somebody in cold blood."

I got real cold myself. Damn it, if my fingers weren't freezing. Strange, considering how much my blood was boiling. "That's what happens when you rub out a politician or rich man's wife and they want the case closed fast so it doesn't get in the way of them taking over the world. Pay off everyone, cops, government, and it all goes away, except the part that gets you what you want. Oh to be rich."

"Lou!"

"Or is it just in the city of San Francisco. Today."

"You're beginning to sound like one of those PSSR jerks."

"I'm beginning to see their point of view. I'm not a joiner, but I sure as hell can see what makes them attractive to folks."

For the sake of avoiding the bigger fight I figured was coming, if not already on both our lips, I lowered my voice, "What if Gus didn't do it? Are you satisfied that someone got caught, guilty or not?"

"*You* got proof? Got pictures? No. Your camera was empty."

"I was chasing a potential witness or killer. Then your boys dragged me out of there and here I am."

"Did you see Gruber *not* pull the trigger?"

There I sat: just a dame, eyes rolling, and a boatload of

sarcasm desperate to be released. "That's the dumbest question I've ever heard tonight. You don't ask a negative."

"Prosecutors do. And *you* are never going to see the inside of a trial room for this case. And *you* are never going to be asked stupid questions by Prosecutors who love to ask dumb questions. You want to know why, Lou?"

"Enlighten me."

"Because *you* are not involved in this case." Hayes stood up, sporting the oddest expression on his face, as if he wanted to take me in his arms? I couldn't accurately read it. It was kinda' disturbing.

"So it's all going under the rug?"

"Yeah," he huffed out with no enthusiasm.

"A cover up."

"Yeah."

"Who is asking for it?"

"Lou!"

"Oh, for the love of God, Hayes, can I at least know who is screwing Gus, Mrs. Landis, you, and me over?" The volume on my voice was up too far so I took a breath before speaking more. "There *was* something," I started gesticulating at invisible concepts darting around my head. "Something was wrong with the crime scene. It was there. Too obvious if I could just remember. I didn't have time to figure it out. Hayes, if I could —"

"No! Absolutely not. No way am I letting you go to the crime scene. End of discussion."

Bossing me around? Nothing sticks in my craw more. He ought to know that by now. "What's the full official story? The big lie?"

I never thought I'd see someone who wanted to wash their own mouth out with soap. Bet Hayes wanted to take a long bath too.

"Augustin Gruber escaped from a mental ward — possibly with an accomplice, assaulting and killing two guards in the process, then wandered around, taking 'Crawlers, until he almost made it to the Presidio Army Base. Before he got there, he saw a woman entering a home in the avenues, followed her, assaulted, then shot her. His brother is pushing for a plea of insanity."

NO REQUIEM FOR THE TIN MAN

"He is?" I asked. "Dr. Frederick Gruber?"

"Gus says he doesn't remember anything and doesn't believe he did it."

That's when my head started whirling. I reseated myself on Hayes's desk. I didn't care if that bothered him or not. "Her husband was told. He knows she's dead and now he's taking the opportunity to campaign on it."

"I wasn't personally given access to the mayoral candidate but that about sums it up."

"I've got to go back to that house."

"No. There's no reason for you to be there."

Think, Lulu. "You said Gus's brother is pushing for an insanity plea. What about his sister? What has she got to say?"

"Oh," that perked up Hayes, "Mrs. Weiss believes wholeheartedly that her brother Augustin killed the woman. Naturally, she didn't explain why."

"Naturally."

I waited, letting the silence between us do the dirty work. Hayes might be annoying, infuriating, and frustrating, but he was damn honorable. Lying about a murder to sweep it under the rug? Yeah, that was gnawing at his innards like a dog on a steak bone.

The *Pemberton Detective School Manual* covers interrogation techniques. Sometimes silence can be more powerful than a question than a worded question.

Hayes snapped under the weight of the quiet guilt. "No, Lou, you can't go back there. You don't have a reason."

"I left something there."

He staggered back like I'd slapped him. "You what ... wait ... can it be traced to you?"

"Absolutely," I lied. Actually, it could be traced to someone else, and that was worrying me quite a bit.

Hayes bit back every cuss word he wanted to use. Couldn't figure as to why. He'd cursed in front of me before. Hell, I'd let out more than my fair share of cussing in front of him. Still, it was his office.

"Alright. I'm taking you back there, Lou. Supervised."

"Fair enough," I grabbed my motorbike helmet. "The cops done with the place already?"

"They didn't waste a lot of time."

"And yet they're leaving no stone unturned, except for every boulder."

"Sarcasm is unladylike, you know that Lou? Is your *something* inside the house?"

"Technically, outside."

"All the better. I take you back, you retrieve what you need, and then we leave. We don't even have to go in."

"Sure," I fibbed again. "Whatever you say. Let me get my *something* and then we'll leave. Honest."

Maybe.

CHAPTER NINETEEN

... Or maybe not.

-Lou Tanner, P.I., 1935, Personal Journal

"Lou? Lou! Damn it, Tanner. Do you hear me, woman? Get the hell out of there."

He was waiting at the back door like the childhood buddy who never wanted to do anything naughty and was always afraid of getting in trouble. Me? I was the one who never listened and got everyone in trouble.

"Hold your horses." I said, turning on a flashlight and strolling through the front room. It's hard to whisper loudly, even though I didn't think we needed to be all that quiet. No one was there.

The bungalow was typical. Low ceilings, white painted plaster walls. Feminine curtains in a floral print popular a couple of years ago. Same overkill of flowers used in the bedroom. I didn't even want to know what the toilet looked like. A couple of bookcases but nothing of note in them besides a few older populist titles. The tomes had been picked up at a secondhand shop by the wear and tear of them. An upright piano of equally used condition leaned against the interior wall, draped with an old shawl, and settled with a fake vase filled with fake flowers. Hardwood floors with cheap Persian-like rugs. The smell of gunpowder and cordite was gone, but death still stank up the place. You can't scrub that out when you don't bother to try.

The cops were gone. Long gone. They'd torn the place up for show. Music from the piano was thrown on the floor but when I lifted the piano bench, no one had bothered to look inside. Two neat and tidy stacks of song books. Untouched by law enforcement.

Movement behind startled me, but gave off a familiar sense, so I resisted the urge to shoot first, ask second.

I found Hayes glaring at paintings on the parlor wall. "What," I asked.

"Too neat — too quick. And these," he pointed at an unattractive oil painting in a dull wood frame. "These haven't been moved."

I gave him my best, innocent sounding, "oh?" as if I wasn't already ten steps ahead of him.

He continued, "Murder is over *love*, *hate*, or *greed*. Unless there isn't a reason, like madness. But even if you're sure it was one of the first two, you always check to see if *greed* was involved."

"You're saying no one checked to see if there's a safe behind any of those pictures."

Was that a smile he sent my way? "Yeah."

"The toss-job is fake. They did the bare minimum and went home."

"Yeah."

I sauntered over to the ugly painting and drew my finger along the full length of the frame, lifting a thick smear of dust away. "No one's touched this in months."

"Notice that they're perfectly straight too? I don't know any cop who puts things back that perfectly after a search."

"Know the lead detective on the case?"

Shaking his head, he replied, "Nobody I recognize. Like I said, not your pallie Bennie Rollins, who wouldn't do a crap job like this."

I leaned into Hayes's ear. "I don't even see fingerprint powder on the frames, cabinets, switches … nowhere." I pointed the flashlight beam at each item as I ticked it off my list.

"Nasty stuff — gets everywhere." He turned his head too quickly.

All of a sudden, we were nose to nose.

In the frigid air, his heat swept over me.

This job comes with a lot of "why" questions. With me,

plenty of those are about why I do the things I do. Like, why I didn't move back from Green Eyes when I was so close. In the dark it wasn't possible, but I swear I could see those little gold flakes in his irises again. Or why was I still giving any man who likes to boss me around as much as five minutes of my time, let alone the hours I give to Hayes?

Those big green eyes of his widened. His lips parted as if he planned to say something smart but couldn't decide which brain provided the remark. He stood there, leaning over me, lips at the ready even though he might not realize they were.

He was getting warmer in that cold bungalow.

Or was that my imagination?

Yeah, warmth was unlikely in that cold, murder scene, cover-up bungalow.

I snapped back to the here-'n-now. My case had gone sideways, but it was still my case.

Regina Landis might or might not be an adulteress, but she didn't deserve to be murdered and tossed away to obscurity. Gus Gruber, former doughboy, rated better than being made to hang for someone else's crime.

I took a step back.

Hayes jumped back to reality, too.

"We may have to have a talk," I said, no doubt throwing him off kilter. "Another time. Let's find what the bad cops wouldn't."

"We … um …" he swallowed and cleared his throat. "We can't tell anyone if we do find the murderer."

"Come on."

"But." He smiled, crinkling up those experience lines on his face. "Maybe I can use the information to help Gruber."

My whole body brightened, and I smiled back.

"Maybe. No promise, Lou. Maybe. And we still won't be able to say anything. Not really."

"So, I do this for my own satisfaction. I hate loose ends and unfinished cases."

I shimmied around him and took up my spot in the door of the bedroom. Of course, everything significant had been removed:

Gus, Regina, the gun, the shoes, her jewelry, clothes, and purse.

All that was left was the big stain on the carpet and an indentation where Gus had been sitting on the bed. The mail had been pushed around. Knowing that Hayes had me covered, I got a bit lower to the floor.

Nothing under the bed. So the chances were that the coppers took the men's shoes, arriving at the same conclusion I had: they weren't Gus's. Gus had his own shoes on. So, who did they belong to? I squeezed my eyes shut, forcing everything out except the memory of the room. The shoes. They were about Gus's size. Expensive, but worn. Not worn out, just worn. Squeezing my eyes began to give me a headache, and I didn't have aspirin powder at home, so I opened them.

Ah? Caught in the duvet that had been bundled on top of the bed. Pieces of paper, big and small. I shook them loose. A receipt? Part of one, at least? Laundry. Not much information on it, but it was a start.

A larger piece of paper?

Just a torn piece of a single sheet. I recognized it. It had been folded in half. I swear, it was the same as the one residing in my handbag at home. I pointed the light onto it. There wasn't enough to determine for sure, but it appeared to be that same PSSR invitation I was handed in Fisherman's Wharf. Maybe. I'd have to compare it to the one I had. If it was, what the hell was it doing here? And knowing how much the police were against the organization, how did it get missed in their search?

Turning my flashlight to skim along the floor, a glint caught my eye. Gold. Ah ha! The lighter. Under the table that supported that ugly Chinese dragon vase, behind the leg, covered by a big leaf that had blown in or been tracked in. My, my, my. So careless. If I was finding this with a flashlight and a few minutes, how was it missed by the forensic boys?

I took off my glove and carefully scooped it inside. Prints — always protect evidence that might have prints. Sadly, more poking around without proper equipment didn't produce anything further. "You know, this place is still a cache of evidence. Can't you do something to get the blue boys back in here?

Hayes stood behind me, following the path of my flashlight as I did the search again — like I did when everything was still, dare I say, warm.

Books crashed to the floor!

We both jerked back and took up defensive positions. The flashlight beam trembled along with my hands as I whipped it back and forth, searching for the source of the crash.

"Cat? Big rat?" he asked.

"Maybe we shook something loose." I gulped in air until I could control my intake.

"You don't scare so easy."

"After Powell Street? I've been jumpy." Glancing over at Hayes, he appeared unsettled too. "What's your excuse?"

"Flanders." He didn't need to say more.

In the side parlor, piles of books scattered across the floor.

"What a mess," Hayes grumbled. "What a —"

He made a sudden bee line to the middle of the room and started a crazed search through one of the many piles of books.

"Hey, what are you doing?" Oh, but that question got answered the minute I stepped into the room. Gun smoke. Cordite. The pile of books centered in the room? Just the right size to cover a body.

I had to wonder if he would appreciate being coffined in literature. He'd always presented himself as a fine, educated man. Then again, do dead men care? Dr. Frederick Gruber wouldn't. He didn't have time. The single shot entered his forehead and I didn't want to look at how it exited the back. His expression was mildly surprised.

As we unburied him, I could see he was in fashionable togs, but no shoes. That explained the shoes in the bedroom. Of course, they were close in size to Gus, Frederick was his brother, but they were too posh for a hospitalized veteran. What was Dr. Gruber doing in the bungalow?

Green Eyes flung the book he had in one hand clean across the room. It smashed into the wall.

"I take it you know who this guy is? If not, I will introduce you."

He didn't answer. I'm pretty good at guessing. Hayes went to stand in the doorway, pressing his hands against the frame like Sampson pushing the temple pillars apart.

My brain went into evidentiary mode. I lifted Frederick's shoulder.

"Don't move the body."

"I couldn't if I wanted to, Hayes. But he's laying on something. It might be important."

He smashed a fist into the door frame and turned back to me. "I'm calling the PD and you're getting out of here. I'll handle this."

For a moment, I wasn't sure what I was looking at. I honest-to-God prayed I wasn't looking at what I thought I was looking at. "Hayes?"

The G-man started digging through all the piles of books he'd tossed aside. "Where the hell is the telephone?"

"Hayes?"

"They have to have one."

I sucked in any revulsion I had to the amount of blood and worse from Gruber's head shot and rolled the doctor onto his stomach."

"Jesus Christ, Lou! I said, don't move the body!"

All I had to do was point.

Uncovered, and in slightly better light, it was worse than it appeared before. And damn it, I was right.

Two bundles of dynamite, a detonator, and a timer. The clock-style timer hands were about to meet.

All I remember was an arm lifting me off my feet. Hitting the door frame as I was carried at a run. Helping to shove open the front door. Feeling grass, then sidewalk, then —

The Powell Street bomb all over again.

This time the shock wave hit instantly, blowing me over. As I grappled with space and time, big hands yanked me into the same space I'd hidden Howie's Aerolift bike. Glass, debris, and the bike fell onto us.

NO REQUIEM FOR THE TIN MAN

When the wave had ridden over and dissipated, we were left cling to one another, Hayes and me, life rafts in an ocean of lost sound and fiery images. I crawled in under his coat. I think he was trying to crawl into his hat, but at least he was trying to take me with him.

His heart or mine? Ours? Something was pounding harder than a jackhammer and I've heard quieter from a steam engine whistle. I didn't want to let go of him. He was alive. I was alive.

We both reacted to the sirens. Fires in this city are no joke. The whole fire brigade must have been descending on us.

Hayes pushed the motor bike off of us. "Will this dingus run?"

"I sure as hell hope so."

"We're leaving." His voice was stone cold, yet a little shake got into it. One I knew he wouldn't appreciate any comment on.

"We can't. There may be people hurt out there."

He gave me an entire lecture with a glare from those green eyes. This was no time for me to be a sap. Sirens equal help. Help for those in need. I wasn't able to do anything better than they could.

We can't be seen.

Until Hayes can work his magic with the cops, I can't be seen.

I'll never be able to explain away my presence here twice, each time ending in a disaster.

Gawkers. More and more of them arrived until there was a serious crowd around the burning bungalow.

There goes all the evidence to clear Gus.

Well ... not all.

Hayes pulled his fedora down hard and climbed over the back fence. I quietly wheeled the Aerolift motorbike out into the crowd, asked a couple of questions as if I knew nothing at all, then straddled the bike to drive away casually. I had to go get Hayes.

Fluttering down from the sky came pieces of leaflet. I knew that paper. Hundreds of pieces fell on the crowd.

Chapter Twenty

"*Dick*. I'm a Private Dick. You can say it."

"*Detective*. You took me there to look. We looked. Now I handle the evidence, okay? All up-'n-up. For Gus's sake, everything has to hold up in court. Agreed?"

The sides of my mouth nearly reached the asphalt.

"Lou?"

Hell of a place for an argument. Smoke rose from the bungalow on 41st and the sirens never stopped. Yet, we were far enough away now. I brought Hayes here to clear his head and to show him where I was delayed by the Garbage 'Bot.

Apparently he thought I'd brought him here to argue.

Fog blotted out most of the treetops but the wind still made its presence known. The park was free of humans, in theory, but the flora and fauna were doing their nightly thing all the same.

Every once in a while, Hayes had to shake his head, which made steering the flying horse a real challenge. Stopping for a break in the Park was a good idea overall.

"Agreed, on two conditions," I said, not only unwilling to argue but not willing to fully surrender my collected evidence. It was all that was left. The cops weren't sharing what little they'd bothered to obtain. Gus was taking the fall for someone and now Frederick was dead.

"I know better than to say, 'shoot.' Go ahead, Lou."

"One: you give me access to this stuff," I indicated one of my prizes — the lighter.

"So long as I have them, you got access. What's number two?"

Oh damn, he was leaning over to me again. Rugged. Weathered. Still too pretty. I don't handle pretty with half the brilliance I handle your average .45 pistol.

"Two: I get to give you a lift all the way home."

"Fine. But only to the Federal Building downtown."

I mocked being aghast. "Don't you ever sleep?"

"Only when I'm not stalking alleyways for blood to drink."

"Humph. No fair. You stole the punch line."

"Aww," he said with absolutely no sincerity. "And I have a condition for you?"

"Me?"

"Don't!" He actually wagged his finger at me. "Don't you dare bat your eyelashes at me, woman. It's been an awful night."

"Would I do that to you?"

"Yes. You already have. I've got a list of the times."

"A whole list? Green Eyes, I'll need a copy of that list to believe you."

After he recovered from cringing at being called Green Eyes, he grinned snidely. "Would you like it alphabetically or chronologically?"

"Alright, alright. What do you want?"

He narrowed those eyes at me. "You drop me off downtown, then you go home and stay there."

"Hayes —."

"No 'buts.' I haven't finished clearing your name and I don't want the cops picking you up until I've cleaned up the mess you're in. Got it!"

I saluted like one of those chorus girls wearing a sweet little version of a uniform.

He got close to me again, but I held the salute.

And if I thought he was getting close in that moment, it was nothing compared to the ride home. His head fit on my shoulder — his reach perfectly encircled my waist. Hayes barely fit behind me and I suspected he resented having to take a back seat to a skirt. Ah, he'd get over it. There wasn't anyone around to see him trundled off by a dame. Besides, he insisted that I leave him two blocks from the Hall of Justice, insuring that no one would ever know.

"Thanks."

"Anytime, Hayes. Just ask."

"Now. Go home, Lou, and lock your door. Don't answer it

unless it's me. Don't even open it for Marley."

"More orders. You love giving orders, don't you."

"You betcha'."

Dismounting from the bike, he gave a last once-over, whistled, and muttered his admiration.

"Why, thank you Big Boy. If tonight had been less exciting and horrible, I'd be tempted to say you're pretty swell too."

I gunned the motor and sped away, certain he shouted something about "I was talking about the cycle!" It would have been the perfect exit, except ...

The boom.

Green Eyes spun around and stared east.

I slammed on the breaks. *Oh God! Not another bomb!*

Two glowing orbs, either of which could have been mistaken for the moon, floated beside the unfinished Bay Bridge. I swear a hand reached out and ripped cables out of the suspension section before whatever it was retreated behind rocks and structures like a bad child afraid of getting caught.

Descending behind Yorba Buena island into the dark waters of the Bay, the orbs blinked, then vanished. Yet they left a tremendous wake that anyone could see in the lights from the Oakland port facilities reflecting off the waves and the sudden flailing of ships in the harbor.

The bridge damage looked small from up on Market, but I knew from my inside source this set back the project by months, if not years.

I glared back to Hayes, expecting him to be as shellshocked as I was. Instead, he was a man as terrified yet fuming as anyone I'd encountered. Left to my vivid imagination, the Agent who turned on his heel and marched toward his office, knew more than he was sharing with me. About the glowing orbs. About the booming. About this whole business with ... well, damn near everything.

Vulnerable. Yeah, that's the word I was thinking of. I gunned that flying horse and high-tailed it out of there with a plan.

I hid Howie's Aerolift cycle in what I call a secure place. A small garage on the edge of Chinatown near Sacramento and Kearny.

No Requiem for the Tin Man

A little garage owned by a friend, with a big, snarling and drooling dog next door. Then made my way back to my office instead of directly home — in case I was being followed. Fine, call me paranoid, but from the moment I left Hayes at the Federal Building, I had feeling someone was tailing me. And I hated that every pop and bang jolted my nerves, making me hop like a Mexican Jumping Bean.

My best paranoid scenario was that some smooth new gumshoe looking to learn the trade by copying me or stealing a case out from under me was glued to my keister, so I decided to play it cool. I strolled my little-ole-self down the sidewalk, then out into the street, as if I would cross it, but then whipped around on my heel. I know these blocks well. Well lit, few cars or doorways to hide with.

Nada.

Not a person on either side of the whole street. And quiet too. The street a few blocks up was busy enough, but not so much that it provided cover for a rhythmic squeak. The fog horns out at the Gate were singing like a choir deep inside a cathedral, but all that was present was that squeak.

Movement? In the shadows.

A little 'Bot was lumbering along at a medium pace with empty milk bottles in a padded basket, to avoid loud glass clinking at the unholy hour of 4 AM. It's morning route, programed into its little brain the night before. One wheel was slightly askew, which accounted for the squeak.

Yeah, no one was there. But the feeling in my gut didn't go away. I wasn't too far from that thoroughfare. Maybe I could spot my tail in the busier intersection.

Pulling my collar up against the damp, I rushed up the other side of the street, keeping close to the parked cars that I might want to use for cover or protection.

At the intersection, I darted over to the 'Crawler stand and pushed the call button. A beam of light shot up into the sky, blockaded from getting too high by the fog. Didn't matter too much if the beacon didn't reach the heavens, it still managed to do the job of alerting the taxi system.

Squeak.

I spun around as the little 'Bot passed me.

That wasn't possible. I all but ran up here, and that little, squat robot was trundling along. How?

My thoughts were interrupted by the stunningly immediate arrival of a 'Crawler. The egg-shaped, white vehicle pulled over on the siding track to the pick-up point, and the passenger door opened for me. That was the fastest 'Crawler response time I'd ever had. Ever.

Getting inside, I gave the address to my office on Market into a brass horn. Some operator, way off down near Fisherman's Wharf, calculated the cost and programed the vehicle. Once the coins were officially received in the meter, the door locked and we were off down the rail system that would work its way over to Market near 9th Street.

Did I feel guilty that I'd promised Hayes I'd go straight home? Not one bit, 'cause I hadn't promised him anything. I'd saluted him. I'd made no promises. I gestured, that's it.

All the way there, however, the console bleeped and blinked. I thought that at any moment, the damn thing might explode. But, no. I made it safe and sound, albeit via the long way. I supposed the lost five or seven minutes didn't matter. The price was the same and it gave me time to see if anyone was following me. So, I kept any complaints to myself, as I took my receipt and climbed out.

One good thing about the world's slowest elevator: it's the noisiest too. If anyone managed to follow me after all of this, they'd never be able to disguise their approach while riding that thing.

Something cast a shadow across my frosted door, and it moved. Were it Marley, she would have music on. If Sam was there with her, they'd be yakking *and* have the music on. It was too early for her anyway. I left Hayes back at the Hall, so …

A third search of my office? Would somebody's goon or goons be so desperate as to search my office a third time? That's dedication.

I drew the rod from my pocket and carefully pulled back the hammer. Damn good thing it doesn't make that annoying clicking sound they always use in the movies. The doorknob turned. Guess they didn't think to lock the door after they got in. Not too bright

NO REQUIEM FOR THE TIN MAN

these gorillas. Cut rate.

I swung open the door. "Can't you hoods get anything right the ... first time?"

A short, squat, unpretentious 'Bot rotated on its main axis towards me, its appendages clasped politely together. Its head tilted to the side and back, like a Cocker Spaniel, and the round eye-scanners blinked. They do that. It's supposed to make them seem more human and therefore less threatening. Nobody ever explained to them that humans are the most threatening animal on the planet. And humanoid-like, emotion-lacking machines are just as scary.

Yet, this was a small 'Bot, compared to what was available out there. Maybe three to three and a half feet tall. Brushed metal exterior. A little backpack, that gave me a sense that it was childlike. Unadorned arms ending in hands operating with springs and tiny hydraulics. I'd almost go as far as to say it was dainty.

"What are you doing here?"

"I perceive that you are Miss Lucille Tanner? A licensed Private Detective?" The voice box produced a tinny series of pre-recorded words strung together like popcorn for a Christmas tree decoration, all as a response, although I would have expected it to respond to my question, not to ask me one.

"Yeah. I'm Lou Tanner," I replied, keeping my heater aimed at its head.

"Thank you. I am H-JO-NES234, Caretaker Services."

"If you're peddling your owner company's goods, you've come to the wrong place. I can take care of myself."

"That is incorrect." It blinked.

"Say again?"

"You are incorrect."

"About which thing I mentioned?"

"All."

I hate that you have to interrogate every 'Bot for the most basic information. "You're here pushing sales for your owner's company?"

"Incorrect."

"You're in the wrong place?"

"Incorrect."

"Great. Why are you here?"

"I am here with regards to your last statement. Quote: "I can take care of myself." Unquote. This is also incorrect."

"Says who?" I demanded, feeling an urge to plant a swift kick into its backside while pushing it out my door.

"Two million, one hundred fourteen thousand, five hundred and six mechanical beings residing in the Greater San Francisco Metropolitan Bay Area. You are in danger. Your companion human, Agent Christopher Hayes of the War Department, is in danger." The 'Bot rolled forward. "This city is in danger."

Chapter Twenty-One

"Danger, huh? According to whom?"

"Two million, one hundred fourteen —"

"Skip it!"

"Our analysis indicates extreme hazard, especially for you and for human Agent Hayes." Blink.

Reluctantly, since my stomach and banging forehead were still overwhelmed by the situation, I chose to put my heater away before I accidentally shot it. I walked through the office, sidling past the dainty 'Bot and over to the other side of Marley's desk. I sat down harder than I meant to. "Okay, 'Bot, what's your story? I'm not saying I believe you, I mean, me and Hayes are always getting into trouble of some sort. It's the job. So, what do you know that makes today different?"

The 'Bot rolled forward to plant itself right in front of me.

"I'm all ears, 'Bot. What is going on?"

"H-JO-NES234. Not *Bot*. H-JO-NES234."

Sometimes you give people that sharp, intelligent glare that instantly puts them in mind of your quick wit and encyclopedic mind. This was not that time. I must have had my mouth open like a trout for a good thirty seconds. 'Bots don't talk back. They don't sass. Then again, neither do most ladies, and I sure have been picky about my own name lately. Who was I to get this little guy's name wrong? "H-OJ … okay, call me a limited human, but I think that's a bit more than I want to allegator-wrestle at the moment. How about a compromise and I call you … ah … Jonesy? Is that acceptable?"

It blinked at me twice. "Acceptable."

Had I hurt its feelings? Guilt was crawling up my spine, so I added, "And you can call me Lou. Acceptable?"

It tilted its head again — the Spaniel thing. "Acceptable."

"So … I'm in danger? Give me the abbreviated but accurate version of why and why you and your two million relatives think so."

Jonesy settled on its rollers. "I am not authorized to share every detail. I will share what I am authorized to share."

I thought about arguing but this wasn't a case where I could convince the client or witness to cough up more based on a heavy application of compassion or remorse ... or fear of bodily injury. Jonesy was a product with wires and feeds, responding to programming that when it was told to stop, it stopped. End of discussion. Yes is yes. No is no. Black and white, no gray.

"Thank you," I said with a forced smile, "Please tell me what you are authorized to tell me."

The sun was starting to come up, and light was forcing its way into my office, to join everything and everyone else who felt welcome to come in, invited or otherwise. I kinda' felt sorry for Jonesy: wasn't its fault it caught me with its cold-hearted data-unloading prior to my having coffee. Still, it should have known better, coming from a caretaker services company. I grit my teeth and did my best. Jonesy was doing me a favor. In theory.

"Lou. The Mayoral Elections are in three 24-hour periods. We have calculated —"

"All two million of you?"

It started to correct me with the accurate number, but stopped and replied with a simple, "Yes." Blink. "We have analyzed and calculated the outcome of the election to within a 99.789562 percentile. Candidate Rossi will be elected."

"This is good?" I stole a cigarette from Marley's drawer.

Gears whirled as it considered my inability to recognize that 99 point-anything percent would indeed be "good" for a human. Perhaps it recognized my loose attempt at humor and moved on. Perhaps not. "Candidate Rossi is anti-mechanicals according to his speeches and printed propaganda. However, further analysis of the wider collection of informational input indicates that he will not follow through with any destructive regulations that will inconvenience humans who are used to our presence and service. This includes those who contribute large sums of money to his cause and / or will require the calling-in of what you refer to as 'favors' that he is historically known to use for larger municipal projects."

"He says one thing, does another. He says he is protecting human jobs from being taken by mechanicals but knows his rich friends will resent losing their 'Bots and 'Tons."

Blink. "That is what I said." Blink, blink. "This will not satisfy a significant number of humans seeking a violent outlet for their nature or monetary gains. In addition, we have determined that there is a 96.32785 percent chance that the losing candidate will cause this violence to happen so that his name recognition can be increased. His ambitions are not limited to the city and county of San Francisco."

The cigarette slowly took the flame, and I drew in the smoke. Letting that smoke slide out at its own good pace, I leaned forward on the desk. "Jonesy, what you're telling me isn't shocking, but it is disappointing. Yes, humans disappoint me all the time. But you left out one thing."

Blink. Spaniel head-tilt.

"You left out the death of Mrs. Landis and the effect it will have on Mr. Landis, the predicted 'losing' candidate. No ... I don't think he'll have the heart or stomach for a big fight right now. And without Landis to spearhead the American Bund movement, the whole thing will crack in half. Not that I'll cry over that spilled milk. I'm only working for the mook, privately, not for his campaign or cause."

Blink. Tilt. Blink. "There is a 96.32785 percent chance that the losing candidate will cause —"

"No, no. Jonesy. Death close to home changes people. Humans are weird about the death of a loved one. It's emotional." I put the cigarette to my lips but didn't draw. "This is something you don't specialize in. And it's okay. You don't have to. It's not a failing on your part. Death brings up strong, life-changing emotions. One's we can't predict or even anticipate sometimes."

"There is a 96.32785 percent chance —"

"Jonesy."

"We have precisely calculated all factors into our analysis. Even *human emotions*. I am a Caretaker Services Specialist Robot." The little guy was silent for a moment. "I understand death." Jonesy straightened and I swear those gears and rods twirled, or whatever they did. A series of beeps and bleeps echoed in its chest, followed by what sounded like responses. This went on for a full minute. Suddenly, Jonesy backed up. "I am authorized to tell you the following —"

"Did you, just this moment, contact someone?"

"Please quote: Inform Detective Tanner that proofs required are contained in the locked drawer beneath the artificial fifteenth century Ming dynasty vase with the gold dragon. Everything she will need is there."

"What is there?" I stood up, pushing Marley's chair back. "Wait, back at the house on 41st? I searched there. There were no 'proofs' to be found. And I have some bad news for you, bub. That place don't exist anymore. It's been torched, and me nearly with it."

"She must obtain these proofs before they are destroyed. They are all that can save her life, the human Hayes, and all of the City."

"Jonesy?"

"That is all I can tell you. Gold dragon. You will know. All else you already have or will have," it said, then rotated slowly, and added, "after you tidy up." And with that, the 'Bot Jonesy rolled out of my office.

Hell yes, I tried to stop it. Turns out it weighs a few hundred pounds and when it wants to go somewhere, it goes.

Well, if that didn't leave me flummoxed. For all my trouble, I ended up sitting on the floor, in front of the elevator gate, listening to the world's slowest elevator descending to the street. Maybe I should have gone home like Hayes ordered me to.

As if things weren't bad enough, with a client's dead wife on my watch, another kinda'-client being held for her murder, and the death of Dr. Frederick Gruber in a location I barely escaped, I'm not safe going to the cops, and now a bunch of mechanicals are analyzing my chances of survival.

I was headed to my bourbon when I reminded myself, those same mechanicals were prophesying about Green Eyes' survival too. I picked up the phone and opened up my mouth to give the operator his exchange and number. I stopped.

Two problems.

One: if Hayes was out, how do I leave a message with his office? It's not like we have private codes or some such Dick Tracy sort of fallback plan. I'd have to leave him some sort of clue about who called him and how to reach me, without giving the away the whole shebang. Or not leave him a message at all. Fat lot of good that would do him.

Two? I suspected earlier that Hayes was keeping an eye on me. Of course he denied it. Maybe he was lying — maybe he wasn't. But I know to trust my gut. Hayes or not Hayes, somebody had their ears in my office phone.

I hung up. This needed a thorough think-through. My place needed a thorough look-through.

There was something that might not be pertinent to the case, but then it might be the most important piece of evidence. I hadn't given it to Hayes, and I should have been ashamed of myself. I wasn't.

Reaching down my shirt, I removed the piece of paper I took from the bungalow. And the chunk of fluttering debris that rained down on everyone near the incinerating bungalow.

Walking over to my desk, I pulled out my purse and that PSSR invitation. Unfolding everything, I lined up the unidentifiable torn bits with my clean copy. Same paper, same ink, same color, same decoration … I didn't even need to do more, but yes, the marks and figures all aligned. Someone in the bungalow where Regina and Frederick were killed, had invitations to the Peoples Society for Social Relief meeting. Lots of them, that were blown apart and flung into the air. Having an invitation didn't make anyone else a member, any more than my having one, but?

How did the PSSR fit in? Did they fit in? And the meeting? It was a couple of nights ago. Were these old fliers that were left in the house? Who owned that bungalow?

I opened my kisser to ask the question out loud and remembered the other reason I wasn't talking to myself — other than not wanting people to think I'm wacked.

Listening devices. I had some in here. They are best hidden under desks, behind stuff on the walls, or in lamps. They need a source of power too, and therefore need to tap into the electricity of the building.

First up, I turned on the radio, loud but not too much. I didn't want the neighbors complaining about the nutty lady who talks to herself now and then. I also took that opportunity to check the radio for bugs.

All clear.

Guy Lombardo's show. Good.

Slipping off my shoes, I moved around both rooms. Nada behind the few decorations on the walls. Nix on the lamps or the tables they sat on. Nothing under Marley's desk or chair.

Nothing under my chair.

Nothing under my desk —

I'll be damned.

There it was. That lousy package of Gus's. Ragged to begin with, now shredded with precision by a cat's claws. It was jammed up under the left side of my desk. Took me a minute, but I pulled it out, propping it up on my desk blotter. Heavy thing.

It unrolled easily enough.

Newspaper wrapped an inner core of uncut paper sheets.

Uncut sheets of PSSR propaganda. *Gus, Gus, Gus. Did you have a secret life you didn't want your sister and brother to know about?*

I kept unwrapping.

Oh God.

Two identical blueprints. One piece of machinery. A gigantic rivet.

And for a while, I sat there, staring at what was under those torn pieces of the daily rag. Evidence?

Yes, *evidence.*

Of treason.

Chapter Twenty-Two

The radio shut off.

Marley woke me up.

Thankfully, she was only moderately annoyed but mostly amused when I pointed my gun at her, before recognizing her of course.

"Did you sleep here?" she asked.

"Not by choice."

"Well, that accounts for why you didn't pick up your phone at home. Hayes needs to buy himself a watch. He gets paid enough, he can afford one," she snapped as she headed over to the burner and started coffee. "Called me before 5AM."

"That's downright unforgivable."

"That's what I told him."

"What did he want?"

"You. Said he'd called you at home and there was no answer."

I tried not to laugh and sneer at the same time. My mother always told me that was unladylike. "Yeah, I was here." I put my fingers to my lips, then pulled over a pad and pencil. <u>We may still be bugged</u>, I wrote down and turned the pad for her to read.

Marley gave me that, *you've got to be kidding expression* followed by a dramatic rolling of the eyes.

I pulled the pad back and wrote, <u>Visited by Bot. Told me I'm in danger. Not only me. You too.</u>

This time, she gave me her signature, *what the hell* look. I pointed to the radio, and she turned it back on. It would give us some cover.

Signaling her to follow me, we slipped out into the hallway. I figured we could whisper safely there, so long as we paid attention to who might also be in the building this early.

"You were already up at five, weren't you? Sam got called in to work early, didn't he, and he called you to say so?"

"Yes. Are you being a detective or do you know something."

"It was a rough night overall. Regarding Sam? Let's just say Hayes and I observed something odd last night. The Bay Bridge —"

Marley glanced around, as if anyone else was up and about in our office building. "Sam said he knew the damage was bad. Every workman was being called in. Something about sabotage."

"I don't know what it was. I think Hayes does, but he said nothing to me. Walked away. And my evening didn't stop being interesting after that." I proceeded to give her the Reader's Digest version of my 'Bot encounter.

"A 'Bot? Came to see you?"

"Yeah. Hit me with those stats and warned me of danger. Associated with the election."

"Oh, is that all."

"Well … it started with almost being blown up, so it was on par for the course as they say."

"Slim, what the hell are you in the middle of?"

"Nothing." I sounded like a kid who knew her Mom had caught her doing *something*. "Alright, something … big. I don't know all of it. I've got pieces to a puzzle but none of them fit and I don't know what the end image looks like."

Okay, so Marley is my mom sometimes. I whispered the end of the incident between me and the little 'Bot into her ear.

"Gold Dragon, eh? Could it be anymore cryptic?"

"Well, it sounded damn specific at the time. But where I'll find this citizenry-saving Ming vase is still unknown."

"Faux Ming vase," she corrected.

"Right. Now, that's not the only thing. There's a real kicker yet to be seen."

"There's more? Slim, you're putting me in the looney bin, I swear."

I was never so glad my snooping landlady wasn't around. We must have looked ridiculous sneaking back into my office, but quiet was important on account of those bugs I hadn't found yet.

Marley followed me back to my desk.

And I revealed the secret hiding under my jacket. She tried not to gasp. But, she did.

Clamping her own hands down over her mouth, she suppressed all the rest of her reactions. At least all the verbal ones.

Smartly, she started running her hands over the plans. Didn't take her more than a second to realize both sets were the same. The white lines were carefully noted with measurements that boggled the mind. Both plans had pencil marking near the ankle of the main figure, encircling a joint. The words "inflexible joint – rivets crack" was written near it.

I revealed the last item hidden away.

It was that same damn rivet.

"They've made one," she whispered.

"If I'm right, they've made three. Remember? Your Martians?"

Tin Men. Big heads. Jointed arms. Nuts. Bolts. Rivets. If I was reading these correctly, there were power sources and some sort of communications. Hell, I'm no engineer. Who was I to say how the damn things worked. And the only person I knew who might understand these wasn't where I could reach him.

Well, engineering skills or no, I could tell what they were. And how big. The measurements were in meters, which wasn't an unknown language to me. My Pop spoke engineering and science. A little quick translation and I could tell these creatures were huge.

Big enough to have sported what looked like eyes floating in the distance. Forget Marley's theory about Martians.

And brother, they were armed. 'Bots and 'Tons aren't supposed to be armed. At the bottom of the blueprint was a mark. An image I associate with the Pointe. Maybe I was being paranoid, but who else would conceive, build, and arm colossus mechanicals like the Tin Men?

Aw hell, anyone could put that mark there. What if the Pointe wasn't involved. They were pro-Rossi, weren't they? Carlotti was.

The elevator clanged into position.

The gate flung open with a tremendous bang.

Marley's hand whipped off my desk and she reached around her back. Good girl. She produced a snub-nosed gat with plenty of natural gravitas. I had the .38 at the ready.

Neither of us moved.

Heavy footsteps.

Marley sidled up to me and we both took defensive position at my desk. It was heavy enough to provide protection. Both of us could flip it if needed.

Office searched numerous times.

Followed. Picked up by Feds and Political Brunos.

PSSR.

'Bots issuing deadly warnings.

Whatever was pounding its way to my entry door could be anything.

A shadow stretched across the upper glass panel — a silhouette twisted by multiple light sources. Big. Human? Maybe. It grew until it blotted out most of the frosted pane.

The door banged open.

Ole Green Eyes stomped in.

He stopped cold, with his hand still on the knob, when he came to face the two of us skirts … all armed and ready for battle. I think he might have reconsidered some of his choices in life in that second. But, good for him, this was G-Man Hayes. He snapped back to reality right quick.

"Put those things away. They remind me of my Aunt Lucy." He shivered melodramatically and closed the door behind him.

I don't know what Marley was thinking, but my guess was that she was on the same page of the *Pemberton manual* as I was, and relieved we neither of us had to pull the trigger.

"Next time knock, Hayes. A man could get himself shot around here."

"You say that to every guy who courts you, don't you?"

Marley stifled a snicker.

"Sure I do. Just before I show him where I hide all my special weapons. Want to see where the little derringer goes?"

What a prude. His face turned the color of beets, then

mashed potatoes. About four sentence fragments tried to jump from those nice lips of his before he could get one out. "You're … you're lucky I'm a Federal employee and a gentleman."

"Didn't know those were exclusive," Marley called from over by the perked coffee.

G-Man stared at the ceiling, then closed his eyes. Holding up his hand, he kept going, having dug up all the words he wanted to use. "I can't stay. Save the repartee for another time. Lou, you're here, not at home, which I can't say surprises me."

"I had to get my things before I barricaded myself in." Not precisely true, but generally. There were a few things I needed to do before going into hiding. Still, I was getting into a bad habit of telling Hayes half-truths. And he was getting into the habit of accepting them.

His mouth opened but stopped. "Yeah, that … makes sense. Okay. I'll drive you home. We've got to go. Now. Hurry up. I assume you've hidden your ah …" he stalled as his gaze darted over to Marley.

"It's alright, Big Guy. Marley hasn't seen it yet, but she knows I was borrowing a *flying horse*. Yes, I've hidden it."

He started to get all twitchy again when I handed him the note I'd given to Marley earlier. <u>We may be bugged.</u>

He was mash potato white again.

I gave him the other note and I thought he might have a stroke right then and there. He pinched the bridge of his nose so hard it left fingerprints I could have used as evidence.

I waved him into my office and while he stared slack-jawed at the contents of Gus's package, I poured bourbon into the coffee Marley brought to him. He took the whole cup in one, long, desperate chug.

With a woman dead, the city's politics on the verge of being handed over to fascists, and robots apparently running a secret brotherhood in the background, we were staring at proof of something far nastier.

"Oh God. Lou. I only wish I was … surprised."

"What?"

Hayes moved faster than I expected. He took one of the plan sets, wadded it up into a poorly-executed, folded square, and stuck it into his coat pocket. He then pushed the remaining plans and the rivet toward me. Pointing at those, then me, then pretending to ride a motorbike, he told me exactly what he needed next. Truth be told, his plan was a good one. And one I suspected he'd thought of long before this meeting of ours.

Well ... I kept secrets from him. I shouldn't get all offended and such if he keeps them from me. It's the game we have to play, even if I'm not always happy about it.

We both turned to Marley, who mimicked not seeing anything at all.

"Thanks for the coffee," he said, adding, "Slim."

"I'll take that ride home. Would you mind a couple of stops on the way. Groceries. Pick up wood for that old fireplace of mine. It's gonna' get cold this week and I'll be sequestered."

His face twisted up in a question. He knows I don't have a fireplace, old or new. I waggled the <u>bugged</u> note again. The nod he gave at least satisfied me for now that he understood. I don't want anyone beyond him and Marley knowing where I live. I'm being paranoid and leaving false clues for anyone listening over the latest Cole Porter tune.

"Yeah, I can do that."

Marley gasped, then tried not to giggle in victory. Spinning around to us, she held up a small package of wires and something close in appearance to a light bulb.

A bug. She'd found it.

My instinct was to smash it underfoot.

Hayes was a little more thoughtful. He took it before I could act, held it delicately in two fingers, examined it closely then dropped it in my coffee. We backed away from the cup and watched it from the other side of the office. "Water isn't their best medium for listening."

"Why don't we simply destroy it?"

He gave me a raised eyebrow.

"Oh. Silly me. Because we shouldn't let them know we're on

to them. A wise decision."

Hayes glared at me. "See. I *am* a smart fella."

I stuffed my set of the plans down my shirt, after I gave him my back to look at.

"Alright, Lou. Where is it?"

"Weren't you watching, I just stuffed it ."

"You know what I mean."

Did I? "Oh." The electricity reached the top floor at last. "That 'it.'"

Hayes pursed his lips and glared. I wish he wouldn't do that.

"Might as well show him," Marley said, walking over to the coffee mug with the device. Holding the mug as if it was radioactive, she took it to the coffee pot and threw a cloth over it.

I signaled Hayes to follow me. At the back of my office, in the bottom next to the radiator, I fussed with the wainscoting. It slid loose. "When I first found this, it wasn't so easy to open. It would push aside enough for," and I glanced back at the amused feline sitting on my desk, "Not My Cat to get in and out. I wondered for a long time how he kept getting around in the building and outside."

Green Eyes knelt down next to me. "What is that?"

"The old dumb waiter shaft. Complete with dumb waiter."

Laying on my back, I reached in and pulled on a thick cord, lowering a level platform. "Back, before the first War, these were apartments. The dumb waiter was for deliveries and laundry. After the War, the place was repurposed into a theater and offices. The shaft was closed up."

The platform leveled at my floor. Several of my boxes were neatly arranged on it. On top of all those, was one mean looking weapon.

Before I took it out of the shaft I gave Hayes the once over. "You're asking because you need it."

"Yeah."

"You're headed to the Pointe?"

"I don't know yet. I'm hoping not. It's the last place I want to go."

"I'm glad to hear you say that."

"Why? Lou, you don't even like me."

"I don't," I said too sharply, seizing the weapon and dragging it out of the hole. "Like Nora used to say to Nick, I'm used to you, that's all. Who will I fight with if you're not around?"

Hayes's forehead furled. "Marley?"

"She doesn't fight fair."

He took the Lightning Gun in both hands as I put the wainscoting back into place and checked for any signs that indicated it had ever been moved by anyone except me.

The Westinghouse 4-21 Lightning Gun. Never touched one of these until Hayes brought one to a party I was forcibly made to attend. Technically, it belongs to the government via Kit Hayes. After that particular case, I found myself in possession of it. That was a long story. I hadn't found the right moment to return it. To be honest, I wasn't sure what that moment would look like.

The electric gun was slick, hefty, and I can say from experience, able to fire more rounds than your average pea-shooter. Nasty rounds. People called it a *Zapper* for good reason.

A man with an earnest voice and too much enunciation started in on the news. While Hayes paced my office, wearing a path in my floor with his anxiety, I packed away all the ammo I could find into my satchel.

"Come on, come on," he sputtered. "We have to go."

"What? Are you on the lam now? Cops after you too?"

Marley perked up to that statement. "Ah, Slim, you didn't get into more trouble did you?"

The radio news was awash in doom and gloom for the upcoming special election. Clearly the station was pro-Rossi. It certainly had plenty of time for Commandant Carlotti of the Pointe to brag about how he was friends with Rossi. Funny … I can't recall him saying that Rossi was a good Mayor, only that they are friends.

The radio host continued his report. "… and now, with the death of Regina Landis, word on the street is that Lucas Landis has a significant card in his hand to play. Sympathy for the Bund candidate is increasing, and Landis has stated that this has only strengthened his resolve to make San Francisco safer. He is working with police to …"

NO REQUIEM FOR THE TIN MAN

I faced her and gave her the respect one gives a trusted partner by looking her straight in the eyes. "The cops think I have something to do with the Landis murder. It's complicated. You're gonna' get a lot of questions. They may come and toss the place. I'm sorta surprised they haven't yet."

She planted her hands on her hips. "You coulda' led with that piece of info, ya' know. We've been bugged. 'Bots. Secret plans. And, now a murder."

I started explaining, like I have the bad habit of doing, when she held up a hand. "Get outta' here, Slim. You didn't murder anyone. But you do owe me an explanation on how you are connected to Landis. I know it ain't political."

"Damn well better believe it's not."

Hayes made some noises and my elbow found its way to his ribs.

At street level, Hayes had parked his fancy, technologically altered car under an oak tree on a side street. The midday sun was barely visible through gathering clouds. While the news boys were all worrying about the run-off election falling to the American Bund and Lucas Landis, no one was giving any attention to the Autumn season fading and rainy season arriving.

CHAPTER TWENTY-THREE

Some days you wake up with a bad taste in your mouth. Some days taste bad overall: the smoke-filled air, the food you manage to scrounge together to make-believe is breakfast, and the news you overhear your landlady complaining about, when she isn't asking about the rent.

Out towards the Bay, a heavy cloud of gray smoke hung low over the water. Must have been a fire down on the piers somewhere. By the time I got dressed, caught a passing Nightcrawler, and arrived on Market Street, it seemed like the whole of the Embarcadero had developed a smoking habit. Fire bells were clanging chaotically.

At 12th and Market, the 'Crawler stopped dead in the middle of a pack of vehicles. I was feeling like prey when I was given a prerecorded notice that an emergency was underway. I tossed my coins into the meter and jumped out, running. The fact was all automation had frozen and effectively halted any traffic into downtown.

The smoke was rising from the south side of Market Street, which crossed off my office as being the source, much to my relief. However, I had an investment in one place that was right in the middle of it.

Howie Evans's stand, his livelihood and pride, was a pile of charcoal and splintered wood, breaking apart ever more as the firemen blasted water on it. Lumps of fried paper scattered the sidewalk, crumpled and blackened sheets ripped away to flutter down the empty street. A few feet away lay a long bump, covered with a white cloth. A body.

Oh God. Howie?

I shoved my way forward, sometimes using my badge to make some headway, mostly using my elbow. I think my brain was trying to exit via my throat the whole time. I couldn't take my eyes off the white sheet. *Oh God.* This wasn't a time to blithely describe a bump-off or a punched ticket. A man was dead. A good man. A man with a name —.

"Mr. Evans. Can you tell us your whereabouts at six o'clock this morning?"

I nearly fell over I turned around so fast.

Some Ward-Bond-looking guy, complete with rumpled overcoat and outsized chapeau, wide jaw and unforgiving eyes, crowded Howie both physically and verbally.

He's alive. My friend wasn't laying under a coroner's sheet. I'll admit it, it took a good, full minute before sensation returned to my knees and arms. Give me some idiot with a mid-caliber roscoe staring me down any day over the loss of a friend. The blue boys were chewing his ear off and Howie was alive to have his ears to be chewed.

And I knew Howie could handle some dime store harness bull with little more than an afterthought. *Thank God.* My stomach returned to its normal but anxious position in my belly.

But if Howie wasn't the dead body, who was? And was Howie standing up to a grilling because the cops thought he might have killed the stiff? While I don't believe in fate, I do believe in taking advantage of an opportunity from the universe when offered it. To paraphrase that older Cole Porter song, I need to do that voodoo I do so well.

I flashed my buzzer to the confused coroner's helper and got as close as the smell would let me. The coroner himself, one Frank Harper, barely looked up while managing a sly grin.

"Honest? A real live Private De-tect-tiv." His accent was so strong, it almost helped overwhelm his sarcasm and the burnt flesh scent.

"Honest to God."

"How the heck ya doin' there, Lou?"

"I'll be doing a lot better if you don't shoo me away and if you know who the victim is? I'm assuming death by smoke inhalation?"

"Ha! It was the third degree an' worse burns that done 'em in. But despite all that, we could kinda' tell who he was. Had one of them Hunter's Pointe uni-forms on. Boss gone an' asked the Pointe if they could help identify 'em. One Com-man-dantee Carlotti called his pallie Mayor Rossi and here I am. Dragged me outta' my office before I done finished my coffee."

No coffee? That was unpardonable.

"Bad idea if ya askin' me. The less the Pointe jack-booters stick their noses in PD business, the better."

"You've got your ID then?"

"Yep."

"Come on, Frank. What else do you know?" Eyelash bat. Bat. Bat.

"Well ..." He looked around quickly. The crowd was getting bigger and closer, but whoever he was checking for wasn't in view. "I put 'em at about thirty years old. Six feet tall. Healthy weight ... originally. Can't say much more 'til I git 'em him on the table and open 'em up. I'll take a peek with the fluoroscope too. Maybe his bones'll tell me somethin'."

I put my hand sweetly on his shoulder. "May I call later to ask about results?"

"Well ...uh?"

"It's important to me, Frank." Bat. Bat. Smile.

"I gotta' tell ma' bosses what I learn first, of course."

"Oh, of course. I wouldn't ask you to do otherwise."

"Y'all, uh, thinkin' I might find somethin' interesting in them bones?"

"Yes. If someone lit a fire next to you, and you were in a small shack, why would you stay in it?"

"So yer sayin' he didn't have a choice about leavin'. Dead before being burned?"

"Um hmm."

"As opposed to bein' unconscious? Either one would keep a man from running away. I will look into all of that. Thank you, ma' dear."

The crowd was getting too close, too squirrely, and too vocal.

Frank gave himself a quick scan of the crowd, then leaned over to me. "Pretty riled up, these folks. Ya might want to take yerself out of here, Lou. Call it a hunch, but I get the feelin' that things are gonna' get messy right quick."

"Frank?"

"Don' make me spell it out for ya, Lou. Live Negro man, dead white boy in a uniform. Heard those two done argued first."

"Howie's never argued with anyone that I know of. Cool as a cucumber sandwich."

"So, ya know 'em. All the more reason ta' git outta' here."

Frank's warning came almost too late.

The so-called crowd looked more like a military recruiting reel. I didn't need cold evidence to know the Pointe was out on the hunt, likely due to the PD call about the burnt body. Commandant Carlotti must have turned the troops loose. And normally, I couldn't give a damn except these jokers were plenty mad.

At Howie.

Lynch mob mad.

Mad enough that Frank dropped his paperwork into his kit, pushed it closer to the body, and grabbed my arm. "This ain't no place for a lady."

"Haven't you heard? I ain't no lady."

Don't know who said what to whom after that. Experience told me Howie hadn't moved an inch or spoken a word. He's too smart for that. I wasn't trying my usual sassy games either. Sure, I can take a couple of mooks, but this was a mob of whipped-up young men, all edging toward the police with murder in their eyes.

The cops weren't so thrilled about the situation either. Four in their big blue woolen overcoats stepped forward, Billy clubs slapping against their hands. Another row of cops set up right behind them. Frank kept urging me to the other side of the body.

We all got the surprise of our lives when the Pointe boys pulled out slap-sticks of their own. Shorter, thicker, and easily concealed apparently. Some fool with more stripes than most shouted obscene slurs at Mr. Evans, something sounding like "get him," and the entire street erupted in a fight.

I yanked my arm free and kicked the legs out from under Frank, forcing him to the ground near a fire plug. Anything was protection. And bless him, Frank was a lab rat by nature, not a fist fighter.

Pulling any kind of a gun would be stupid, even when a pair of guys knocked me to the ground, rolled over me, throwing punches as they went. But the rod I was carrying was heavy enough to make my pretty little lady purse into a weapon.

The Pointe boy had a cop pinned down. Frank grabbed the boy's jacket at the back, pulling until it pinioned his arms, while I swung like Joe DiMaggio. Purse and pistol cracked against the attacker's face. He went down, hard.

A thick, uniformed arm wrapped around my neck and lifted. The ringing blasting in my ears while I was sucking for breath spared me whatever abusive words he was heaping on me. Vision doubled. I clawed. Scratched. Flung the purse wildly behind me. No air. Kicking. Wasn't helping.

The mook let go.

I landed on the pavement.

Above me, in duplicate at first, I watched Howie pound the wits out of my assailant. It wasn't a fair fight, Howie was faster, smarter, and stronger.

The cops swooped in, peeling Mr. Evans off the man who meant to murder me. The Ward Bond cop separated them, spoke harshly to the boy then fairly to Howie. I didn't catch the words but the tone was unmistakable. Just as fast as Howie arrived to save me, the cops swept him away from the fight.

Two wagons of heavily armed cops leapt into action at the same time. People were running in all directions. Civilians. Angry men. Pointe boys.

Plenty were overwhelmed by the police and found themselves unceremoniously lying on the ground, being given a lovely new pair of bracelets.

Me? I stared at the stiff that had been kicked several feet from where it once lay. In unison, Frank and I crawled back to it and did our best to replace the coroner's sheet. Whoever he was, he was some mother's son and the least we could do was give him a bit of dignity in death.

Pain shot up from my knee. I yelped and rolled onto my hip.

No Requiem for the Tin Man

Jammed into my kneecap by its tack was a large, enameled pin. American and Nazi flags crossed. A piece of burned uniform was also embedded into that hole.

My stockings had a tear in them now. Nothing I could repair. Ruined.

Blood seeped out. Hurt like a *sonofabitch*. Must have hit a nerve.

Frank grabbed over his kit. A pair of pliers and a continuous string of apologies later, he yanked out the pin. He didn't think it went into the bone but said one of those new tetanus shots was required. I think I mumbled something about not wanting to be a test subject. That tetanus medicine hasn't been around long enough for my comfort.

"Up to you, Lou. Don't come haunt me if you die of diphtheria, pertussis, or tetanus."

Thankfully he had a bandage and some gauze in that kit. The alcohol that he cleaned my puncture wound with had me chewing thru the inside of my cheek and wishing he'd let me imbibe it first.

Just as Frank was about to toss the pin and scrap away, I seized his wrist. "Evidence."

He turned the pin over, eyed me pretty sternly, then agreed.

Yeah, I told him. *I know that pin.* I held out my hand. "Mind if I have that first?"

"I don' know. Will you let me get ya fed then home?"

Frank could be a real swell when he wanted to. He kept apologizing for his wheels being *the meat wagon*. Honestly, I didn't mind. The stiff was in the back.

The coffee and sandwich was more necessary than I wanted to admit. I'm not the sort of gal who goes out with a guy just to get a free meal or easy booze, so I made sure Frank understood this wasn't a date. I thanked him all the same.

Carefully patting his mouth clean, he kept talking. I didn't mind that either. The more talking he did, more I learned.

I did some talking too. Frank was listening and I couldn't count on that by any others at SFPD. Maybe Bennie Rollins, if he wasn't in a tight spot and had to put his badge ahead of our friendship. Frank was willing to relay my story to the right ears, so I filled them up with my theory about Gus Gruber not being the killer. Check the gun for prints and print direction. Gus was too far out of his nut. Drugged or medicated. He knew and liked Regina Landis. He wasn't an asylum escapee but a patient under care. That sort of thing. Frank heard me out. Didn't say if he believed me or not, but he gave me the fair hearing I'd never get from anyone else at the downtown station right now. Frank was a fair man.

And he wouldn't shoot me over a rumor.

We'd left the coroner's office and headed to a local emergency care facility. My knee was looking angrier than a dislodged hornet or my landlady on rent day.

When Frank was off making some move on a nurse he had no intention of following through with, I indicated the drug store across the street and left him to it.

The little Ma-'n-Pa place had what I needed. Packets of aspirin powder and a telephone booth. They had stockings, but that wasn't in my budget yet. And they might not be.

"Tanner Investigations," Marley's voice sparkled when she picked up my call.

"I'm amazed you made it in to the office. Have they unblocked Market yet?"

"Slim?" The change in her tone grabbed at my gut. She was scared. "Oh, thank God. Where are you calling from?"

"A drug store near St. Mary's. Give me an hour and I should be to you. A friend will drop me off if I ask him. He's heading back to SFPD"

There was a period of dead silence on the phone. "Did you get arrested? Tell me you didn't get arrested?"

"Nobody nabbed me. I went to see something at the morgue." The booth was cramped and I shifted for unachievable comfort. "There's been a terrible development near us."

"I heard that Howard Evans's news stand was burned down, and a mob showed up to lynch him."

Taking a deep breath, I proceeded to give her one very truncated version of the events. While she was stammering about the rot eating its way through the police, not that I'd dispute her, I gave it my best shot to assuage her fear. I only managed to turn up the volume.

She cut me off fast. "Something weird happened while you were playing nice with the coroner." I could tell she was fishing out a cigarette from her purse. "Sam and me — we were barred from going into the office — into the Fox building altogether. By boys out from the Pointe."

"Where'd they get *that* authority?"

"Who says they got any."

"Did either of you get recognized?"

"Don't think so." She paused, lighting up.

"Searched the office did they?"

"Yeah. We got your desk righted after they left. Slim, they knew where to look for … the 'cat's toy.'"

The bundle. How the hell did they know I had it and where it had been? I must have asked that out loud.

Marley answered. "Not from me. Nobody's talked to me. Sam doesn't know. That leaves the *two of you*."

Me and Green-eyes.

In case someone was listening in, yet again, I added, "I'm glad you don't know nothing. It's best that way. You and Sam are to keep out of the know. You hear me?"

Pause. "Sure," she stammered a little at first. "Sure, Slim. Whatever you say. But I'm here for you if you need me."

"I do, Irish. I need you to tell me who owns the bungalow on 41st Street. I need you to get ahold of our favorite agent. And then I need you to go on holiday. You and Sam are to head up to your Mother's. Up north, right?"

Another pause. "Okay, Slim. I'll head to Mother's. She won't mind. She's put Sam up before. But …"

I let the quiet fill the void between us. "You're safest there."

"I'm safe wherever me and my .38 Colt are."

"That's my girl! Now, leave whatever you find out for me on my desk, and get that man of yours up north. Understood."

Last pause. "Yeah. You be careful, Slim."

"Be safe, Irish."

Yeah. She'll be okay. Her mother of sainted memory died five years ago. I went to the funeral and burial. A lovely affair, outside Ventura — *down south*. She still has family down there. One thing was for sure: Marley O'Brien didn't need a job right now nearly as much as an armed escort. In Sam, she'd have the equivalent as they both head south to the Los Angeles area.

Frank spotted me and sauntered over, hands in his pockets. "Find what you need?"

"Not yet, but if I can keep the pain under control, I should be able to piece everything together without much distraction."

"You're gonna' let me in on anything you discover, right? You'll be straight with me. I can tell the regular cops for you. You know I'll do that."

I took his arm and let him help me out of the confined phone booth. He was a nice enough fella and I could use the help gimping along, for now. Boy-howdy, for a little pin hole, it hurt. Now I know it hit a nerve. "If you'll do me a favor and drop me at my office, I'll give you all the dope on the way."

And I did. I was straight with him. Frank was attentive but kept his eyes on the road. Balancing on the precipice of a San Francisco hill while shifting to first gear is an artform.

Okay, I was straight with him, but I did leave out a few glaring things: the contents of Gus Gruber's bundle and their current whereabouts. That was one set of cards I planned to play close to the vest. I wasn't being cagey or dishonest. This was to keep Frank safe. To keep him alive. The less he knew about that, the better.

As promised, he dropped me outside the Fox Theater, and I limped my way up to the office, I was pleased to see that Marley had packed up her beau and herself and left. Correction: I was damn-well relieved.

My best associate left me notes. She hadn't been able to reach

Hayes. The police were still looking for me. The PSSR was on the hook for the bombings, including the bungalow at 41st. They hadn't identified the body yet, or who might have been in the bungalow, but the current theory was that a PSSR bomber got caught in his own work.

Nothing is worse than evidence-lacking speculation.

As expected, Marley had pulled a few strings and learned who owned the house Regina Landis died in. Color me thrown off my game, whatever hue that turns out to be. I would have bet anything that the place was owned by the late Frederick Gruber.

I would have lost that bet.

It wasn't owned by Gus either.

Nor either of the Landis's.

It was a Corman Weiss who had signed the escrow papers. The late Corman Weiss, who then left it to his dear, bereaved widow.

Elsa Gruber Weiss.

Chapter Twenty-Four

Every time I walk into danger, I tell myself I'm walking into the lion's den.

That's not the entire truth. I usually tell myself to keep on walking and not stop.

All my wit and sass couldn't come up with the right descriptor this time. SFPD headquarters was a flurry of madness. There were news hawks and crime owls, and plenty of legal vultures, all waiting their turn to pick at the still-living corpse of Howie Evans.

I was not in my Sunday best, and despite my Myrna Loy looks, it was any wonder I caught the eye of more than one chum in the bunch. Never mind I was limping, I knew the bandage was hidden under my trousers. I came dressed to fight or flee, whichever was the wisest move.

Their eyes bored into me like termites on a log. The twitching that overtook my hands could only be hidden so much by my clutching a purse. Were they glaring at me because of the outfit or the familiar Hollywood face? Or did they recognize me?

Lou Tanner, cop killer?

Chin down so far it almost disappeared into the silk tie around my neck, I peeped out from under the brim of Uncle Joe's hat. The chaos rang in my ears like pots and pans falling from a great distance onto a tiled floor. My heart throbbed under that silk tie. I knew to keep moving. If I stopped, someone might take more than a passing notice of me, and then the questioning would start.

I hadn't been here since the business with Milton Somerset. I hadn't dared and Kit Hayes wasn't wrong to do his damnedest to protect me from the vengeance other cops would take out on me.

Yet, I needed to see Howie. To make sure he was alive and not getting the abuse I feared.

I needed to find Bennie Rollins, to get him onto this case, whether he liked it or not. He was the only cop I could count on.

NO REQUIEM FOR THE TIN MAN

"Hey, girly girl. Little Miss P.I.?"

Oh Hell, I knew that voice. Rotating on nerve-locked legs, I faced Junior-cop Jefferies, the chum I met at the Woolworths. Same snarl. Same demeanor.

"You got some moxie showing your face in our office."

"What? I couldn't be here because I miss sparring with you so much, I just had to come to you?" Well, at least my sarcasm isn't scared.

"You need to shut your yap, hussy. Knowing your kind, you're here to hang out with that nigger commie —"

"Jefferies!"

The desk sergeant's voice was ten times louder than it should have been since he was standing a couple of feet away from us. "We don't talk like that in this building. Not to no one, certainly not to women. You're wearing a uniform that has meaning in this town. Live up to it — or get out if it."

Junior Jefferies straightened up into a soldierly stance and backed away. The sergeant took his place. A bit roundish through the middle, he was nonetheless imposing in a serious way, certainly enough to bring back the commotion that had frozen when he'd first barked. With a jerk of his head, he sent Jefferies scurrying for the back of the room.

The man then rounded on me. "You know, Sweetheart, you probably should have waited another six months at the earliest before dropping in."

"I couldn't wait. Junior-boy, over there, was right about one thing: I know Howie Evans and I am worried that he isn't getting a fair shake."

"Ah, you need to trust us."

"I trust *you*," I flirted despite my gut squeezing at my lie. "It's the potential lynch mobs I don't trust."

"You don't need to worry your pretty little head about that, Sweetheart. Some of them Pointe boys tried rushin' the joint this morning. Didn't make it past me." He pointed his big thumbs at himself.

Weakness grabbed at my legs. "You're kidding. What a

palooka move? How many were there?"

"About 30 of them." His grin was huge and comforting. "All youngsters. A bunch of young punks. Thought they were impressing someone up the command chain."

"Not so impressed when he has to come bail them out."

"Got that right, Sweetheart. Boy-howdy, their boss was pissed off —" His face tightened and pinked. "Excuse my language. Their boss was 'cheesed!'"

I sidled up to that big 'ole lug, with his big 'ole smile, trying to be amiable not cheeky. "I'd like to see Mr. Evans. Can you arrange that?"

"No can do, Sweetheart. He's off limits."

"Oh, come on."

"Why not?" a nasty sounding voice said. It was none other than Carlotti, himself. I wish I was surprised. Despite the sharp creases and polished brass of his uniform, he leaned against the near wall, lighting a foul stogie. His eyes patted me down for more than weapons and his lighter caught the light, flashing it in my eyes. Cheap cigar, cheaper brass ornaments, gold lighter.

The desk sergeant straighten up. "Sorry, sir, but I have my orders. We have to keep him all wrapped up an' safe-like."

I folded my arms and did my best to ignore Carlotti. "But I'm not one of the lynch mob."

"Says you. Oh, an' I believe you. But if something happens and I'm the one who let someone in down there, it's my job. Sorry, Sweetheart."

"Oh, go ahead and let her visit her boyfriend. She isn't able to do too much damage, now is she?" Carlotti gave me a smile that convinced me he wasn't worth saving if the ship started sinking. Gold lighter, eh? Like the one Landis tried to foist on me? It wouldn't surprise me if Carlotti was playing all sides. Typical of the militia.

What was surprising was the security around Howie. It wasn't like the flatfeet to put so much fencing around a Joe Average in the cooler, even an unknown, un-rich, un-connected, Joe Average. Of course, Joe Average didn't generally incite mobs of uniformed boys to attack a police station either. Or …

No Requiem for the Tin Man

Were they keeping me out — because I'm ... well ... me? The dame involved with Milt Somerset's death.

Carlotti huffed something vaguely like a laugh, exhaled a huge plume of smoke, and wandered off like he hadn't a care in the world.

Only way to find out was to get to Bennie Rollins.

"Bennie? Yeah, he's around here. I'll get someone to escort you to his office. So's you don't get messed with by Junior or his like."

"I appreciate the generous effort."

"Think nuthin' of it."

I sat as close to the front desk as I could. The buzz around me was palpable. It might be election time, but it wasn't any different from any other day at the station. The sergeant had his radio going. Sounded like Landis's campaign was in trouble, if you trust polls and interviews. The sympathy vote hadn't earned him enough love to overcome questions about his actual politics.

As a little 'Bot scurried by with stacks of mail, I couldn't help but think of Jonesy. I hoped he was right — Rossi wins but doesn't do anything repressive to them. Yeah ... I'll say it ... they deserve better.

A moment later, a kid in a fresh but oversized uniform and deep frown arrived. I don't know what his opinion of the San Francisco Seals baseball team is or what he thinks of politics, but his expression told me everything he thought about me. He bothered only to gesture to me to follow him. Maybe the kid thought he was being all brains and stuff, but I know the downtown station well enough to know that Holding was down the hall and to the left. So when he turned right, I stopped at the junction of desks. "Wrong way."

"Look, toots. You want see your commie boyfriend or don't you."

So, they were letting me see Howie after all. Why all the denial before? And what was with the name calling? I bit my lip. "You're a tad young to be jumping to conclusions without evidence or experience."

"Don't take much to assume."

"Young man. You never heard the old saying? 'Assume' all you want, it'll only make an 'ass' out of 'u' or 'me.' I'm not gonna' be the ass in this case. Your call if you want to be. You're a big boy."

Not the brightest bulb amongst the streetlights, that kid. He was squishing up his face the harder he concentrated on making sense of what I'd said to him. Shaking his head, he gestured impatiently. "Just follow me. You gotta' get one approval first."

Fine.

At least he opened the door for me.

This wasn't Bennie's office. That was back towards Holding, unless he got it moved. This was simply a room. Inside waited a spartan desk, one ugly lamp, a folding metal chair that promised discomfort, and a man puffing dramatically on his pipe. Cheap tobacco. The rest of the room was dark. No windows.

"Sit down, Honey."

"I prefer standing."

"Not with that hole in your knee, getting infected. Doc Harper told you to get a shot." He lit his pipe and the glow of his match illuminated his deep set, black eyes. "Serves you right, trying to interfere with a police investigation into a homicide. You should stick to missing dogs and necklaces."

"Probably. I still prefer to stand. Gives me the feeling I'll be able to leave whenever I want to."

"You're not going anywhere, Honey."

"I'm not? Gosh, and here all along I thought I kept my own calendar."

"Don't try to be wise with me, Honey —"

"Then quit calling me 'Honey' and ask me what it is you dragged me in here to ask."

"You giving me lip?"

"'Giving you lip' implies that I'm actually addressing you in some fashion, like answering a question. So ask."

"Sit down!" He landed both hands on the table with a bang.

"Shove off, before I call a cop."

"That's rich."

"Nix the 'Honey' moniker, introduce yourself like a

gentleman, and ask your damn question. If not, I'm leaving, and it will take one hell of a lot more man than you to stop me."

"Sit down!"

"No!"

The door flew open and my heart's grip on my chest loosened a bit. Bennie Rollins, looking more fit than the last time I saw him, rushed in. "Geez, MacCormick. We can hear you two outside. What's going on?"

MacCormick stood up and backed away. "We need to arrest this woman."

"For what?" Bennie and I asked at the same time.

"Accessory to murder. I can think of a few other things. Pretending to be a licensed private investigator. Hindering an active investigation —"

I pushed on the bridge of my nose hoping the head pain that was pounding in my sinuses might go away if I applied more pressure. Seemed to work for most of the men I know.

"Horse feathers!" Bennie shouted at him. "I know she's got a valid license. I know she's a straight shooter."

"The hell! She isn't being straight with me."

I planted my hands on my hips like I wanted them to grow into a garden of fury. "You haven't asked me anything."

Bennie glanced over at MacCormick with a raised eyebrow. "Sounds like we all need to sit down and talk." Before I could argue preferences, Bennie pulled the folding chair out for me. A real swell. "Say, Lou, I had a nice chat with Frank over from the examiner's office. Interesting theory. Not sure I buy it, but I'll give it a gander."

"I appreciate that."

I took the time getting settled in the uncomfortable chair to breathe deeply. Bennie fetched another chair from outside the door for himself, leaving MacCormick seated on the other side of the desk.

"Are you a member of the Nazi Party or the American Bund?"

"No!"

"Are you a member of the Communist Party?"

"No." I looked over at Bennie.

"Do you sometimes entertain men in your home?"

Bennie interrupted, "okay, that's enough."

MacCormick ignored him. "Are you now or have you ever been a member of the People's Society for Social Relief?"

I snarled at MacCormick. "I'm beginning to wonder if I shouldn't. But no. And until meeting you, it never crossed my mind."

Bennie was right there with me. "I said 'enough.' Whaddaya' doing here, Mac? Using up SFPD resources for one of your little witch hunts?"

I leaned over to Bennie. "You saying he does this all the time?"

"Oh, so he didn't introduce himself. That's sort of in the law, you know. You're supposed to identify yourself when questioning a witness or a suspect." MacCormick opened his mouth, but Bennie beat him to it. "Lou, I'd like you to meet Inspector George MacCormick of Army Intelligence. He ain't no cop."

"He ain't no gentleman either," I said to Bennie until I turned all my ire on the stooge with the pipe. "War Department? What the hell are you really doing?"

"Rollins, this woman has information she's keeping from us. From you."

"Is that true, Lou?"

I was about to spit. "Other than accusing me of being a socialist or a lady of the night, he hasn't said or asked anything worth anything. How about we start talking truth and facts."

"Okay, Honey, try this question: where's Christopher Hayes?"

Holding up his hands and trying to shush the pipe-smoking G-man, Bennie waved at him, making a slashing gesture. "Ix-nay on the Ayes-hay! Holy moly, Mac, he's even less popular around here these days than she is."

"So I've noticed."

"What about Hayes," I stammered.

MacCormick puffed for a second. "I was getting' nowhere. Hayes isn't calling me back. His name and rep weren't getting' me anywhere. I dropped your name and finally shook some cooperation out of this place. At least *you* were useful for something. All you've managed to do so far, little miss detective, is support the Nazi Party, cheer on the PSSR, bat your eyelashes at Agent Hayes and get him killed."

I went cold. Meat locker cold. Can't-feel-my-hands-anymore cold. Green Eyes was missing and maybe dead? If I had words, they were long gone. Bennie and MacCormick kept on arguing, I don't know about what. All I could do was think about Hayes: his rumpled hair and big eyes … "How long?"

"What?"

"How long has he been missing? And are you sure, very sure, he's missing? Maybe he doesn't like you anymore than I do, and he isn't returning your calls."

"Honey, we're sure. We know what we're doing."

Ice got replaced with fire. "Oh, please. You couldn't find and arrest a rooster on a farm for crowing at sunrise."

"Lou," Bennie scolded.

"Hey, don't 'Lou' me. This goon has been cracking his knuckles at me from minute one. He has yet to ask anything useful, and he's lost one of his best agents."

"Honey, you wouldn't understand. This business is too big for you."

I looked him over. "I'm too big for you, if I was even willing to stoop to being seen with you in public."

"That's a lousy crack, Honey."

"Come over here and I'll put a matching crack in your empty, little skull."

Bennie burst out laughing. "She will, Mac. She will too." He placed himself between us, just in case. "Lou, why don't you take the lead and lay it out for us? You're good at that."

MacCormick's face screwed up. "Are you kidding?"

"Nope."

"I'll do the asking and she'll answer. I don't need some cheap tail —" He stopped mid-sentence to take a breath. I guess he figured out that he was outnumbered in here. "She works for a Nazi."

I spoke up. "What does that have to do with Hayes?"

"I'll ask the questions."

"'Cause you're so good at that."

"Have you no shame, you, working for the Nazis?"

"I don't work for them, you mook."

"You work for Lucas Landis, Head of the San Francisco Nazi Party!"

"I'm working for a man who wants to know if his wife cheated on him. Now it's a moot point. She's dead."

MacCormick snickered. "You killed 'er out of jealousy?"

"No."

"You croak the broad on his orders?"

"Are you nuts? No."

"Did Landis make you sign onto the Party or did you go to him for the work on your own volition?"

"I took a job from a guy who said he had work for me. That's how I see it, that's how I treat it."

He started repacking his pipe. "Awfully convenient and easy. Just ignore the politics."

"I don't like politics. Never have."

"Say, Lou," Bennie leaned in, "why that case?"

"'Cause she's a Nazi sympathizer, Rollins!"

I leapt to my feet and turned on MacCormick so fast he stumbled back three steps as my folding chair hit the floor. Even Bennie stood up in fear.

"Alright you two wiseasses, listen up. I'm gonna lay it out for you real good, and I'm gonna' use small words so even you, MacCormick, can keep track. I'm doing what you two mooks should be doing instead of playing footsie with me. You can cut the 'Good boy — Bad boy' routine you cooked up earlier. No! Don't deny it. Neither of you believes I'm a Nazi, a Communist, or a murderer. Hayes maybe straightened that out a day ago. But now he's missing and you need my help to find him, only I didn't know he was missing, so that plan didn't work out so good." I glared at Rollins. "How am I doing, Bennie?"

"You've always been swell at this. Keep goin'."

"The skinny version? I'm broke thanks to Milton Somerset, a

crooked cop and corpse found on the losing end of a bullet. Jobs dried up for me. You Johnnie Law types closed ranks and got the word out that Hayes and me killed him for no good reason. He was crooked and didn't deserve his badge. You ought to be ashamed of yourselves."

"Aw, Lou —"

"Zip it! I'm talking. You wanted me to talk, well, now I am. My case is a matter of keyhole peeping. I don't like my client, but I don't have to. Don't think I've haven't had a few tough moments wrestling with this. But I know what I'm doing and for whom. I don't work for the American Bund. And yeah, I can put things into tiny bottles and choose to open only those I want to. I have to in this business. It's the only way to survive. Sometimes good clients come your way. But for most cases, by the time a shamus is needed, things are bad. So I don't get the best of the best. If I want to pay my bills, I hold my nose and take what comes."

I waited for MacCormick to open his trap. No? Good.

"Now, for the record, my client's politics disgust me. But if I make a contract with the Devil himself, I'll keep it. I can sleep at night knowing that fact and that my income is no cleaner or dirtier than anyone else's. Certainly around here. So if you're through wasting time, what do you have so far on Hayes? Who talked to him last? Why are you so certain he —"

"Thank you, Miss Tanner. We'll call you if we need you." MacCormick turned his back on me.

All the noise of the City vanished into a piercing scream in my head. "Excuse me?"

"You're free to go. But don't leave town." He started to light his pipe.

"'Leave town?' With an unsolved murder and Kit Hayes missing? I haven't even been paid for this case and with his wife dead I doubt I will, so leaving town isn't in the cards."

"With any luck," puff, puff, puff, "this is your last case playing detective and you can go do something more appropriate for a girl. It'll be better for you in the long run."

That's it! I'm getting arrested today. I don't care if I have bail money. I'm getting arrested for assault on a Federal Agent.

Puff, puff, puff. MacCormick sat near me, on the desk edge. "What does Landis pay you?"

"Twenty-five dollars a day plus expenses," I said through my gritted teeth.

"That's a man's pay. What do you charge?"

Bennie had to physically remove me from the room. After I showed him my feminine but effective right hook. MacCormick's pipe flew across the room. He spun into the desk. Bennie laughed out loud, grabbed me around the waist, and carried me out to the desk sergeant all while announcing that he was not arresting me, but he might give me a medal.

Chapter Twenty-Five

A 'Ton held out its hand, pointing toward the back of the station. I was to be escorted out. Even Bennie wasn't helping.

I was being tossed out on my keister. The indignity!

I stood up as straight as I could, adjusted Uncle Joe's hat, and walked with pride behind the automaton in uniform. It took me a moment before I realized this 'Ton was designed with a female form.

"Miss Tanner," it's tinny voice said through a speaker near it's immobile mouth. "Please continue to follow me. This is an … unusual route. Unknown likely to you. It is what is referred to as 'the back way.'"

"Bennie's idea?"

There was a longish pause. "No. Mine."

At least it didn't say 'Incorrect.' "Safety measure?"

"Yes. I judged it most advantageous to allow you to egress the station in a way that encountered fewer personnel. Also," it began.

"Also?"

"To use this route, we must pass through Holding."

I stopped and touched it … her … by her smooth metal arm. She maneuvered until she faced me. As an automaton, she was built to be human shaped and pleasing, although she could hardly move fast enough to run and catch a perp. She was pleasant. And thoughtful. Easy to gab with. "I know a 'Bot who has agreed to let me call him Jonesy."

She blinked. I guess that's a reaction they've built into many mechanicals to make them more comfortable. Shame on me. I hadn't noticed so much.

"I believe I know of whom you reference."

"What should I call you?"

"I am called 'Friday.'"

"I call my best friend and associate that name sometimes."

"Why?"

"It's a compliment. It means she can do anything."

Blink. "I shall remember that. Please follow me."

Friday led me to Holding, which was as spartan as one might expect.

One can see into each tiny room. Privacy being one of the first things you give up after being booked. Friday took up watch at the door and by all appearances, gave her approval for my presence to the other mechanicals busying themselves with endless paperwork.

Howard Evans occupied the second cooler from the left.

Four more locked doors down, a pair of 'Tons wearing police livery faced inward, watching the prisoner.

Gus.

Gus sat alone, staring at the bars of his cell, dressed in a gray jumpsuit and battered denim jacket marked with lettering sure to identify him as a prisoner. His eyes were glazed over.

Sap that I am, I started towards Gus and found myself blockaded by a variety of mechanicals. Gus was off limits. He wasn't moving anyway.

Friday redirected me and apologized quickly to the reactive machinery. "Miss Tanner, no one is allowed to visit Prisoner 45 right now."

"Augustin Gruber you mean?"

"Yes. Prisoner 45."

Not only had their clothes and personal items been confiscated, their names had been taken. I stumbled along and was taken straight to Howie's cell.

"I should explain that Prisoner 38 has his lawyer with him.

Unlike Gus, Howie, at least, had a lawyer.

Not that it had done him much good. He and his lawyer both looked like they'd been fed into a meatgrinder. The lawyer, tall and thin, darker skinned than Howie, was sporting a shiner on his left eye and by the way he kept touching it I could guess that it was new.

But of course. Two negro men inside of police property? Alone. Unprotected. With all the modern thinking and mechanical observation, how was this still possible.

And why was I not surprised. Infuriated, but hardly surprised.

Smacked around, if not worse, and neither appeared to be astonished by their circumstances. At my arrival, Howie *was* amazed. "Miss Tanner, what in the world has brought you here? You shouldn't be here."

"Neither should you!"

"What do you mean?" the lawyer asked. "Mr. Evans has been accused of murder. I'm his lawyer."

Friday allowed me into their cell. "Please don't think me self-centered, but I've been thinking and the only conclusion I can reach is that you are here because of me. Or rather, because of something I'm involved in."

Howie allowed a little grin to play on his face. "Possibly. Is it *that case* you're working on?"

Shame wound its way through every fiber in my muscles and hurt so badly I could have cried. Hell, my eyes got watery. I nodded. "The only way I can figure it is ... well ... the bike you kindly leant me? I hid it while tailing my mark, but the case went sideways and I didn't get to retrieve it for a couple of hours. Someone must have noticed it and reported it to the police thinking you were involved with another crime. While you likely have an alibi for your time when *that* crime was committed, your frequent magazine buyer ... *me* ... and borrower of the said vehicle does not."

"Miss Tanner?"

"Yes, I was working on *that case*." I had one hell of a time looking him in the eyes, but I had to. I owed him the straight truth. Seeing the swelling on his cheek, the remains of blood in the rim of his nostril? I'd never owed someone so much before. I'd screwed up and he'd paid the bill that came due. "Mr. Evans. I am so sorry. I had no intention of getting you involved, but it looks like I did anyway. Intentions be damned, I owe you more than an apology." I started digging around in my bag for a tissue or a handkerchief.

"I'm a big boy. I could have said 'no,' and I knew something was up when I leant you the bike."

"And that there is the other thing. I should have told you more. I wasn't straight with you."

"Maybe. Maybe not. Sometimes it's best not to give away all the secrets you know." His lawyer agreed in silence.

"Truth? I was and still am ashamed."

"Oh?"

He was playing with me. Maybe that was the coinage he wanted in payment for my being such a heel. Fine. His hurt, his compensation. "I keep telling myself that the means is just a way to the end. That I could separate client from their world."

For a moment he looked meditative. I don't know how he could. Me? I'd be grumbling about how much pain I was in. But Howie? He'd been around the block a few times too many. "We tell ourselves things that sound like reason and truth. Sometimes they are. Sometimes they're our way of making the cock-'n-bull more bearable."

"You're not going to start spouting wisdom like Charlie Chan are you?"

The lawyer smiled, "Lawyer's job is like Detective's," he said jokingly. "Many times, client stinks."

Howie snickered. "And Lou here got a real snoot-full of sewer. I will vouch for her, she wouldn't have taken the job if she didn't have to."

I opened my mouth. "How?"

"A woman's beautician and manicurist aren't the only ones she shares everything with. Her newspaper and magazine stand man gets the details too."

"True," his lawyer added, "lots of people tell the newspaper guy what's on their mind or what they've heard. Stories get around this town fast."

These two were being better detectives than me, with my fancy diploma. "Then you both know who I was working for? I swear to you, when I took the job, it was never for his organization, it was only for him, and not because he is who he is.."

Howie's eyebrows met in the center of his forehead, and he scowled. "I was aware you had a ... let's call him a troublesome customer. Like I said, you wouldn't have said yes if you didn't have to."

NO REQUIEM FOR THE TIN MAN

There was a shuffle of feet not far from the other end of the cells, all three of us stiffened, but no one new or threatening entered the area.

"How *exactly* did you know? I need to put everything together and this puzzle is missing too many pieces as it is. And now my friend Hayes has gone AWOL."

Both men were alarmed by that.

"What happened to him?"

"I don't know, Howie. I've got to find him. He has some information that could really bring things crashing down."

Again, the two men exchanged glances and it's a good thing I don't believe in mind reading, because I would have thought they were having a whole telepathic conversation without me.

The lawyer sighed. "You must know about the People's Society by now?"

"Oh, no ... are you kidding me? Howie. You're with the people planting bombs —"

"We are doing no such thing!" Howie held up his hands.

"You both? You're part of them? So, all the accusations that you're part of the PSSR are right?"

Howie shrugged. "Don't be so disappointed. We are not terrorizing this city. We're not violent. Not yet. All we want is justice. Think about it Lou. It makes sense, doesn't it. It should make sense for you too."

Yeah, it did.

"We're smarter than that, Lou. Don't let the radio reports and officials tell you the lie. We are not out there randomly harming people. But I have a good idea who is. And it would be in their best interests for the blame to fall on us."

"I trust you. But understand, it's a little tough. Put yourself in my shoes, Howie. You told me you have eyes and ears on the street. Are you now saying that the PSSR spied on me and that's how you know about my case?"

The looks again.

"Howard? Tell her everything," the lawyer commanded.

Howie sighed. "Yes, but not exactly, Lou. Gus, over there?

He is one of ours. He's one of the founding members of the People's Society for Social Relief."

You could have picked my jaw, lips, and teeth up from the floor. "Gus?" I pointed down a few cells to the drugged-up man being kept on suicide watch.

"I'll explain later exactly how he fits into the PSSR. For now, let's just say, Lou, you don't owe me anything. I sent Gus to you. With his package."

"What!" I shouted.

"Lou!" Howie's voice was sharp but whispered. "Shhh."

"Tell me what happened. I've already been here too long. I'm guessing you have three minutes if we're lucky. Two or less if we're not."

"I'm not feeling lucky tonight," the lawyer mumbled.

"Me neither. So, start singing, you two."

The lawyer took over the story. "We've been hearing rumors about plans between the Pointe and Landis's Campaign. Gus Gruber used to work at the Pointe, being a veteran. They always hire veterans, except veterans like me." He rubbed the skin on his arm. "Gus called me because I've known him since the War. He called to say that he'd found something terrible that needed to be brought to the authorities but was in danger of being caught. I arranged for him to call me again and went to talk to Howard. Howard suggested we send him to you. That you could help."

"Tick tock. We're down to two minutes." I glanced over at Friday who nodded in agreement.

"That's it."

"Do you know what's in the bundle?"

"Neither of us do."

"Okay, let me give you the rest of the run down."

Howie held up his hands again. "No. The less we know, the better. I don't know about my litigator friend here, but I'm only so brave. If I don't know it, I can't spill it."

Friday walked up. "Miss Tanner. Someone is coming. I believe they are bringing in new persons under arrest."

"God help us if they're more Pointe boys."

NO REQUIEM FOR THE TIN MAN

The lawyer winked. "They're being kept separate from us. This handiwork," he circled his face with his hand, "was the work of an overzealous, low-end cop. It all got stopped by some roly-poly fella with a mustache."

"Sounds like Bennie Rollins. I'm not surprised."

"We're fine for now, Lou. You," Howie pointed at me, "have work to do."

Howie and the lawyer both offered me their hands to shake. And I shook them, gladly. As I left Holding, I took a moment to look back, praying this wasn't the last time I'd see Howie, Gus, or the lawyer —

Alive.

Chapter Twenty-Six

Screw it. I made a bad decision. I have to fix things.
Make it right.
No one else can do that for me.

-Lou Tanner, P.I., 1935, Private Journal

I didn't wait for an appointment.

According to Pemberton's *P.I. Instruction Manual*, a good shamus needs to have numerous skills, amongst them: lock picking, defensive driving, basic accounting, and in my case — the willingness to get scuffed up while breaking into an old warehouse via means that can't be discussed in squeamish company.

Translation? I was quite a sight for Lucas Landis when he got back to his office from an evening of condolence gathering, vengeance declaring, and money-making crocodile tears.

Having too much experience with death and dying, I was originally prepared to cut him a lot of slack, yet the smirk on his face as he ambled in and the jovial sound in his voice, as he wished his Chief of Staff good night, convinced me to toss away my scissors. That damn Bund membership pin glittered from his lapel. The armband he slipped off with too much ease had a swastika on it.

No slack cut for him. I almost scared him to death, which felt deliciously satisfying.

"Miss Hein ... no ... it's Turner, isn't it?" Landis wadded up the armband and jammed it into his pocket.

"Tanner."

"I wasn't told you'd be here tonight." He edged back toward his office door.

"Why don't you sit down, Mr. Landis. We need to talk."

"Oh? About what?"

"About why you hired me. The truth." So what if my voice was far beyond sarcastic. Sure, why not. I was fit to be tied ... pissed in fact. "Cheesed off" wouldn't cut it anymore.

"Uh ... why, to confirm that my wife was or was not cheating on me."

I crossed my legs in a mannish way, calf perpendicular to the knee, which had finally stopped hurting so much, and I poked a cigarette into my mouth. I was still in the necktie, rough trousers, boots and waistcoat. Of course I left Uncle Joe's fedora at the office. I wasn't risking that on whatever detritus might decide to fall on me while breaking in. Yeah, like I said, I was quite a sight.

Landis scooted over to me and did the gentlemanly thing by lighting my snipe with one of his fancy gold lighters. Tempting to blow smoke in his face, I held off. Mad or not, I was still grasping at professionalism.

Just as fast, he retreated behind his big desk, putting it between us.

"Nothing else?" I asked as I blew out the smoke.

"Why no. Nothing else at all." He shuffled papers without reading them. Stacked them, then replied them. The coffee cup and saucer were moved at least three times. I honestly expected him to start dusting the curtains and flags behind him.

For a man in mourning, he looked incredibly lively. Black suit, black necktie, and an armband to be clear that he was checking off all the official efforts towards public grief. The lack of circles under his eyes, the easy laughter and comments he'd made before he met me, was giving off a different appearance.

"You seem a bit nervous, Mr. Landis."

"Only a day and a half before the election."

"How are you doing?"

His shoulders relaxed. "The newspaper polls say I'm ahead. Not by much, though, but enough to rout Rossi. It was close last time, but this time, I'm sure we'll have enough votes to make the result undeniable."

I drew in another mouthful of smoke. "I wasn't asking about the runoff election. I was asking about you, in your unfortunate circumstances." I went ahead and made myself quite comfortable leaning my arms on his desk, cigarette clamped in my lips, and got myself a closer stare at him. He started into those paper piles again. Oh, I could have let that go on for hours, but I came here for answers. "No, Mr. Landis, I had nothing to do with the death of your wife."

I didn't realize he could open his eyes that wide, nor did I expect to take so much pleasure from seeing him freeze in place.

"I'm ... I'm sure you ... didn't ..."

My eyebrow raised automatically but I still managed to keep the laugh I wanted to bark at him deep inside.

He was up on his feet in a second. "Were you worried that I thought you had ... oh, now I understand. Of course, Miss Tanner. No wonder you seem quite put out with me." Landis sighed a bit too heavily and strolled over to his decanter bar. Those shoulders of his, however, did not relax. "You thought I wouldn't pay you because the rumor said you were involved with poor Regina's death. I assure you, Miss Tanner, that will not happen."

The pop of the crystal top to the decanter was muted but welcome. Since I suspected I wasn't seeing one single sawback, a drink would be the minimum he owed me.

Then again, if he offered me any of his rancid lettuce, I wasn't taking a bite. I wanted nothing to do with his tainted money. Marley was safe for now, and me? I'll always survive.

"You will be paid," he said as if reading my mind. "I can assure you of that. Shall we have a drink together, Miss Tanner. You can tell me what happened and what you have learned, and I will, I promise, be completely on the level with you."

The liquid was deep bronze in color and gave off a strong smell. Cognac. He handed me a short glass and poured one for himself. Once seated, he raised it slightly. "If you will permit me: to Regina. Regardless of your findings, she was still my wife."

I waited. There was no way in hell I was drinking a thimble's-worth of that hooch until he drank it first. And he didn't disappoint.

Half his glass disappeared in a nervous swallow. Still, I wasn't about to sling back the whole thing. I sipped like a lady.

Damn, it tasted good. Of course he kept the good stuff.

"Was she?" he asked with a slight choak in his voice.

"Cheating on you? I cannot confirm one way or another. There wasn't enough time. There was, however, enough time for me to decide that your wife was a caring person. And I have some other theories."

His expression molded into something that I didn't think one could rehearse. Soft. Lonely. "Yes. That does sound like Regina. She took on every sad-sack case who cried in her direction. Tell me, Miss Tanner, do you think that's why ..." He let the sentence falter.

"She died? No. No one invites murder, Mr. Landis. No one looks for it."

"But Gus killed her. He was one of her sad-sack cases. And, I admit, I thought he was taking up too much of her time, too. It didn't help that he was ... is the brother of Elsa Weiss. I owe Elsa so much. Can't go complaining under those circumstances."

"And Dr. Gruber?"

"What?"

"Gus is Frederick's brother too."

"Oh, yes." He smoked for a long minute. "Frederick's untimely passing is very disturbing too."

I watched him for a moment. "How do you know Frederick is dead?"

The glass rattled against his teeth. "It's all over the news."

Interesting. "They haven't identified the body."

"Didn't you do that for them? You saw. You worked with the police at one time. What's your best guess about their confidence that they have the right man."

Fine. Change the topic. But I heard you slip up. "I believe they have the wrong man, and I told them so."

Well, call me surprised. I startled him.

"You ... spoke with the police?"

"Absolutely. Mr. Landis, I was a witness and for a while, they thought I was an accomplice. You know the rumor that ran around town so fast? I was obligated to talk to them at one point or another, about their theory that I might have done it. People think Private Investigators aren't subject to the law, but that's just in the movies and the pulps."

"Forgive me, I was under the impression that you ... um ... you, like other detectives, aren't always on the best terms with the police."

"Whatever gave you that idea," I said with too much sugar. "But this time, I needed to present my side of what happened or end up in the clink. Besides, they were headed in the wrong direction for a while. Let's call it my civic obligation to provide the police with all the information so that they won't waste taxpayer money."

"But, they don't believe you're an accomplice anymore?"

A low knock rapped on his door.

"No. I'm happy to say, they are very confident that I am not."

"And you told them you don't think Gus did it."

His hands were shaking something awful now. The lip of the decanter rattled on the side of his glass. I could see the waves in his glass as he refilled it.

"I believe I have convinced them to look elsewhere."

Landis glanced down at his own hands. He gripped his hands to stop the shake. "That means Regina's killer is still out there." He suddenly glared up at me. "I have to catch him." Landis was on his feet again. "You may not believe me, Miss Tanner, but I loved Regina."

"And Frederick's killer?"

Another knock at the door made us both tense.

"Miss Tanner. I think it might be wise if I took things from here." He opened a lower drawer and pulled out an envelope. "Our business is complete."

The envelope was tossed over to me. It had my name written on it. It was slightly fat. Sealed.

I stared at it and then him, up through my eyelashes. "I didn't complete my case for you," I stated while keeping my hands locked in place.

"Please take the payment."

NO REQUIEM FOR THE TIN MAN

"No." I didn't want his money anymore.

"You answered a question for me, just not the one I originally asked. You should be paid."

"If not the original question, what question did I answer?"

The door creaked as it opened, and I can't say I was amazed when Elsa Gruber Weiss skulked in. It was her turn to be shocked. "Fraulein Turner?"

"Let's stop beatin' our gums and settle this here and now, shall we?" I drank deeply from the glass and landed it heavily on the desktop. Call it *Dutch Courage* if you must. "When I first came in here to meet with Mr. Landis, he knew perfectly well what my name was. You, Mrs. Weiss, know perfectly well what my name is. Tanner. I'm Lou Tanner. You had to look it up so you could find your brother at my office address. So stop with the horse-feathering. I'm not insulted — I'm annoyed. And we have much more important things between us than using childish name mockery, don't we. Like, for instance, who really killed Regina Landis and your brother Dr. Gruber and why."

Landis sat down rather hard.

But Elsa? She moved those lips from a smile to a sneer. "I was wondering when you would say something."

"About your brother? My condolences, Mrs. Weiss."

"No. Frederick was stupid. The foolish games I was playing. I really haven't much use for you overall, but you were … are somewhat funny to laugh at. I was hoping you were long suffering sort. It prolongs the game."

Cold hearted bitch. "So you were, huh? You might have been waiting a long time, sister, since I tend to be overly patient with clients. But I've developed a notion that you two were never my clients in the first place."

"No, no," Landis began swapping glances between us girls. "I genuinely wanted to know what my wife was up to."

Elsa's hand slammed down onto his arm, but her eyes stayed glued on me.

I made a scorn-face of my own and finished my drink. "Thank you, Mr. Landis. That may well be the first truthful thing you've told me. Well, other than the fact that you genuinely loved your wife, Regina." I kept a close watch on Elsa's face. "You deeply and completely loved her and *no one else*." Yeah, call it a gut feeling I was chasing, but men like Lucas Landis and his organization don't tend to put women in positions of control or authority. Like Elsa. Not unless they have to, or they have an overriding emotional need to. Landis was what I'd call *the easy blackmail sort*, so I was counting on Elsa's reactions to confirm it.

Elsa didn't disappoint. That nasty look of satisfaction she wore as easy as a pair of old gloves turned into loathing fast. It took her a few moments to catch herself and juggle those lips back into a more familiar sneer. A little thing, but I noticed it.

"Mr. Landis," I gave him my full attention. "I don't know if your wife was having an affair, but you were. Nothing meaningful ..."

Elsa snarled.

"... but let's just say, the feeling of ... of guilt ... you projected ...whatever she was doing wasn't so ... obvious that ..." My vision doubled, then returned to normal. "That it would ... harm ..."

Oh no.

My lips and tongue were feeling thick and uncooperative. My thoughts had miles between them and stringing words together was close to impossible. How had he done it? He drank the same booze he poured for me. Now he seemed fine while I was wobbling?

Like trying to get home on foot after the whole night had been swallowed bottle by bottle at a bar, I focused hard on speaking clearly and moving deliberately. "Sorry, I lost my place in the script. Got too far ahead of my thoughts. If your wife was doing something indiscreet, she had the good sense," God, I needed to avoid words that started with "s," "and decency not to be obvious about it." I put a hand out to steady myself, as my legs got a rubbery sensation. "You should take that as a sign of respect, at the min ..."

That muddiness that leaves you unable to drag yourself forward? Like you're stuck in quick sand? It had a stranglehold on me. I found a chuckle had wormed it's way out of my mouth. Resting on both hands now, I flashed my eyes over at Elsa then back to Landis. "Before I fall down, what was it? What was in the drink?"

Elsa checked over her bosses shoulder to the tray of decanters. "If he gave you the new Jägermeister, it was Cyanide. If he gave you Napoleon Brandy, then he must have taken a liking to you, Miss Tanner. That is only Laudanum or possibly Chloral hydrate."

"You drank that Mickey Finn too," I slurred, trying to pinpoint which of the two of him was the real Lucas Landis.

Both of him smiled weakly. "I've developed a tolerance to Laudanum. Takes quite a bit more than that to affect me anymore, let alone compromise me. Too many years of falling back on its …" his voice faded away even though I knew he was still talking.

Makes sense. Sorta'. Kinda'. Maybe. I sure wish the floor had been closer than it was. Hitting it didn't hurt now, but that wasn't the case later on.

High heels strolled over. Blurry, but I knew they were hers. The scummy bottom of her shoe playfully pressed on my neck.

"You should get used to this, Fraulein *Turner*. It's the future."

Chapter Twenty-Seven

Knockout drops made from Laudanum. A special brew of Laudanum. Spade told me about those once. I think it was the time the bunch of us, including our hosts the Charles's, were trapped in the penthouse of the Mark Hopkins. Power out. Elevator sitting on the first floor. Case of scotch open and emptying fast. Sam Spade could hold his liquor, but only when he chose to. The memory came back to me in waves of nauseous colors and recalls of swatting away impertinent wandering hands.

Knockout drops. None of my limbs could move. Muddy was no longer strong enough to be my word of choice. If that drunken gumshoe Spade hadn't only spun a tall tale from a web of hyperbole with the purpose of hitting on me, at least his aggrandized fable included a general timeline.

Based on Spade's story of his being drugged plus other things I knew, I figure I landed on the floor twelve hours prior to a vague memory of waking. Someone slapped me, held me down, and stuck a needle in my arm. Out I went ... again.

That's what I got for not keeping my yap shut.

My best guess was that I'd completely lost Monday.

With each thought taking about five minutes to get from one ear to the other and back, it was any wonder I ever opened my eyes. My ears, much to the chagrin of my throbbing head, were working just fine.

Two people were having themselves a warm if not heated discussion on the other side of the wall to the room I was occupying.

"She says Gus didn't do it." That was Landis. He sure was a whiney little punk off stage. He clearly saved his best performances for his adoring crowds. He also got help from his staff, like Elsa, to make sure he didn't screw up and look like a fool. "And what happened to Frederick?"

"Lower your voice." Elsa? Yeah, that was Elsa. Hitler, Jr. in a skirt. *God damn it*, I'd made a mess of choices and decisions. I never should have … ugh.

"She told the police."

"Oh, they won't believe her. I told you, they think she's a cop-killer and will do anything to get her alone in one of their jail cells or interrogation rooms. That's what the lower species do to settle affairs. We should leave them to it."

"They wouldn't. She's a lady!"

"Oh, hardly. She has no family of importance. She carouses with Jews, Negros, and the Irish. And she's no longer of any use to us. No one will believe her."

"But if Gus didn't kill Regina —"

"Then someone else figured out what that turn-coat wife of yours was doing and took matters into their own hands. Lucas, what does it matter? The Regina problem is solved."

"And Frederick?"

"My brother was a heart-sick ass. He followed her around like a puppy and got himself killed."

"Elsa, love … what happened —"

The door opened and I held my breath, holding as still as possible.

"Lucas, I know what you are thinking. You're blaming yourself for Regina. But she brought it all on herself, just like that stupid trollop in here did." I could guess she meant me. "Like that nigger with his newspapers and conspiracies against good, honest people. He'll get what he deserves too."

"Someone may blame *me* if it turns out to be one of our members who took matters into his own hands."

Elsa's laugh chilled me. "Nonsense. You never told anyone to kill your wife any more than you told that stupid boy to attack the nigger and his news stand. We are safe from blame. All we do is tell our members *who* is conspiring to ruin the American Dream. Can we help it if they take matters into their own hands?" The mockery was thick.

Their footsteps banged louder as they approached me.

"Still out," Elsa said, disappointment dripping from her

words.

"Another loose thread."

"So what?"

The whispers dropped to a smear of sound between them. I couldn't pick out the words any longer. Maybe the drug was still working on my head.

"Leave it to me," she said sternly. I didn't like hearing that from Elsa. "The polls have opened, Darling. You were showing better as of yesterday. Regina's death is playing well with the average voter. You look strong and vengeful, ready to bring the sword down on crime. It's what they want. The people here want a vital, powerful commander who isn't afraid to do what is necessary. They're tired of having to settle on this or that. They're tired of losing no matter which way they decide. They want simple, guided lives. They need us to rule for them. As for Regina? In the end, she ended up doing you more good dead than alive." There was a long pause. "Too bad you didn't ask your little detective about the package."

"Did he have it when you found him in her office?"

"No."

"Then I say she doesn't have it and never did. How many times was her office searched —"

"Lucas, I love you, darling, but sometimes you are the fool." She twisted her heel away from me. "Come along. You need to finish dressing. You have a meeting with your Chief of Staff in ten minutes. Then off to the Civic Center to make a show of casting your vote. You'll need to look strong but bereaved."

"You're coming too?

"No, no. You're the candidate and now widower. You don't need a woman on your arm. That will look bad. You need to play the bereaved yet strong avenger. The manly widower. I'm going to get Hans and have him take that trollop out through the basement to dispose …"

The door shut.

I didn't wait for her to finish the last of that sentence. I sat up, ready for the pain that rang my ears and banged my head like the Bells of St. Mary's. My hands were cuffed behind me, ankles tied with

NO REQUIEM FOR THE TIN MAN

a winter scarf, and something silk stuffed in my mouth.

The room was spinning and taking my stomach for a ride. At best, I had a minute or two before Elsa and whoever the hell Hans was, came back. Squeezing my eyes shut, I shimmied my wrists under my tush, wiggled my arms past my hips, and got my hands behind my knees. I could reach the knot in the scarf and managed to free my legs. With sufficient amounts of desperate bending, I twisted my leg free. Plenty of wrestling freed the other leg, but it didn't take as much manipulation before my hands were up in front of me and my legs were useful.

Head spinning and cuffed wrists, I wasn't fighting my way out of this. The silk tie was spit out right quick and I bumbled my way over to Landis's desk. He had to have some piece of artillery in one of his drawers.

Something arrived at the door.

The only thing I could find was a letter opener. It was nasty looking but who was I kidding.

The knob turned.

The door opened.

I dropped behind Landis's desk, clutching the opener.

Silence was all that filled the room, although outside all sorts of excitement cut through the peace. A much smaller-sounding crowd, minor compared to the one I'd encountered first visiting this place, was gathering voter details. Cheers would occasionally erupt from the auditorium. I did my best to hold my breath. The door closed.

Wheels squeaked.

A 'Bot?

Taking an awful risk, I peeked out from my hiding spot. The back half of a squat little robot was holding still in the middle of the office.

"Miss Tanner?"

I didn't reply.

"I am H-JO-NES234. We have met."

"Jonesy?"

"That is correct." He swiveled towards me.

I slowly crawled out from my spot and watched him tilt his head in that spaniel style. "What are you doing here? You're sure a sight for sore eyes, but I'm not sure why you're here."

"You did not follow our instructions, thus it was determined that one of us should attempt to bring the proofs required to avert the violence to you."

"As you can see, I was detained from that purpose." I held up my cuffed hands. "Any chance you can fix these bracelets?"

"You are not wearing bracelets." Blink.

Be literal. "Handcuffs."

"The handcuffs are not broken."

I opened my mouth in frustration, when Jonesy added, "but I can surmise there is a 95.4835 percent chance you would desire to have those removed."

Only 95% chance? What did Jonesy think I liked?

A little door opened in the 'Bot's body and a tray of keys slid out. Checking inside, there were various skeleton keys, standard looking sets, and yes ... one set of handcuff keys. He held them in a pair of pincers while I did a bit of contortions to unlock the cuffs. They'd been on me pretty tight. I felt the difference in circulation almost immediately.

"Okay, Jonesy. If you're here for so-called proofs, where were *you* going to look?"

"Behind you."

Well, I'll be damned. Jonesy was right. On the credenza to the back and right of the big desk was one, ugly, faux Chinese vase, with one big, gold dragon. The decoration was printed, not painted. Obviously fake. "Mind if I borrow these," I asked, taking the pincers away from the 'Bot. "Would you also mind watching the door?"

"The door is not going anywhere."

"But someone might try to come in. That would not be good for either of us."

Long pause and head tilts were followed by, "Agreed." He wheeled himself closer to the door.

Pemberton's *Lock Picking* chapter didn't cover using pincers but I had enough knowledge of what to do that the credenza drawers weren't too much of a challenge.

In the drawer directly under the vase, were several files. One of them held correspondence with the Hunter's Pointe Militia concerning how the City could be cut off from the rest of California in an emergency. How this would disrupt shipping on the West Coast, handing control of the largest commercial potential to the Bund. How the Pointe was prepared to take control of all military installations in the immediate area.

Yeah. It went on. And on.

To destroy both the Golden Gate and Bay Bridges further isolating San Francisco from *invasion* by the United States.

Oh, it was more complicated than that. But I'm not a military expert. I'm just a voter and taxpayer.

The bottom of the drawer wiggled.

Under all that horror waited one more. The title page was all I needed to see.

The New American Reich.

"Lou. Several persons are approaching. I estimate five."

The manifesto had been edited. There were initialed notes. That was indeed proof. Handwriting could be identified. Maybe there were prints too. I snagged the winter scarf, then carefully wrapped the correspondence and manifesto up in it. The less I touched them, the better.

The door started to open.

Jonesy slammed his little squat body into it.

His head turned to me. Was that panic?

Chapter Twenty-Eight

Jonesy kept the door blocked. "Lou Tanner. Explain how you entered this building. We did not detect it." Bang! Those on the outside tried to push their way in. I'll bet someone is hurting: Jonesy is heavier than he looks and the door barely budged.

"I came in through those ducts," I pointed to the grate in a side panel.

"You must egress by the same route. Take the proofs with you. This is essential to the continuance of peace in this city and county."

Whoa. Hold it. "Jonesy, you can't fit through there. We have to find another way out."

"Incorrect."

"What?"

"You and you alone must leave."

I started knocking on the walls to see if Landis had his own private exit. Hey, it was possible.

"You must leave," he repeated.

"Jonesy ... no, I won't. You could be —"

"Harmed?" Blink. "I am not alive."

"You're alive enough to want your brethren to have peace and quiet."

His head tilted. "An interesting concept not appropriate to consider at this time. However, logically, you must take those proofs to those you deem powerful enough to stop the destruction of this city."

I tucked everything under my waistcoat. "Jonesy?"

The 'Bot was slammed forward by an attempt to open the door. He did not budge and the attempt failed.

"Jonesy, will you be alright?"

"There is a high probability that I will."

"You're not giving me a number."

"It is best I do not."

I bent down to pull the grate out of the wall. "Hey, Jonesy. Thanks."

"Thanks will not be required if you succeed in your task."

"I'm saying it all the same."

Oh, I knew this duct too well. Wasn't I just here? Wasn't I just forgetting this cramped, filthy tube. The grate slipped back into place. Like hell I was making it easier for anyone to find where I'd gone.

The bad news? Crawling along the metal length of my escape route made plenty of noise, not to mention irritating my pin-stabbed knee close to intolerance, so I hustled along as fast as possible.

The good news was that anyone following me would make plenty of noise of their own. I'd hear it.

Jonesy was fine. He'd merely tilt his head and blink. They'd probably not even bother with him. They'd probably assume the little caretaker was looking out for the Landis office. Maybe they'd assume I'd already escaped. It would take them some time to figure out what path I'd taken.

I was calling Jonesy "him?"

Reversing my mental treasure map, I worked my way back and down. Stopping to listen. They hadn't followed me. Not yet. But that didn't mean I wouldn't have a reception party waiting for me.

Where the air and garbage ducts all dumped out into the Bay, I changed my route. The paper I carried couldn't get wet while all bets were off for me. Risking the stench of fish, I worked my way along a water line that fed the cannery.

Above, shouting and raging pierced my hiding spot. Something was up. But before I could escape further down the line, the tunnel narrowed to the point I'd either have to swim or drown.

Fine. I could handle this. Another grate pushed out to a prize spot — right behind stacked rows of garbage cans. With no possibility of dignity available, I crawled out on my hands.

A pair of big mitts gripped my shoulders and I was flying sideways into the cans.

"That's her, Hans. Hurt her."

Oh. It's you.

Elsa folded her arms and stepped back, unsure of her footing in the mud and uneven ground. "Hurt her. Do anything you like to her."

Hans was huge. His hands were bigger than my head and I pictured my head exploding under their squeeze. He reached down. I scrambled back, kicking dirt and muck on his black uniform.

I made him mad doing that.

He stomped forward, swinging and grabbing for me. I dodged and fell and did anything to avoid his grasp.

Some of the Bund came over to stare or point.

I got onto my feet and faced the berserker. Elsa must have found him in Casting Central, stored under *Scary Villain's Henchman*. Bald, scar under the eye. Six foot, forty-seven. Twenty-five tons. I don't know. I knew if he got his mitts on me, I was dead.

He grinned — I think that was a grin — and crouched down like we were at a girl's school wrestling match and he was some sort of obvious ringer.

I don't know nuthin' about wrestling as a sport. I was on the downside of a slight slope. Mud everywhere. Trash and debris.

And protestors?

I'd been so focused on Berserker Hans that I didn't even notice the crowd forming up behind me.

No uniforms. Many dark-skinned faces that would never find acceptance in the Bund auditorium. Their signs read, "Equal pay – equal rights – equal citizens!"

Dear God, it's the PSSR. Was that a 'Bot or two amongst the people when I glanced over my other shoulder, to make sure I wasn't imagining things. The People's Society was here, of all places and times, here!

An important rule for Private Investigators: *don't take your eyes off the guy who wants to turn out your lights for good.*

Hans was at me in seconds. I ducked, but only in the nick of time. He was so close I could smell what he devoured for dinner on this breath.

So … I did what any red-blooded American woman would do.

No Requiem for the Tin Man

He was close enough that I twisted sideways and planted my size-seven shoe right in between his knees.

Not a good choice. I only made him angrier.

Dropping and rolling, I pressed the manifesto under my shirt to my skin with one hand and with the other, I picked up a garbage can lid. His fist crashed into it. And for a moment, I thought he felt something.

Nope!

But Hans took his eyes off the dame who *didn't* want to die today. I swung the lid and smashed his jaw. More luck than skill, the blow threw him off balance and backward.

The protesting crowd was on him and racing towards Elsa. Panicking — well, I would have — Elsa ran for the warehouse entrance. Some of the uniformed men and women joined her, seeking refuge. Some uniformed men joined Hans in the melee.

I was grabbed from behind. Yet again.

I spun around, hoping it was Hayes — ready for it to be someone bad.

A 'Bot with a red cross on its front blinked its eyes at me. Saying nothing, its hand appendage enclosed mine and I was dragged out of the middle of the scuffle.

Whistles blew, sirens erupted all around us. The cops were arriving.

Another pair of mechanical hands helped me to stand.

"Miss Tanner," the red cross nursing 'Bot began.

"I gotta' get back in there." I'll admit I was excited about making my opinion of that so-called American political party known. Jubilant in fact.

"No. That is incorrect." The helper 'Bot slipped in front of me. Its tinny voice was higher and more feminine. "You are in danger."

"So is everyone in that fight. Outta' the way!"

"No. You must take the proofs away from here."

Damn. The 'Bot was right. I couldn't get caught with these by anyone in the Bund. Staring a bit longingly at the fist fight, I bit my lip and agreed. "Say, fellas. You've got a 'Bot in there that needs your help. H-something. Yeah, H-JO-NES234. I call him Jonesy. Anyway, he was stalling those Nazis —"

"You are incorrect."

Relief. "He's already out? Safe."

"No."

I shook the red cross 'Bot by the shoulders. "Is Jonesy out of the building?"

"Yes."

"Then he's safe."

The two turned to each other, blinked in unison, and the helper replied. "No."

That terrible pang you get in your stomach, when bad news is all you're hearing? That's what gripped my insides. How was little, silly, all-too-literal Jonesy not safe? And why did I care? He was just a …

After another blink, the 'Bot said, "Follow us."

Down an alley, where we'd been able to *flee*, which was how it seemed to me, we found a handful of mechanicals of varying size and function. They stood in a circle, facing inward.

Dread was coursing through my veins now, as if we were on the fields of Flanders with the smoke starting to clear. Who knew what we would find? They knew. I didn't.

The appendages had been torn off. The body of the 'Bot I'd known as Jonesy had been stomped flat. No lights worked. No whirls or blinking. Scrap metal was all that was left. Berserker Hans had trashed the little thing, not realizing that it was …

Jonesy was dead. Not destroyed or decommissioned. Dead.

Tears pricked at my eyes a bit. Through the blur, I found the other mechanicals watched me. I whispered something unhelpful and pathetic, such as "I'm so sorry," to the beings that were said to have no emotions. And I wanted to say something more. More tender. More compassionate.

Would they understand? Would they want such words? Did any of them need the condolence? If any did, they didn't tell me. They turned on their various wheels and treads and left.

NO REQUIEM FOR THE TIN MAN

Market Street was eerie, although I couldn't quite put my finger on the reason. People were milling around, confused, speaking in hushed tones. Many of the storefront's constant neon lights were off. The grand façade of the Fox Theater was dark. Getting up into my office wasn't the problem I anticipated, and that was unsettling too.

The little Helper 'Bot who'd shown me Jonesy's remains, followed me upstairs and had plopped himself down in the corner of my reception area and proceeded to do absolutely nothing. I suspected he was watching me and quietly telling all his fellow mechanicals what I was up to.

The phone rang, jarring my nerves. "If it's some wisenheimer selling something, I'll send him off with a flea in his ear," I told my little Helper. I was too tired to even cuss, as much as I wanted to.

The phone rang a second time.

I picked up the phone. "Tanner Investigations."

"Lou?" It was Marley. "I had a bad feeling I'd catch you here."

"Hey, Irish. You all settled in?"

"No. Not even close."

That was not what I wanted to hear. "Where are you?"

"Heading back. No one's allowed to leave the City. I'll explain it when I get there. We're stopped at a gas station that has a phone. Everyone's been calling someone to tell them what's happened."

"What is going on?"

"There are Pointe guards everywhere and they've blockaded all the roads out. Trains are stopped —"

"Hey lady! Hurry up!" the voice called near Marley.

"Settle down, chum. I get my minute too," she shouted back. "This guy's gonna' kick me off in a second. Let me do the talking! Nobody can leave. I tried calling Hayes. He's missing. Been missing for a while. Lou?"

"What do you mean? No one's seen him at work?"

"Nobody knows where he is, Slim. Sam's been a real jewel. He's been stopping every few miles or so to let me call, but now we've been cut off. The Point boys are armed for bear. Somethings about to happen. Something bad."

The line went dead.

"Marley? Marley?"

Helper 'Bot stirred. The whirls and groans coming from him left me thinking of a big dog waking up.

"Alright, friend. I don't suppose you can reach out to all your compatriots and find someone for me."

Helper blinked. "That is possible."

"Do you know who Christopher Hayes, Agent, U.S. War Department is?"

Blink. "Yes."

"I need to locate Agent Hayes. Do any other 'Bots or 'Tons have eyes on him." In case that was too much of a broadly-worded request, I added, "Can one of you tell me where he is right now? And if so, please tell me his location."

"I will attempt to obtain this information. Will it be helpful?"

My head dropped. *Patience, Lulu.* "Yes, please. This information is of extreme help to me."

With that, and another blink, Helper began an internal dialogue with mechanicals far and wide. I took the moments to swap out my togs to something less destitute looking and less likely to have ammunition falling through holes in my pockets. Forget breadcrumbs — I leave trails of bullets.

Where was Not My Cat? For a few minutes of panic, I checked all the places NMC might hide. Nada. With any luck, the feline was hiding somewhere in the basement of the building. I wish I could join him.

Fresh shirt and trousers, mismatched as I never intended to wear them together, still, I felt cleaner. The quick towel bath helped, but I was sure there were things in my hair I want never to see or confirm.

In the process of changing, I pulled all the collected evidence together and laid it out on my desk. I had a good idea of what was going on now. Hayes needed to know.

Dread is a real animal in this business, and when it sinks its teeth into your gut, the feeling is as real as any other sensation. Where was Hayes? Of course I could trust him to take care of himself, couldn't I? He had the Westinghouse Lightning Gun. That alone should give him all the advantages. So why was I scared? Yeah, *scared*. Terrified.

For him? For me? *He's a big boy*, I kept repeating like a bad song that gets stuck in your head. Who was the one to come get me before the cops arrested me for murder? Who did I turn to when the bungalow exploded?

Better question: hadn't I sworn off men? Hayes was a man. So why did I keep thinking about him? All we ever do is argue and flirt with absolute hostility.

The cobwebs and pudding between my ears wouldn't shake out. I applied some medicinal Old Forester.

If the bourbon didn't bump-off my fear, it stood a damn good chance of killing any infection in that stupid pin hole my knee picked up earlier.

I glared at my evidence collection. Plans for giant robots. Letters from Landis to the Pointe. Those would be helpful to the Prosecution. However, the manifesto was the real prize.

The New American Reich.

I didn't want to touch the pages, thinking my prints might mingle with those of stupid, ambitious people. The paper was interesting, too. Fresh. But not perfect. This had gone a few places, been read, and then there were the notes. Obviously, the initials under each showed approval of the changes. I couldn't quite work out the letters of the initialing.

Taking a careful gander at the back page, I considered if this was less a manifesto and more of a contract or quote. An agreement between parties. If so, then signatures might be had on the back pages.

I had no idea how bad that bad could be.

I let go of that document in seconds. It hadn't just been

handled by stupid people, it had been handled by monsters. Perhaps Landis wasn't as stupid as I was dismissing him, since he knew that an act of treason this big would need the guaranteed support of … of … a big monster.

Landis had signed the manifesto with a flourish.

Elsa Weiss even put her signature on it.

The biggest signature wasn't legible, but it was possible to figure it out.

The big monster himself.

Adolph Hitler had signed this.

If they know I have this, they absolutely must get it back or else. Germany was a threat but for the most part, the nation was behaving much like its neighbors in the international arena. Rumors came over with immigrants that the German government was starting within its own borders to carry out its plans for conquest. Anyone like me, like Howard Evans, or any number of the friends I could count, were unwanted national baggage. And, we would be dealt with as such.

This was what the American Bund was bringing to my City. And someone at the Pointe was helping.

Yeah, I knew who it was, too. That wasn't a tremendous bit of detective work. Anyone with eyes, ears, and two brain cells to rub together and keep warm with could figure out that Rossi had a turncoat in his midst.

"Miss Tanner?" Helper wheeled over to me.

Took me a moment to snap out of my doomsday mindset and recognize the little 'Bot was talking to me. "You find him?"

"There are three items I believe you should be made aware of."

My head started pounding. "Quick, man, out with it!"

"I am not technically a —"

"The three things! Now."

Blink. Blink. "We have located Agent Hayes."

"Thank God. He's okay?"

"No. That is inaccurate. Although he is not dead, he is not in control of his situation. I calculate a 94.625% chance he will not —"

I snarled, although I didn't mean to. "Where!"

"Agent Hayes?"

"Yes!"

"Downtown. Last reported on Sansome or Geary Streets."

I know for a fact that my heart skipped a beat. I certainly stopped breathing momentarily. "He's on the move? Okay. I can find him."

The little 'Bot started again. "There are three items —"

"You covered two. Spill it! What's number three?"

"You are about to receive an unwelcome visitor."

Chapter Twenty-Nine

Hans and three other Bund goons kicked in my office door. Shouts. Cursing. Things knocked over. But they found nothing. Before the sounds were muffled completely by the building, I swear I heard Elsa.

Helper and I barely fit inside the dumb waiter. I'd shoved him in, so he was lying on his side. Me, with all those boxes already there, barely fit in after him but I wasn't leaving him to fend for himself like I'd left Jonesy.

Quietly, I lowered us to the basement floor. A coal tunnel leads into the back of the Fox Theater. Helper could get out that way.

He gave me vague but acceptable details about where I could find Hayes. I could leave Helper now. With instructions to act like one of the mechanicals operating the theater, he would not be in any danger.

Not like Jonesy.

Sprinting along the tunnel, I found the back exit using my amazing detective skills — it was marked with a neon sign. Every theater, even for motion pictures, has a back door. And no surprise here, it opened to a garbage filled alley.

I didn't bring an overcoat, making me stand out a bit. I'd even left Uncle Joe's fedora up in the office.

Checking the documents stuffed down my shirt and buttoned against my skin to keep them as dry as possible, I joined the crowds milling around under the unlit neon sign.

The F-Line trolly was stopped in the middle of the street. People who were smarter than me with their umbrellas waited for the trolly doors to open. That was my cue to take an exit from the theater crowd.

I made about four steps out to the sidewalk when Inspector MacCormick and Bennie Rollins blockaded me.

"Lou? Whatcha' doin' out here without your rain gear?"

"Escaping the goon squad in my office."

"Aw, who's pestering you now?" MacCormick grumbled.

"Nazis. Say, Mister," I started in my bright, co-ed innocent voice, "ever see Adolph Hitler's signature?"

I swear both Bennie and the G-man creep both jumped on me to shut me up. Some kid turned around to see what was happening. "Beat it, kid. Ain't none of your business," Bennie swaggered effectively.

"Would you like to see it," I whispered triumphantly to MacCormick.

"I dunno' about him, but I sure do," Bennie cut in.

"Then let's high tail it to downtown. We need to give Hayes a hand. He's in trouble."

That made MacCormick perk up. He started waving frantically.

The San Francisco skies opened up, sending movie goers and the rest of us scrambling for cover. For the record, I was never so glad to be in a government car, dry and warm. I handed everything to Bennie, glaring at MacCormick to go ahead and try me. "Okay, Miss Tanner. Rollins says you're good at laying out the facts. Show me."

"What are you, from Missouri?"

"In fact, I am."

Well, he had me there. "Here's the whole scoop. Put on your running shoes because this is a doozy of race, and you'll need to keep up or get overrun in the final stretch."

"Hold up, Lou. First tell us where you got these?"

"I stole them." Neither man balked at my confession, so I kept going. "From Lucas Landis's office, when he was off kissing babies for last minute votes and leaving my demise in the hands of some of his Teutonic friends and Mrs. Elsa Weiss."

MacCormick whipped off his hat and ran his hand through what was left of his hair. "I swear to God, Tanner."

"Trouble follows me. Sometimes it's my fault and sometimes it isn't. Now are you going to shut it long enough for me to tell you what's what? And are we saving Hayes or aren't we?"

In an act of momentary brilliance, MacCormick closed his trap and let me have the limelight.

"Gus Gruber, the guy you've got in the jug? He's with the People's Society for —"

"The bombers?"

The car swerved around pedestrians piling out of another Market Street trolly. The rain was cutting the driver's view in half.

"Is this your story or mine? It's mine. Keep your trousers on, brother, I'm getting there. Gus brought me," I pointed to the folded blueprint, "that information wrapped up in a package. He took it from the Pointe where he used to work. It ended up with me because Howard Evans knew I'd get it to the right hands if Gus couldn't. Those are plans for some serious weaponry. Nation destroying weaponry."

"City destroying, for starters." MacCormick whistled at the blueprints. "But could they build anything this big?"

He wasn't asking me, but I answered anyway, being a know-it-all-kinda'-gal. "They already have. We've seen them in action. The big orbs in the sky near the port? The destruction on the Bay Bridge? Yeah, its them. I'll bet my life on it."

Bennie began pressing his fingers to his temples as the car took another swerve. "How does Regina Landis fit into all this? And you?"

"The big wigs in the American Bund knew they had a leak. Landis himself refused to believe it was his own wife, so they hired me on the false premise she was having an affair … with the other person they suspected was the leak. Dr. Frederick Gruber. Gus's brother."

"They killed Regina?"

"As sure as I'm sitting here. And they killed Frederick. It was his body in the bungalow when it blew up."

"Why didn't the police figure all this out?" MacCormick stared at Bennie.

"Ease up, brother. Bennie wasn't assigned to the case until late in the game. Besides, there was an insider in Mayor Rossi's office who did a little whispering in the dark and put the finger on me for her murder. Somebody working with Landis and the Pointe, as well as Rossi's office."

"Carlotti," both men said at once. Yeah, that one was obvious. "I swear, he didn't do much to hide."

Bennie shook his head. "I always figured he was playing both sides to get the best position. But these?" He held up the correspondence. I knew Carlotti's name wasn't on it. The man was nothing if not duplicitous and consistent about it.

That's when the car shuddered. I thought it was the wind. There's always wind in downtown around Bush and Sansome, and the Montgomery Street Aero and Transit Station. Big wind tunnel —

We were hit again, hard. Slammed.

The car suddenly spun wildly down the slick trolly lines, bumping over a Nightcrawler track, and rolling twice before skidding to a spinning stop almost to Bush.

That's when I got it through my thick skull.

We didn't make it.

CHAPTER THIRTY

Forget the annoying pin-prick hole in my knee. Forget the aches and pains. At this point, there was no part of my body unbruised. I started laughing like Peter Lorre. Two bombs. Crazy brawling mob. Secret plans. Murderous Nazis. And it was the rain and a slick road that killed me?

No. I was still breathing and hurting. Not dead yet. Even the rain wouldn't snuff me out tonight.

Neither MacCormick nor Rollins were moving. Breathing, not moving. After trying several times, I couldn't find a pulse on the driver.

Crawling out on what had been the roof of the government sedan took a herculean effort. My hand touched something cold ... metal ... solid. Pulling my arm back out of reflex, I rolled into a seated position to see what it was. With my back against the crashed vehicle, I hoped that we hadn't hit another car. Squinting, I saw it through bloodied rain.

The foot.

Bigger than the car I was propped up against.

MacCormick's jalopy wouldn't ride again — not with the giant dent in its side and the rest of the damage.

The foot shifted, then stopped.

I held my breath. As though that might do any good.

The Buick sized foot linked to a thick, metallic calf ... multi-geared knee ... thigh ...

Rain-water poured down the entirety of the colossus. At the top, two huge lamp eyes stared straight ahead, casting a beam of light much like the searchlights outside a Hollywood opening. No such joy or excitement would follow those beams. Strapped to its arms and back were guns. Big guns. Guns we never thought existed.

It didn't know I was there at its feet.

Too small.

NO REQUIEM FOR THE TIN MAN

Too insignificant.

Daring to move my head, jerking inch by inch, I checked to see if either of my living colleagues might come to or make an unfortunate noise.

They were out.

Damn it, they both needed an ambulance and hospitalization.

The thing didn't move, but sirens were starting to approach. I gave our Bluecoats credit for a good fight, but none of them was ready for this …

A Tin Man.

It rotated its upper torso to shine its eye-lights in the direction of the approaching sirens.

I scrambled around the front of the car and inched along the upside down front bumper. The opposite passenger door was partially open. My hip wedged it open further. First one out was MacCormick. Skinnier. Closer to the door. His coat was buttoned up good and made well enough for me to use it to drag him free from the car. Then I hauled him by his arm to stack of tables near a closed restaurant.

Bennie was further inside.

The Tin Man maneuvered the lower half of itself to align to the sirens.

I crawled halfway through the door, snagging the scattered evidence. Then I yanked on Bennie by his coat, sleeve, suspenders … anything I could grasp. He didn't move so easily. Bennie was one big man. This had to work. It had to!

I got part of Bennie out of the car.

The Tin Man bent down to grasp the Buick.

I pulled with all the strength I had.

Tin Man lifted the Buick as if it were a toy.

Green Eyes popped up behind me, wrapped an arm around my shoulders, another around Bennie, and let gravity do the rest.

We fell only a few feet as the car rose into the air. Tin Man tossed the Buick at the cop cars. Some swerved — some didn't.

Vehicle crashes have a particular bone rattling, nerve grating sound. This was multiplied by one hundred as the Buick smashed into the collection of cops.

Hayes and I hauled Bennie over by MacCormick.

Both men still had pulses, though I sure as hell couldn't figure out how or why. Talk about dumb luck. Somebody was sure looking out for them.

And for the man I now stared at.

G-Man Hayes was never a snappy dresser or one of the swell set, but here he looked like someone had worked him over with brass knuckles and a tire iron. That poor mug of his was only free of blood due to the pouring rain constantly washing him down. He looked how I felt.

He hefted something heavy, showing off to me that he was still in possession of the Lightning Gun.

I don't know why. Maybe because he had a bigger peashooter than me. Maybe because I was so happy I was alive, along with Hayes, Bennie, and yeah ... even MacCormick. Forgetting the Tin Man, I laid one on Hayes's lips. A big wet one, although the weather didn't allow for any other option.

He didn't fight me.

Maybe he was happy we were alive, too.

I had no idea what I to say when we unlocked our lips. Tin Man apparently didn't like being ignored.

An explosion rocked the air from across the City.

"Potrero Hill Power Station," Hayes declared. "I knew they'd go for that first."

"In a pig's eye! That station's protected by —"

An orange cloud rose in the distance. Street by street, in succession, the lights went out. All that illuminated my city were car headlamps, flashlights, and Tin Man's eyes.

"Never mind," I groaned.

We looked at our patients. Bennie and his G-Man buddy were safe enough, there in the dark. 'Bots, the helpful and medical kind, started swarming out into the streets. They each had little lamps that were nothing compared to Tin Man's but they were enough to zero in on the two men at our feet.

Christ, what now?

NO REQUIEM FOR THE TIN MAN

A couple of those little 'Bot fellas were brave enough to make a dash under Tin Man and over to us.

Hayes and I must have been thinking the same thing. No words. We made a wounded dash out into the street, making sure the Tin Man's beams found us, and then headed up Sansome, running for our lives.

Chapter Thirty-One

Tin Man took one step for our every twenty-million, panic stricken, running strides.

Hayes snatched my wrist, yanked me to the left and up Pine Street. Any other time, we'd come to righteous glares if not verbal blows over such a move. But not tonight. All I cared about was achieving enough oxygen through the desperate gasps of air to keep me moving and thinking.

Releasing me, Hayes spun around to see if Tin Man was still behind us. He held the Lightning Gun tight against his shoulder, soldier style.

I passed him on his left, as we arrived at the Stock Exchange Building. "That thing going to destroy it or only make it mad?"

The dark air above us sparkled with strange lights. Reflections. A big shape. Twisting. Getting bigger.

A shiny, silver, 4-door Packard.

Hayes let something harsh slip out. We broke apart, diving in opposite directions as the vehicle crashed between us. Splinters of glass and chrome sprayed out as shrapnel. I covered my neck and head. Hayes rolled even further away from me.

Tin Man locked its beams on Hayes.

"Keep moving!" He shouted, standing up, and taking a wildly wide shot at Tin Man. I'd forgotten how amazing that artillery was.

A bolt of piercing white light shot out of the muzzle, blowing Hayes backward. The electric blast sizzled past Tin Man's "ear."

"Come on, you piece of scrap!"

Bright eyebeams tracked Hayes as he headed down a narrow alley that cut between Pine and California.

Tin Man followed until the buildings stopped it. It couldn't fit in between. Watching Hayes, for a moment longer, it turned back towards Sansome and stomped away, taking the long route after him.

Through the alley, I could see Hayes waiting for him. Hayes

was shouting at Tin Man, drawing the behemoth's attention. The beams on him grew brighter and brighter until he turned and made a dash for it.

The new quiet was strange and I knew it couldn't last.

I hate it when I'm right.

They call it *Chicago Lightning*. It's the nickname from the days of prohibition when rum runners would light up Chicago nights with gunfire. Tommy gun gunfire.

So charming.

Bullets sprayed in my direction.

I hit dirt.

Chips of the Stock Exchange burst off the building and poured down on me like hail from an obscene thunderstorm.

I shot blindly into the darkness.

No one else was there ... except Elsa.

How the hell did she find us? Or was she even looking for Hayes or me? Was she following the Tin Man? Of course she was, she knew all about them.

Despite the quantity of bullets, we both missed. The bits and pieces of the Stock Exchange didn't – some razor sharp bits sliced me up as if someone had dropped me into an industrial grinder. My arm felt shredded, although at this point my imagination was working plenty of overtime.

Burying my face under a hand and doing anything I could think of to stay still, I kept listening for her. If I couldn't see her, maybe she couldn't see me.

Click. Snap. Another canister of ammo for that typewriter of hers.

One thing on my side: she wasn't good with it. You gotta' know what you're doing with a Tommy Gun. They work great for filling the air with a thick fog of lead. But they also overheat and run out of plugs right quick. Could I use one any better? Not a chance. I'll stick to my pea-shooters.

One thing I had against me: bad luck going up against her good luck. Anyone of those typewriter keys could find me, all by accident, but it would kill me all the same as if she'd pointed it like a precision target shooter. So why wasn't she taking a chance?

I shut up my brain and listened harder. Hefting noises echoed against the building, like those you make when your luggage or grocery bags are too heavy. Elsa wasn't much bigger than me.

A soft, "Oof," gave away her position. Close.

I rolled and fired my last two slugs. Elsa cried out.

I didn't buy into that sob story. I know what it feels like to be shot. I know what comes out of your mouth, whether you like it or not. I know when someone is faking a scream.

I dove sideways.

And as God is my witness, she emptied that Tommy into the front door of the Stock Exchange. Light flashed from the muzzle, showing her face as a twisted kabuki mask of fury.

The gunfire stopped.

No more ammo? Too hot? Jammed?

I launched myself at her and we collided like two locomotives on the same track. My eyes had already adjusted to the dark. Hers, with all that muzzle flare, hadn't. I gave her some elbow to think about while I grabbed her shirt and flung her onto the ground. She wasn't a push over. She swung hard and landed her fair share of hits before she dropped.

Elsa kicked and punched. Almost broke my nose.

I was raving mad. I wanted to pummel her into oblivion. If I knuckled every tooth out of her face, so what! I wanted to see blood. Her blood.

I kept pounding on her until she stopped moving.

Pain shot up from my leg.

I guess she knows how to use a knife.

Chapter Thirty-Two

My leg throbbed like hell. I reached down to hold it.

Three P-29s bomber aeroplanes buzzed overhead, no more than spitting distance from the roof top of the Stock Exchange. Their engines screamed and I held my damp hand over one ear, as if that would help. All that filled my surroundings were sounds of battle pounding its way up from Market Street and the city sirens. The ground kept shaking in a perfect rhythm. Heavy equipment or something more dangerous?

Nice of 'em to show up.

The darkness suffocating downtown wasn't something I was used to.. The power wasn't back up. No chance in hell it would be back after the loss of the generators on Potrero Hill. Somebody knew what they were doing by taking those out early in the assault.

The skin and muscles smarted like a sonofabitch, then burned. I winced and staggered away from Elsa. *Damn it.* She got me. Deep. One long slice across my left thigh.

Knee trembling, foot tingling, at least I still had feeling in my leg. That was a good sign, right?

On the steps of the Exchange, I pushed my back into the granite legs of the Man of Industry statue and collapsed at his feet. He gazed out with those empty eyes and chiseled features into the blankness that might no longer be a city. Come sunrise, I had a feeling we were all in for a shock, worse than the aftermath of the '06 Quake.

The Man of Industry, clutching uncaringly to a freakish looking child, was too flawless. Who among us could live up to his perfection? Or lack of humanity? My humanity was leaking out onto the granite steps, although not too badly? I couldn't tell. The rain was making everything seem worse all the while cleaning up after itself.

Tonight, my City was the goddamned Wild West again, so I

held onto that .38 roscoe in one hand and pressing hard with the other on the shooting pain from my newly acquired, future scar. I was scared. Damn scared. It was cold enough to tease a snowman, but me? I was sweating.

Elsa had her knife and a Tommy Gun. Maybe more ammo. Heaven only knew what else she could hide up under her skirt and I wouldn't be surprised.

A slight crunch. Down — to my left — beyond the stone pots of plants. A footstep? No. But I could smell tobacco. Great, she wasn't down anymore.

"This is exhilarating, isn't it?" she cooed between gulps of breath. She didn't sound so good. Maybe I did some damage. That was a win for me. "What do you think of the *Der Blechmann*? The Tin Man? He is magnificent, wouldn't you agree?" After a moment, she added, "A perfect creation by those who are intelligent ... superior."

Go ahead, sister, keep talking.

"People like Lucas and myself are meant to lead. To command. To govern. You and all those like you need to be governed. By us. It's only natural."

Me and my usually big mouth made a wise decision: we didn't say a word. Another win. Good thing too, my mouth was so dry, I'd need a camel to ride across it.

"I know you are still here, Fraulein. What purpose is there in hiding? Maybe we should do this like the men, say, at the O.K. Corral?" She moved a bit more. Stone crushed under her shoes. That put her in the space between the building and the cement sidewalk, not far from where I left her.

"It is very sad, to see the damage to this city. But we have to start somewhere. War is inevitable and necessary. It is what is needed to cleanse the nation of the pollution that has clogged it up for too long. Don't you agree?"

No, I don't agree. But I wasn't getting drawn out by insults or slurs. I don't give a rat's ass what her opinion is anyway.

"Fraulein," she sang a bit. "I really would prefer doing this the way gentlemen handle things. Much more honorable. But maybe you don't understand that. Your family was more or less New Money.

No Requiem for the Tin Man

And it didn't last. You spent too much of your acquired wealth helping unworthy people. Those who are meant to rule know that you must acquire power and longevity first." I could see some lightness — her white shirt and pale hair — as she started up the steps past me.

I held my breath and gritted my teeth.

She was focused on the pillars of the Exchange's façade. A tiny glint of light reminded me why she was not an easy target. I stayed put — blended into the base of the Man of Industry.

Elsa sprang forward, darting between the second and third pillars. A flock of confused pigeons burst out of the entryway and disappeared into the bleak sky.

She faced the Man of Industry statue.

I had the good sense not to be there.

Beneath our feet, the pounding changed. This wasn't the result of Tin Man anymore.

An ear-splitting screech of metal on metal shredded the immediate quiet, followed by a crash caused by something or things I couldn't even imagine. Behind me. On Montgomery Street.

Elsa burst out laughing, like a schoolgirl discovering Fred Astair or Clark Gable was going to visit her finishing academy. "Excuse me, Fraulein. But you no longer interest me. Go back to your negros and outsiders. I must see this!" She started a staggered jog, then running. I had no idea how she could see well enough to move that fast. Maybe she didn't care if she fell over something. "This! This is how we will deal with all of you!"

Chapter Thirty-Three

Like the idiot I am, I followed her, stopping to clutch my leg. No, I didn't shoot her. I should have — but I was out of bullets, couldn't see well, and was hobbling, so I only followed her up to Montgomery.

I would have been a hell of a lot better off if I'd stayed back at the Exchange.

I would have been a hell of a lot better off if I'd stayed back in New York.

Reaching Montgomery and Pine, I was swarmed by the panicking crowds running from something ... something big ... moving down from Market. Having the wits of a gnat on occasion, I didn't join the foot race for safety. Sheer frenzy might have carried me along despite my wound. Nope. I stood there, glaring into the darkness until my eyes hurt.

Some schmuck slammed into me, didn't bother to apologize, and kept running. Pushed back into the side of the building for support, I counted myself lucky, I was out of the way when a phalanx of bluecoats arrived out of the shadows, all uniformed, lit up, and armed. Cop car headlamps turned on. Flashlights were readied. They were shiny as hell. Cocky as hell. God, I hope their moxie wasn't for naught.

The Boys in Blue lined up, facing south, towards Market Street, two lines, staggered. Tommy guns at the ready.

A whump ricocheted down the echo corridor that was Montgomery Street, accompanied by a hard jolt of the asphalt under my shoes.

I pressed my back against the building, pushed on my burning thigh, and peeked around the corner. Sure, like that would protect me from whatever was —

Another grotesque thump was followed by a crash of stone and brick, and yeah ... more ground shaking.

No Requiem for the Tin Man

The stomping and crashing grew louder. Damn if the shaking wasn't footfall. Heavy footsteps.

My heart throbbed in my throat. Pushing the freezing cold stone, I forced my legs to move, gimping across the street. Every breath was so shallow I was getting dizzy from the failure to inhale successfully. Trembling, I leaned out from my new hiding spot, dreading to look.

The Boys stayed in place but many had eyes the size of saucers. Some handled their gats with anxious fingers. Others rubbed or prodded their faces as if trying to make sure this wasn't a hallucination, that it was really happening.

The footfall stopped. Even parts of the sky blacked out.

I recognized Senior — from the Woolworths counter, that uncomfortable morning only a few days ago. And there was Junior, too. Junior looked like he might need a change of trousers sooner rather than later. Back at the Woolworths, I would have laughed. Tonight, I couldn't blame him.

I hated to see them there. Never mind the lousy encounters we had, I didn't want to see them or any of the others injured ... or killed.

Senior shouted a command. The Boys snapped to, alert, and aiming.

I dared to look down the street again.

You know that saying about *deafening silence*? I've got a new saying and definition now. Only debris settling, a cop sniffing, and my own pulse rushing through my ears broke the quiet.

Then gears in motion. Hydraulics engaged. Metal on metal. Two sets of bright yellow lights opened about three stories up. Three sets.

Eyes.

A fire truck arrived on the northern end of the block, its red lights creating a horror story of the scene. A search light was switched on and swung down the street. I covered my eyes before it fried them out. As it passed me, throwing me back into anonymous shadow, I sneaked a view of what the spotlight landed on.

Metal with a dulled effect, some by harsh brushing or chemical burning, the rest by black paint. Yellow eyes glaring out mindlessly at a target well beyond the cops and the firemen, and the crowd clustered some blocks away. Dull flashlights, by comparison, revealed people clinging to one another, pointing, shaking their heads in disbelief.

I looked again at the metal.

At the Tin *Men*.

Now I could see them. Complete. The head to body ratio was outsized, even with the shoulders supporting clavicle and bicep armor. The arms were truncated, as was the torso. The legs were better proportioned for the head and clearly capable of stomping holes in the flimsy roadway.

Senior the Cop shouted a command that was immediately drowned out by round after round of gunfire. I plugged my ears. Those Chicago typewriters opened up and sprayed a deadly wash of bullets into the chests of the Tin Men. Muzzle flash was equaled with sparks where bullets struck on metal.

Nothing penetrated the Tin Men's armor. Numerous dents remained but no damage.

Senior called for them to halt. That terrible silence returned.

A palm-sized moth flew into one of the yellow eyes, drawn to its demise by the light. The eye blinked.

The moth was long gone.

Senior screamed out his order again, his voice hoarse and terrified. Machine gun fire blasted again, and I buried my head under my hands.

The Tin Men never so much as moved.

A horrible crackle, like the noise you get when tuning a radio, ripped through the air. A dim incoherent voice. I didn't catch what it said.

Ten seconds later, I could guess.

Banging. Clanging. The Tin Men started to grow. The legs lengthened only a bit, but worst of all, they expanded, revealing an array of missile-appearing objects within the reach of fingers. Arms extended. Hands widened. Shoulders broadened. Weapons or things that could be lethal appeared.

NO REQUIEM FOR THE TIN MAN

They didn't stop. More and more. The Tin Men kept growing until they stared down at us from even with the ninth floor of the Aero-Rail Transit Station.

In unison, they stepped forward and their combined weight landed into their left feet. The buildings and ground rattled. Their right feet landed properly, this time rattling our nerves. Some of the Boys retreated a step or two.

I stayed right where I was on the ground, too stupefied or too stupid to move.

My perspective did nothing to lower my heart rate. The Tin Men were colossal. Fully expanded, they were sized correctly. The first thought that rolled across my brain was that they looked like futuristic soldiers. These things were not 'Bots or 'Tons ready to serve the needs of the average housewife.

Without warning, they began to stomp. Hell, "stomp" wasn't even the right word. They were shaking the ground so hard, I fell down on my face and covered my head again.

Pieces of the buildings around us began to fall. The cops couldn't stand, wabbling like fools in some old silent reel, and screams burst forth from the watching crowd.

The goliaths tramped their way forward, crushing cars and stonework under feet. Nothing was stopping them.

My hiding spot wasn't safe. Struggling to my feet, I glanced down Montgomery to pick the best way out.

Junior the Cop, was left in the middle of the road, staring at them. He opened fire with his Tommy. What an idiot. All he got for his trouble was a light show of sparks. Then his ammo ran out. He shook his weapon, then pounded it on the street surface, as if it had jammed.

Coherent thought was not involved. Bodily sensation was not involved. Running full bore at him, I slammed into his body. He was like a side of beef hanging in a Chicago slaughter house, but I moved him. My .38 skittered out of sight. We slid only a couple of feet.

A Tin Man's foot dropped onto the exact spot Junior had been standing.

I yelled something harsh at him. It may not have made any

sense, but it was good and harsh. He looked dumber than that proverbial deer in the headlights, shocked by the sheer damned luck we weren't crushed.

My body decided at that moment to remind me of its current condition. I yelped in pain.

Junior cursed and ran for his life.

I shouted more unladylike cursing myself and crawled over to a pile of debris to clutch my leg.

Junior was long gone. The creep had left me with his artillery but no ammo. My delicate, feminine adjectives were aimed less at the pain and more at the departed cop.

To their credit, a pair of Boys in Blue, scrambled out of their hiding place and headed my way. One reduced my pain by using their collective ties to wrap the wound on my thigh. The other provided me with a set of rather imaginative descriptions of Junior my mother would never have believed were anatomically possible, all while helping me to my feet.

With the Tin Men heading up California, they located an emergency nursing station. While their radios were abuzz with cries for assistance and commands to hold the line, so too were there reports of civilians and doctors coming out in droves. No one was going to stomp *Our City* into the ground.

Oh God, I hurt. I'd rather be shot. I could say that from experience of being shot, too. One of the Boys let me lean on him. My hearing was a little dazzled but from what they were saying, I was a hero now. Saved a cop from being crushed to death. Oh goody for me, I hope there's still a city to keep working in. At least some cops won't be furious with me anymore.

And someday I'll have to figure out why I did what I did. Oh yeah … I'm a sap.

Almost forgot.

Chapter Thirty-Four

Makeshift nurse's stations were popping up everywhere I was told while resting at the one established at Pine and Kearny Streets. Each time the P-32s buzzed over, everyone — including me — ducked. As if that would do any good if the bombers accidentally dropped their loads on us instead of the Tin Men.

Which apparently had been happening elsewhere in San Francisco. P-32s are not bombers, one doctor told me. But there were local and could be up flying fast.

Smoke was rising from most of the buildings in downtown. Small business or big corporation, it didn't matter. All the shaking. All the shooting. All the bombs dropped on the gigantic metal monsters or by accident. Everything suffered in the wake.

My City by the Bay was looking much like it did after the '06 Quake. I saw the photos. I've talked to folks who were there.

Several of us peered around the remnants of a two story building to stare across the open vista of the California Street lot. The bankers hadn't decided what to do with the land. It was too valuable to build on and too valuable not to build on, so no one did anything except mow the grass.

A P-32 swept in, and I swear, its wings were inches off our heads. A metal container dropped from its belly and skidded across the lawn. The resulting screams were ear splitting and in seconds the nurse's station was empty.

Me? I was the unarmed dame with the fresh stitches in her leg, dripping wet hair, and a stupefied look on her face. I couldn't run far if I wanted to.

Thinking that maybe the leftover building might offer us some protection, a small handful of us peeked out at the container: an olive drab canister that continued to settle. O. X. Y ... ?

"Oxygen," one of the remaining doctors sighed. "He dropped it to lighten his load."

I could have used some of that oxygen. It wasn't a bomb after all.

Another P-32 strafed the length of California Street, from the top of the hill down toward the Tin Men, still loitering between Montgomery and Sansome. Three sets of beams locked onto the aircraft as it overflew them.

The few of us at the remnant building started to run the hell out of there. This was no place for a lady, let alone a human being. I stopped to look again. Some notion was bugging me, gnawing through me like termites on wood. Bullets weren't working.

The Lightning Gun would.

So, why wasn't Hayes using it? I hadn't seen that they'd gotten him. He had to be safe — he had to be.

Uncle Joe told me that the one thing police academies and detective schools can't teach is gut instinct. You either have it, or you don't. He'd tease me back in the day, because I was this darling little girl in pig-tails who could make tea, recite poems, secretly swear like a sailor, and had the most amazing gut instinct.

My gut told me to turn around.

So did Elsa's.

One of her goose-stepping goons was propping her up. Hans, all big and stupid looking, had the real focus of my gut upset.

Hayes.

My G-Man Hayes.

His overcoat was missing as was his usual expression of confidence. A serious bruise had formed under his eye and traces of blood sat in the corners of his nose and mouth. That's my G-man — he'd given them a fight.

He'd lost, but he'd given more trouble than not.

I'm such a smart detective: I could tell he'd been a problem because they'd handcuffed him too. That would make him mad. It also meant he wouldn't do much use to me in this situation.

"How is your leg, Fraulein *Turner*."

That again. "It's fine. Six stitches, a shot of something real nice, and it's all good. Next time, do your job better and go for a ten-stitch slice."

NO REQUIEM FOR THE TIN MAN

One of her goons snickered. I grinned. Hayes grinned.

Elsa didn't like any of that. "Knives are for peasants." She said. "Westinghouse electric guns. Those are for well-equipped armies. I'm looking forward to passing this one," she indicated the Lightning Gun held by a goon, "to the right hands."

"You mean your Pay Master, brown-eyed, brown shirted, brown-nosed Hitler? He's kinda' short and not quite Aryan isn't he?"

Her face squeezed into a furious red scowl.

Hayes, on the other hand, looked curious.

"Fraulein, you have documents. By the poor fit of your clothing, I can guess that they are on your person. You see, it is easy to be a detective if one is born with natural intelligence and superiority. Now, we will make a trade."

"We will?"

"Yes. Your government agent for the documents."

Green eyes flashed at me. "Lou?"

"Don't ask," I warned him. The less he appeared to know right now, the better.

But Elsa had already worked that part out in her little Nazi brain. "Oh, you can tell him. You give me the documents, then there is no evidence. You and this man, both of you being of suspect character to the police, and you being completely doubtful to Rossi and his ilk, will never be able to convince anyone that the evidence ever existed."

Hans pulled Hayes up by his arm and settled the muzzle of a big Luger next to one of his pretty green eyes.

"Give me the document, Fraulein. I have no use for him ,or you either."

"So, you'll kill us."

"No," she replied in the sing-song tone of hers. "I want to see you suffer from disappointment. I want you to have to fail under the Landis regime over this city … and parts beyond. I want you to watch as the Bund moves out swiftly, in both power and popularity. I want the police to catch up with you and give you your just desserts. To kill you now would be no fun at all."

"But Hayes?"

"You can have him. He can suffer right along with you. Impotency is as painful as any failure."

"Isn't this where you spill the beans. Where you tell me your whole grand plan?"

Her face screwed up again. "No. You're the detective. You figure it out. I have no more time for you. The document, or his blood mingles with the grass."

"Don't!" Hayes shouted only to have a hand clamped down over his mouth. He struggled against it all, but Hans was about half a foot taller and half a ton heavier. Two goons were happy to help.

There was nothing I could do.

Damn it. I couldn't pretend Hayes's life didn't mean anything to me.

There was only one possibility to save Hayes — and only one.

Chapter Thirty-Five

I unbuttoned the top button of my waistcoat. Carefully, I removed the blueprint of the Tin Man from my shirt and held it out.

The rain was subsiding but still dampened the document. A goon ran forward, snatched it out of my hand, and took it back to her while I rebuttoned.

"This is but one document, Fraulein. Give me the other."

"I don't have that on me."

"Search her!"

"Try it, you mooks, and I'll break every bone in your bodies."

Hans made a grunt to remind me that he was willing and able to shoot Hayes.

"Does he know how to talk? Look, chum, don't get fussy on me. I know the drill. You still have Agent Hayes. We haven't completed our transaction." I held my hands out slightly, which protected my torso from view. "I have the document you need, Elsa. But I hid it. I knew it was too valuable, with all those signatures."

She actually rolled her eyes.

"What? You don't believe I knew the manifesto's importance? Or that you can't believe Lucas Landis insisted on signed proof that when he commits treason against the United States, he has absolute assurance that Adolph Hitler and the National Socialist Party of Germany will back his play?"

"Perhaps a little of both."

"Well then, keep your stocking's on, sister, 'cause we're not far from where I hid it. That is, if your friends at the Pointe and their big metal babies haven't destroyed the joint yet."

"Or your ridiculous airplanes haven't accidentally bombed it."

"Touche. Shall we go?"

"Where?"

"Just over there, edge of Chinatown."

I had to ignore Hayes. I couldn't read what was going on

behind his eyes. He was fuming at me, but embarrassed. Humiliated.

I gimped ahead of them, although not by much. I felt one of them breathing on my neck.

The Tin Men were holding court at Montgomery and pounding the snot out of the buildings closer to the Bay. One of her goons helped drag me across California's two cable car tracks that looked utterly destroyed by P-32 strafing. This town would need serious reconstruction. The 'Bots and 'Tons were right: Rossi would win the election and he would definitely clean things up.

The pain killer started to wear off by the time we reached my little hiding spot, the small garage. The dog next door barked wildly. Hayes had marched like a dead man walking in the big house. God, how I wanted to know what he was thinking and to tell him what I was planning.

The side door opened easily enough. I turned on the tiny, dim, overhead light. Inside were car parts, tools, a tarp covered object of large size, and lots of grease. There was a hole in the roof I didn't realize was there. If I got out of this alive, I'd need to talk to my friend about security.

Elsa pushed her prop-up goon aside and followed me in. Hayes was added to our company along with Hans. The others stayed outside.

"No more stalling. Give me the document."

"Look, Elsa —"

"I'll have Hans skin Agent Hayes, alive. Would you like that?"

Hans smiled. That was not a pleasant sight. He'd like hurting Green Eyes. He'd love it.

The document wasn't worth it. Nothing was more valuable than Hayes's life. Not a job, not an office, not a diploma. Marley had survived bad situations with crummy employers before, she could do it again. She was strong. Sam would be strong for her too. Hayes? I couldn't see him killed. Not even for this. We could still stop Landis and the Bund. This was just some evidence. We had more.

I reached down my shirt.

"You had it the whole time?"

"I needed to know how serious you were."

She gave me some bamboozle about her intentions, but I cut her off.

"Look, sister, what would you have done? Huh. Maybe nothing. What do you care about except telling everyone how superior you are. Haven't seen any proof of it myself. All I've seen is a cold, ruthless murderess who took out her boss's wife and her own brother."

Elsa staggered forward. "What do you know. I killed Regina because she betrayed Lucas."

"Horse feathers! You killed her because you wanted Landis for yourself."

"Perhaps. But she was also working for that pathetic gang of hoodlums. The 'People's Society,'" she mocked. "A disorganized band of ne'er-do-wells, nobodies, who want everything given to them for free. They think they're entitled to everything I have. They want to replace me and destroy me!"

"No," I said. "No, they don't. They want what they want. They want to be treated as human beings. To not get called names or told they can't eat here or walk there. We all want a chance to become our dreams. What the hell is so wrong with that?"

"What is wrong is that it is against the proper order of things. People are made to either rule or be ruled. There's no in-between and changing places. Lucas understands that."

I was all set and ready to argue, when I remembered I'm a detective. "You two betrayed Regina long before she betrayed Landis. But he isn't in love with you half as much as you are with him. How long can you hold him once he's king of the city?"

Elsa straightened her shoulders in offense.

The dog next door kept barking and barking.

I charged ahead. "But you're not still lovers, are you?"

"We have chosen to put things aside for now."

I let a little lopsided grin dance on my mug. "You mean, Landis stopped the affair because it put his campaign at risk, he wasn't committed to you, and he realized that he still loved Regina. You framed Gus so he has no idea Gus *didn't* kill her. He can never find out you murdered the woman he truly loved, can he? If he does, then he'll push you away forever. As for Frederick, you were willing to murder him because Freddie liked Regina enough to make it his business to keep her in line. Regina had her own ideas, going to all those PSSR meetings or supporting Gus. Freddie started confronting her. They started fighting about it publicly, in restaurants for example. That made him a liability. So, Freddie had to go."

There is something horribly frightening when an angry person suddenly goes stone cold. "I never liked Frederick. No backbone. Using him to make the PSSR look bad was, well, easy. Lucas knows about Frederick, but …" She smiled.

"… But he thinks Frederick's intentions were to get Regina for himself, not to get her to leave the PSSR. That's why Landis sanctioned his killing, along with the bombings. The only thing poor old Landis didn't agree to — the murder of his own wife."

"Brava. Give me the damn document or you can have Agent Hayes's skin to keep warm with."

Shit.

I held out the document, regardless of Hayes protesting. Of course he protested. I would have too.

I backed into the tarp covered object.

"Fetch it," she ordered Hans.

Hans moved forward. I grasped the tarp with my free hand. Dropping to my good knee, I swung my arm out and the tarp flew out in a wide arc. Hans ducked but was too big to avoid the spread of the tarp.

Hayes kicked the door shut. Following through on the momentum, he landed a sweeping kick to Elsa's legs, dropping her like a rock.

Hans was flailing in the tarp when Hayes rushed him. The two landed on the floor with a big thump. I stuck the manifesto back into my shirt where it poked out partially and went to Green Eyes' aid.

Elsa reached over me and seized the document. I spun around on her and grabbed what I could of the papers. We wrestled back and forth, yanking and pulling, until she let go, nailed me with a right cross, and tore off about one half of the manifesto.

Rushing to the door, she couldn't open it. Elsa banged

furiously on it, demanding the goons open it. They were shouting something about the dog.

I grabbed the object under the tarp. The real reason I came here: Howie's Aerolift bike. Dragging it upright and over towards the center of the garage, I was about to find a tool to use on Hans when I got an eye-full of Hayes registering his complaints with Hans's service. Apparently, the room service was less than agreeable. Hayes stomped on the Nazi, right in the *want ads*, and broke his jaw with a hard cross-kick. Not bad.

Elsa's goons rushed in.

I swung a heavy wrench up from the floor, connecting with the first goon's chin.

Hayes still had his hands cuffed behind him; he shouldered his way into the other goon, who in turn slammed into Elsa.

Hayes could only pull that move a couple of times, and he'd used chit number two. I awkwardly crouched by Hans and found the key to the cuffs. I'm pretty quick with that sort of thing. "Get on the bike!"

"And go where?" Hayes demanded.

I looked at the hole in the roof. We looked at each other. Hayes looked at the ground.

Starting the motorbike took a moment. My G-man kindly kept one of the goons off us. As the chain-smoking tiger came to life, Hayes found himself in possession of the Lightning Gun ... again.

"Stop losing that!"

"Are you starting a fight? Now?"

Maybe I was. I was staring at the control panel of the Aerolift and watching the blinking lights fade in and out of my vision. That dog next door wouldn't stop barking but that was our fault for making such a fuss. Why couldn't I see and remember the controls? *Damn it. How do I fly this thing?*

"That is as far as you go, Fraulein!" Elsa shouted.

Chapter Thirty-Six

Elsa backed up to the side door. She had the Luger pointed straight at us.

"As I said, Fraulein, I have no more use for you."

She opened the door to leave. I figured Hayes and I could fall off the motorbike but she could keep shooting at us, depending on how many bullets she had.

That damn dog.

That damn wonderful, slobbering, protective, 130 pounds of worked-up guard dog.

He came through that door like a tank and landed on Elsa. She screamed and dropped her weapon. The dog did what it was trained to do: it stopped a human with a gun. Snarling, biting, and clawing, the dog attacked Elsa with furious glee.

My friend and his neighbor rushed outside. I didn't know or care if Elsa lived. Me and the G-man had more work to do.

I faced the control panel again and recalled the brief lessons Howie had given me. With Hayes yelping behind me, I hit the right buttons.

The Aerolift Motorbike lived up to its name.

We jolted out of the garage through the hole, which wasn't the right size for us. It certainly was by the time we exited. And, yeah, we were both a bit worse for the effort. And, yeah, I scratched the paint job.

We spiraled up into the air.

The rain might have been letting up, but at that altitude and speed, we were soaked in seconds.

Did I ever mention I hate heights.

Green Eyes wrapped his arm around me and hugged tight. At first I feared he, too, was no fan of heights, then I remembered that I had told him about my acrophobia.

I hate to admit it, but I felt safer. Only a little bit, but a little

NO REQUIEM FOR THE TIN MAN

does count. Fighting a throbbing leg, an airsick queasy breadbasket, and an aching everything, I gently turned us into the wind, and down California Street. Seeing the damage from above made me more nauseous and brutally cognizant of potential company from the P-32s.

Instead, we got a view of the Tin Men.

One rotated its body towards us.

Eyebeams locked on and I blocked the light with my arms.

"Go around the building so I can catch it from the side," Hayes called into my ear.

G-Man and G-forces grabbed my midsection as I banked the Aerolift over and flew us in between two buildings. Rounding the skyscraper on the right, I kept the turn until we were approaching the Tin Men on Sansome.

Hayes let go of me and used my back for balance. He hefted the Lightning Gun to his shoulder.

I brought us around to slow at California.

Hayes fired.

The lightning bolt went wild and we bucked with the recoil.

"Damn!"

"Hang on," I called out.

I moved the Aerolift up and out, then gunned the engine at high while locking the gravity function in place. I had no idea if this dingus could take it.

Tipping the nose down slightly to compensate for the recoil, I was about to tell Hayes to take another shot. He was ahead of me.

The zapper produced a bright blue-white flash that zipped across the air, catching the closest Tin Man at the jaw connection to the torso.

I don't know if Hayes meant the shot to go that way, but it was perfect.

The Tin Man's head snapped to the right. It's eyebeams shut off. One by one, all it's lights turned off.

Tearing metal and one horrible squealing, ripping noise was followed by the head crashing to the street.

The Aerolift started beeping at me. I'd overheated it. Lights were flashing and sparking. I had to put us down before we fell out of the sky. We landed hard, but safe enough, skidding a portion of the way. Hayes jumped off the motorbike and ran back to the corner to see what else might happen.

At this point, I hurt too damn much and was likely to throw up. Still, I managed to do a good impression of Bela Lugosi in hobbling over to Hayes.

The Tin Men stood there.

"I know that sound," I whispered to Green Eyes. "The radio sound. They're communicating with someone."

"I can't get another shot like that last one without the bike." He glanced back at the Aerolift. "Any chance?"

"I think I broke it."

Metal on metal again.

One of the Tin Men picked up the head of the destroyed one. The other operational Tin Man pushed something on the body, which then compressed. Together, they carried it.

Like a fallen brother they carried it.

We flagged a cop car. Hayes still had his buzzer and he flashed it while announcing firmly that he was from the War Department. And that's how we followed the Tin Men. With Howie's broken bike in the trunk of the cop car, two astonished policemen, one beaten-up Federal agent, and a wounded Private Dick of the female persuasion.

The Tin Men walked, not stomped, down to the Embarcadero, past the Ferry Building.

We followed.

They walked like a funeral procession along the route to Aquatic Park.

And we, along with a growing number of police, followed.

They crossed Marina Park and Crissy Field.

We were forced to stop.

Turning west, the Tin Men stepped out into the waves crashing along the bay shoreline. The sunset prodded its way out from under the rain clouds, casting them in a shade of orange.

The surreal scene, begged one to wonder how surreal is surreal when one is talking about Tin Men and the destruction of downtown

NO REQUIEM FOR THE TIN MAN

San Francisco, left me in shock as well as awe. The Tin Men turned again, heading towards the new San Francisco to Marin bridge.

"Did they destroy it?" One cop asked.

Before anyone could answer, the depth of the channel between the Marin Headlands and Fort Point became apparent as the Tin Men dropped significantly. Only their heads showed, then only the wake of their movement.

Then nothing.

Someone at the Pointe had set them loose, but who? Carlotti was the first suspect. I was convinced. But why throw them into the ocean? What a waste of resources!

I for one was too tired to deal with it anymore.

The Tin Men were no longer my problem. At least for the moment.

Hayes asked that the cops take me back to my office, dropping him back in Chinatown. He had the right to Hans and Elsa. Theirs were personal crimes against him and crimes against the U.S. He could have them.

They couldn't drop me too close because of damage, so I limped one block.

That was the longest block.

The Fox Theater was destroyed.

Some of it was still standing, but most of it was gone. The part that was gone included my office. All three floors were rubble at street level.

My office.

The frosted glass door with my name on it. The photographs of my parents. Case files and research. My desk. Marley's desk. My diploma and my badge. Uncle Joe's fedora.

All gone.

Oh God. Not My Cat.

I ran to the rubble that was still smoldering in some spots. I didn't know who or what hit the building, but no living thing had walked away from this.

Over on the street were meat wagons for theater goers that stayed inside for safety and didn't escape.

Not My Cat.

Of course people are important. Every body bag was someone's brother or sister, husband or wife.

Not My Cat.

I sat down on a piece of limestone brick and stared up the street. My leg didn't hurt anywhere near as much as my heart did.

A pair of yellow dots fluoresced in the sewer opening across Market. A black streak darted across the first half of the street, crept through the transit islands in the middle, then dashed over towards me.

Those yellow dots peeked up over debris, showing that they belonged to a whiskered face with upright ears.

In fear of scaring him off, I held out a hand and made kissy noises.

He checked both directions and ran over to me.

I picked up Not My Cat and held him. He'd never been big on being held, but tonight, he was the world's biggest fan of snuggling. And he'd get fish tonight if I had to mug a fisherman. And he'd never have to sleep outside again. And he was coming home with me …

I avoided anything regarding the election until the morning. Didn't have the energy to care. At least I found a way home. No one dared argue with me about having a cat in my arms.

Not My Cat was *My Cat* from now on.

Of course he slept on my wounded leg. But to be fair, it felt kinda' good.

CHAPTER THIRTY-SEVEN

Things change. Sometimes, it's a damn shame.

-Lou Tanner, P.I., 1935, Personal Journal

Lucas Landis won.

Making a Special Radio Announcement in the early evening of Election Night that he would stop the so-called People's Society bombers, reveal the killer of his wife, and that the Tin Men were there to protect the City, hence when things got out of hand it was *he* who had them sent away, Landis gained the sympathy vote. Plenty of people getting off work, who were already scared by the whole business of the Army bombing the hell out of us, ran to the polls at the last minute. The disaster worked in his favor.

He beat Rossi to the microphone by ten minutes. As I've said before, "Timing is everything." Rossi's speech may have been better polished and unrushed, but Landis struck the first emotional chords.

Although Landis said he won in a landslide, the numbers said he barely squeaked into office.

Other elections, from that terrible week ago, didn't go the way Landis needed for his total victory. No other American Bund official won a seat or judgeship. There would be no Bund sheriffs or aldermen in power. Only Landis. What damage could he do?

Plenty. I didn't want to think about it. I had more immediate demands on my attention.

Having provided my home landlady the sob story of My Cat, she allowed me to keep him, in the short term, whatever that means. I suppose if he doesn't pee all over everything and scratch the wainscoting, he can stay.

My Cat found a spot in the bay window of my apartment to sun himself and like most of us is still jumpy at loud noises. Jangled nerves would take some collective time for both of us to get over. The whole city was shell shocked.

A knock on my door was the landlady. Ah, how I don't love her visits. I limped over and opened the door with my best "howdy there!" smile on.

She held out a telegram. "This came for you."

"Oh. Ah … thank you very much. You didn't need to bring it all the way up here."

She didn't answer. She leaned in, gave my space the once-over, looked at My Cat snoozing, harumphed, and then left.

After shutting the door, My Cat opened one yellow eye but otherwise didn't move. "Good job," I told him.

The telegram was from Hayes. Lunch picnic in Marina Park. Okay? Why not. The weather was not what I'd call *picnic weather* but this was Hayes. Why not.

I still had my phone, for now. Not needing to worry about Marley's salary or my office rent had taken some of the pressure away, but I was still close to flat broke.

I didn't mind. I made the right choice in the end.

I called cabbie friend Skeeter to see if he would do me a favor. Of course he would. Never fails, that Skeeter.

He dropped me at Marina Park. It was overcast and cool, but not rainy. Work was underway on what they were calling the Golden Gate Bridge. The wind, as always and never ceasing, was blowing solidly. Not too far away, a decent jazz ensemble played.

Green Eyes sat on a nice wool blanket, leaning against a half chair supporting his back. Rumpled overcoat as usual, but a new hat. There was another half chair, for me I hoped, a coffee pot, two cups, some envelopes, a box, and a basket.

"Is this a date," I asked, failing to sneak up on him.

"There you are. Rumor has it you prefer the company of your cat."

"He saved the day a few times, so I thought I owed it to him."

No Requiem for the Tin Man

I let Hayes assist me into the half chair. Truth was, I couldn't have made it into that seat without falling into it. My leg wasn't quite right yet. Better, but it had taken a turn for the worse before it went on the mend.

Okay, I dressed up for the occasion. As if this was a date. Not that I was agreeing it was a date. But, in case I allowed it to become something similar to … you know … a date.

We got past our pleasantries, including Marley living down south for a bit, all the things I lost in the Fox building destruction, and the healing of my leg. Time for some business. "Okay, spill it, Big Guy. Is Elsa talking? What's she saying?"

Hayes stared out at the unfinished bridge.

"Hayes?"

"We didn't find her."

"You waited a week to tell me this?"

"Nothing to tell. There was enough blood in that garage that we know she either bled to death or the dog ate her."

"You didn't punish the dog, did you?"

"No. That's what he was trained to do. Besides, we couldn't find the dog either. I think the owner hid the dog from us so that we wouldn't destroy it. Anyway, we found Hans, with a Luger hole in his brain pan."

I did a fast recall of the events. "We didn't put it there, so who did?"

"Good question. We also didn't find the second half of the paperwork Elsa had."

Oh, that's just great. Now I was staring out to sea with nothing to say, except, "damn." Green Eyes opened the plug on the coffee pot and poured me a cup. After a long sip, I pondered out loud, "So we can't ever prove that Landis was directly working for Germany."

"Nope."

"He's already claimed the Tin Men were the good guys and the Army showed up to create panic or destruction, thus they're the bad guys."

"Yup."

"Elsa's gone, so we have no one alive to finger for Regina and

Frederick's murder, even though Landis gave her the green light to cap Frederick."

Hayes shook his head in disgust. "That makes two brothers she threw away for love or loyalty to Landis. And without a confession from Elsa, or Hans, or Landis — we don't have the evidence to take him down. He's the new Mayor. I'd say that about covers it."

"And I'm back where I started in this mess. Broke and nowhere."

"Nope." He smiled, still looking out at the Bay. "Not quite."

I shot him a glance instead of a question.

He does have a nice smile when he uses it. Hayes handed me a box but refused to look at me. He waved at me to open it. Inside was a darling, lady's fedora. Gray. Charcoal band. Teal and charcoal feather set. "Maybe it's okay if you start your own traditional hat collection. You had your Uncle Joe's, now you'll have yours. Just like you have your own business. I fully expect you to be back in business as soon as that leg heals up."

"From you?" I asked, running my finger across the soft felt.

"Yup."

"Thank you." I pulled the pin out of the cloche I had on and popped on the fedora. Not quite a perfect fit, but a little steaming would fix it. It was as perfect as it needed to be.

Then he tossed over the two envelopes. Cash.

I felt uneasy and embarrassed.

"Rental fees and such," he said without prompting.

"For what?"

"Storage fee for the Lightning Gun, which belongs to the U.S. Government. You kept it safe from improper hands. Use of the Aerolift Motorbike, which I'm sure you'll pass along to Howard Evans if and when he shows up."

"Ah, that. Yeah, the police have no idea where he got to."

"'Not surprised. The lock up was wrecked like half of the city. Everyone was so busy with the Tin Men, they lost more than one prisoner." His nonchalant tone told me he wasn't too upset about Howie's escape. "You think the *Bot Brigade* busted him out of the clink?"

"I wouldn't be surprised but be careful how you ask them. Be very, very literal."

"Oh," he pointed to the envelopes, "and also, payment for services rendered in assistance to two agents of the War Department, one of whom required hospitalization."

"Really, how is MacCormick."

"Grouchy, stubborn, and happy no one knows all the details."

"The same as usual?"

"Yup."

Leaning back against the chair, feeling the breeze, hearing the voices of people talking, the band playing ... I felt for that moment, things might turn out alright. "And how about you, Agent Hayes? How are you doing?"

"Fractured cheek bone. Bruised ribs, but not broken. Cheesed off boss. Otherwise, the same."

"You're welcome."

He glanced my way. He hates saying, "thank you."

We sat there until the cool weather turned cold. The band packed up and many of the picknickers headed home. We San Franciscans are a tough lot and aren't scared off by fog or other weather, but we do know our limits.

Behind us, in his special government issued vehicle, the in-car radio played. With the jazz band gone, the broadcast provided the rhythm for our hopes and fears. Passersby stopped to look inside the auto, fascinated by the idea that a car had a radio. Sure, they weren't unknown, but who had over 130 sawbucks to throw at only the radio when the car itself was already around 500 clams?

Someday. I'd get a nice roadster. Something small, maneuverable, sweet. Who, other than Agent Hayes, needed a radio in their car?

The coffee from the pot was still warm. It was a pleasant moment in time.

Then Landis came on the broadcast.

Rossi was handing over the reins of power soon as was appropriate. A peaceful transition of authority. The new mayor had much to bluster about. He had plans and ideas.

The feeling that things might just be alright were swept away by the chilled wind, and I held on tightly to Hayes's arm.

ABOUT THE AUTHOR

T.E. MacArthur is an award-winning author, artist, historian, amateur cat whisperer, and parapsychologist wannabe living in the San Francisco Bay Area with her cat and far too many books.

She has written for several specialized publications, anthologies, and was even an accidental sports reporter for Reuters News.

Her storytelling dramatically shifted direction from Sci-Fi to the mysterious, one of many lifelong obsessions. Her published works are in the Steampunk, Dieselpunk, Historical, and now Paranormal subgenres of Mystery and Thrillers. "I love them all. Dress me up and take me out dancing - darn near any era will do."

If you want to talk ghosts, Raymond Chandler slang, steam locomotives, and Elizabethan insults? She's your girl.

Please come see what she's up next to at
www.TEMacArthur.com

ABOUT THE PUBLISHER

We are a co-op of like-minded authors working together to showcase our books, and our diversity as writers that embrace over a dozen different genres. We openly encourage and support both new and established authors in pursuit of finding their audience while bringing to you books worth reading.

In this vibrant world of Indie publishing, many authors languish, not because the books they produce are bad, but because the industry itself is stacked against them. Individual voices are easily lost in the din of advertising and most Indies can never hope to compete on the same level as a house author with all their backing. We want to change that, and so Indies United was created to give those authors a home to call their own and bring fresh, innovative, and exciting books to readers all over the world.

Come discover Indies United at:
https://www.IndiesUnited.net

Made in the USA
Middletown, DE
16 November 2025